DREAMS AND SECRETS BOOK FOUR

A HOLLOW SECRET

LINN COLDIRON

Cover Design by Jules Designs
(www. coversbyjules.crd.co)
Book Layout by Linn Coldiron

A Hollow Secret / Linn Coldiron ~ Second Edition 2024
ISBN: 978-1-955200-33-2

10 9 8 7 6 5 4 3 2

To Chika and QB. The reasons these books exist in the first place. Thank you for giving me a safe space to explore my writing.

The Dreams and Secrets Series

Lotus In the Mountain
An Imminent Dream
The Children of Death
A Hollow Secret
The Risen Queen

A Note from the Author

In the process of creating this story, world, and characters, I've spent hundreds of hours researching the cultures involved, including learning Mandarin and living in China for a period of about a year. However, research does not replace lived experience and I, in no way, claim that the experiences of my characters represent the entirety of the Asian American community. The same goes for the indigenous tribe I created for the sake of the story and clans. I created the culture based on my own readings and understandings of Native American tribes, particularly the Shoshone tribe which much inspiration was taken. For lived experience representation, please seek out books by authors of any culture you wish to read about. There is a list of some of my favorites on my website, linncoldiron.com.

Content Warnings

While a work of fiction intended for entertainment, there are darker elements and themes in *A Hollow Secret*. This book contains the following content warnings: violence using fantasy magic, swears and curses, PTSD, attempted kidnapping, mentions of suicide, and death.

Part One

Chapter One

For all of his life, Cody had been an outsider. The weird kid. Every time he'd thought he might've found someone to love him, to care about him for who he was, it had fallen apart. Because there was nothing normal about Cody. He looked different. He acted different. He *felt* different. He was smarter than anyone at school, even the teachers. He was quiet and shy. He was socially awkward.

He could see the souls of other people.

For a while, things had been going well. But everything had fallen apart in less than a week. His friends...well, he wasn't sure where he stood with his friends. They were the only people in the world who had given him a chance. Sure, Derek wasn't speaking to him. And sure, his best friend—the girl he loved—was such a mess that she couldn't be alone. But they were still his friends.

Even Blair. Blair, who had made his life hell for years. Blair, who had poked fun at him and picked fights. He wasn't exactly sure how to define their relationship anymore, especially not after taking on Jae and rescuing Mia. They'd made a break through. They'd talked about their problems.

1

He was still hesitant around Blair, but he cared about her.

Which is why he now leaned against his car, arms crossed, and watched Blair staring at the shimmering barrier which stopped them from entering Sangota. She stood tall, hair down from its braids for the first time since he'd known her. She hadn't explained anything. All he knew is that she had her clan's necklace. An artifact that enhanced her seer powers, and her blue mist, the color of the bright sky above them, was thick and strong.

Cody shifted. The last time he'd seen anyone from Sangota, he'd broken into their sacred chamber and rescued Blair from her grandmother's plans. Which wouldn't be so bad, except they'd also stolen the necklace. Or was it stolen? Blair insisted it belonged to her. If it belonged to her, though, then why were they here?

He didn't know what was going to happen. He didn't know if Blair was going to get in a fight with her grandmother, or if she was going to keep her word and go live in Sangota. Her mist worried him. While it was always a thick blue, it normally swished with her internal battles. Her secrets. At the moment, it was still.

What secret had she let go of?

Just as he was about to call out her name, the barrier between Sangota and the rest of Wyoming separated. For a brief second, Cody saw it. The magical, beautiful world he could have belonged to if he was a full mage. Then it vanished behind the barrier, and Cody focused his attention on the people walking toward them.

Blair stiffened. Her mist shifted. Cody stiffened. His magic shifted.

He didn't want to fight. He knew that the Iravata were close. The eight immortals had not let the kids out of their sight since rescuing them from Jae's fire. Cody knew that if things went sideways, they would help. But he didn't want that. He was too exhausted to fight.

Enola Demini led the parade. Elders. Blair's aunt. Her cousin. More people than Cody would ever imagine coming to greet them.

Maybe they, too, sensed the disaster coming their way.

"Blair." Enola's voice boomed across the clearing.

Cody squinted, focusing on her blue mist. The color was similar to Blair's. Very similar. He hadn't paid much attention to it when they were in the cave, but now he had the time, the energy, and the focus. It was time to focus on the small details.

Cody watched Blair tense. He wanted to help, but she'd warned him to stay quiet. Just like last time.

"Grandmother," Blair said.

"Is your friend all right?" Enola asked, tilting her head.

"That's none of your business."

Cody flinched and whispers broke out among the crowd. Blair's tone was one Cody had heard many times before when she was angry with him.

Enola's brow furrowed. "You steal our artifact and then speak to me like that?"

"You trick me and expect me to respect you?" Blair snapped back.

"Trick you?" Enola scowled. "I gave you what you needed."

But Blair shook her head. "No, you didn't. All of these years... you've been hiding it for all of these years."

Something about Blair's words must have caught with Enola. She raised a hand to her chest, as if feeling for a necklace. The necklace that Blair held by her side right now.

"I don't know what you're talking about," Enola said.

But Blair scoffed, shaking her head. "Sure you don't."

Lyda, Blair's aunt, stepped forward. "This isn't the time for games, Blair. The clan elders are angry with you. If you just give us back the necklace and come home, they'll forgive you."

"It's my necklace." Blair shrugged. "You all said so yourself. It belongs to the current seer."

More whispers, and Cody frowned, trying to figure out what

3

Blair was doing. Why she was antagonizing her family. Why she held her head high, like she knew something that no one else did.

She held up the necklace, letting the jade glint in the sunlight. "It chose me. I can do whatever I want with it."

"It means you're the new clan leader."

Cody didn't recognize the elder who stepped forward.

Blair tilted her head, listening.

The clan elder continued. "I've known you since you were small, Blair. You've always had a mind of your own, just like your mother. But there comes a time when we all must grow up, and this is yours. It's time to let go of your own mind and take care of the clan. You must come back."

Blair merely snorted. "Yeah. Sure. I'll just give up all of my freedoms so that I can come play house with a group of people who are so egocentric they weren't willing to help me save my friend because…why? She's not a mage?"

Enola stepped forward. "This isn't a game, Blair. Being a seer means you hold a responsibility to your clan!"

"You would know, wouldn't you?" Blair's tone took on a harsh quality.

What is she playing at?

Cody glanced between Blair and her grandmother. In particular, he stared at their mists. The mists of almost the same color. Magic that exploded out of them with such ferocity that Cody wondered if they were….

They were….

He gasped.

Enola's face drained of color.

"Why have you been keeping it a secret, Grandmother?" Blair asked.

"Mom, what is she talking about?" Lyda asked.

Enola didn't respond.

Blair continued. "Why haven't you told anyone that you're a seer?"

Still, Enola didn't respond. Everyone else broke out into whispers. Some louder than others. The wave of blue mists shifted, molding together. Pain broke out behind Cody's right eye and he winced, but pushed the pain to the side.

Blair's grandmother was a seer. Cody didn't want to believe it. He knew how alone and scared Blair had been since finding out her powers. Her mother had been so panicked, knowing that if the clan found out, they would take her away. She was the first seer in a generation. In two generations. There had never been another in anyone's lifetime.

This changed everything.

"I don't know what you're talking about," Enola finally said after the whispers died down.

Blair reached into her pocket and pulled out a piece of paper. Cody didn't recognize it. Had she gotten this from the basement? Is that what had called her there?

"*There will always be two,*" Blair read from the page. "*Two seers to counteract each other. Two seers of great power. There have always been, and always will be two seers.*"

Enola sighed. "Blair, that's a piece of paper. Where did you even —"

"You've lied to everyone," Blair said. "But you can't lie to me. I know you've been keeping this secret. It's what you do best."

"Mom, *what is she talking about?*" Lyda asked.

"I'm talking about the fact that seers can feel out other seers!" Blair screamed. Even the quietest whisper could be heard in the silence after Blair's outburst. "I'm talking about the connection we've always had. How you've singled me out my entire life. Taught me spells I shouldn't have to know. Why you're so obsessed with me coming back to Sangota. You didn't find out about my visions

5

a week ago. You've known my entire life! Because seers can sense other seers."

She held up the paper, waving it around. "This paper is not lying to me. It's all the information I've ever wanted about who I am. Information you could have—should have—given me. You could have prepared me. You could have taught me how to control it. But you never did!"

"Blair, this is ridiculous—"

"Go ahead," Blair said, backing away. She held up the necklace. "Go ahead and keep lying to everyone, but I know the truth. You're a seer. It's how you're able to keep such an iron grip on the clan. Everyone always told me you were just lucky. You were smart. And maybe those things are still true, but you're also a seer. You can *see* things, just like I can."

Blair was panting at this point, and the elders were murmuring amongst themselves. Enola glanced at them, but held her head high.

Cody shifted. He shouldn't be here. He didn't know why Blair had asked him to come with. Was it because he had a car? The Iravata could have brought her here without his help. Regardless, he didn't belong. In another world. Watching a family fall apart.

His head stung.

"Enola, is this true?" an elder asked.

Enola waved the elder off. "Of course it's not true. Blair is upset. When she calms down, she'll see—"

"Oh just stop," Blair snapped. "Stop trying to convince me I'm wrong. I've learned a lot in the past few days. About my family, about my friends, and about the Gray Spirits."

A large gasp spread throughout the crowd.

Enola's eyes widened. "The Gray Spirits are not to be trifled with!"

"Yeah?" Blair took another step back. "Well, they were more help finding Mia than you were. They haven't tried to trick me. They haven't threatened to take away my freedom. They, at least, gave me a *choice!*"

"You chose your friends over your family," Enola snapped.

"No," Blair said. "I chose my friend over *you.*"

Blair lifted the necklace. Her mist mixed with it. Connecting them. Making them one. The necklace had chosen her as its bearer.

"I have no interest in being your next clan leader," Blair continued when no one said a word. "I have no interest in continuing our clan's lies and secrets. I'm sick of it. I'm sick of feeling like I'm being pulled in two directions. So I'm giving this one up."

She dropped the necklace. It crumpled to the ground, mist still glowing. Still mixed with Blair's. Cody watched it. Blair was giving it up? Just like that? After everything they'd done to get it?

"Blair, you can't do this," Lyda said.

"Watch me." Blair turned around and headed toward Cody with her head held high. Shoulders back. Eyes vacant.

Cody's gaze flickered to the elderly woman who had deflated. She took a tentative step forward. Then another. Then another. Until she was upon the necklace. Blair opened the door to the truck and got in without a word, but Cody waited to see what would happen.

Enola picked up the necklace. Its mist jerked away from Enola's. Rejecting her.

It wanted Blair.

Enola and Cody made eye contact and her eyes narrowed. He thought about saying something. To promise that he would talk to Blair.

But he said nothing and walked around to his side of the car. He got in and turned it on. He pressed down on the gas and the two headed back to Colorado. In his rearview mirror, he saw the group of elders surround Enola. He could imagine their questions.

He had a million of them.

"Blair?" he ventured.

She didn't look at him, but he saw a tear drop from her chin.

He breathed out through his nose and focused on the road again.

So much had happened the past few days. Cody still had a million more questions. He still had so much that he wanted to know about the Iravata. About what Shubishi had said at the plateau.

Cody wasn't stupid. He could put pieces of the puzzle together that other people might have missed. And if there was one thing he was absolutely sure of, it was that the Iravata were still keeping secrets from him and his friends. Yes, Lady Shion had insisted they'd explain everything. And yes, they'd been given a lot of information. Almost too much.

But how could it have been everything? The Iravata were immortals who had been around since before Earth existed. There was bound to be something they'd left out. Many, many, many things they'd left out.

For instance: who was Cody's father—though he suspected one Iravata in particular; why were the teens involved in any of this? Okay, maybe it was because of Derek being Niran's reincarnation, but that didn't explain why Cody, Blair, and Mia were involved; and they didn't explain why now. Of all the times in the world, of every time Niran must have been reincarnated, why was this happening *now?*

Maybe they didn't know themselves. They were uncertain, just like he and his friends were. They were just going along for the ride because none of them could see the future.

That was Blair's job.

And apparently Enola Demini's.

Cody glanced at Blair again. Her mist dulled, and he wondered if that was from her choice, or from giving up the necklace. Even if the necklace hadn't given up on her.

"Are you okay?" Cody tried again.

Blair wiped her eyes and stared forward. "No."

"Anything I can do?"

"Just take us home."

Cody frowned. "Blair...."

"I don't want to talk about it," Blair said. "I don't want to talk about this, or Derek, or anything that happened. I just want to go home and see my parents."

Cody nodded and kept driving. They had a few hours before they got home, so he turned on the radio and cranked it up, not wanting the silence. Blair returned to her position against the window and together the two of them remained quiet while the car rumbled underneath them.

Chapter Two

Mia wouldn't let go of Derek's hand. She rested her head on his shoulder, staring at the ER bustling about around her.

"Don't tell anyone where you were," Lior had warned her. *"As far as the police and FBI are concerned, you were kidnapped by a trafficker. They got away, but you're safe. You're unhurt and you weren't touched. They won't question you."*

But they had questioned her. The police officers. The FBI. They'd asked her questions, asked her if she was hurt, and they would have asked more, but then a doctor had come in for an exam. They'd stripped Mia of her clothes. Put her in a gown. Looked her up and down as if she'd been assaulted, and then ran a million tests.

In the end, they'd found nothing wrong with her, save for a few bruises. Jae had been gentle with her, except when he hadn't been. He hadn't hurt her, much. Besides, it wasn't her body she was worried about. Or, would be worried about if everything wasn't so numb.

Derek squeezed her hand. She didn't look at him. It was hard to do so, lying in a hospital bed. But she squeezed his hand back to let him know she hadn't gone completely catatonic. That the words of the Iravata hadn't completely destroyed her and everything she knew about the world.

"Mom and Dad will be here soon," Derek said. "What are we going to tell them?"

Mia didn't respond. She looked at the IV sticking out of her arm and thought back to the night that started all of this. When Derek had been the one in the hospital bed, sick as a dog.

Derek squeezed her hand again. "Do you want to be left alone?"

Mia's heart raced. She sat up, staring at her brother with wide eyes, and he flinched.

"Sorry, sorry," he said, free hand flying to his chest. Mia jolted back, bowing her head. Sometimes, when the two of them were talking, when it was just them, she forgot that he could literally *feel* her emotions. "I won't leave you alone. I'm here."

He was there. But Cody and Blair weren't. Jae had wanted to kill Derek. Cody and Blair were the only reason that he hadn't succeeded, and Mia wasn't sure that the two of them were safe together. Derek had been more energetic than usual, but he was still prone to exhaustion.

Growing pains, Adelia had said. His magic was growing, and he was always exhausted. He seemed to be okay now, but she wasn't sure how safe she felt with her brother. Even with the Iravata standing by, in case something happened, Jae could easily walk into the hospital and take her again. She hadn't even seen her parents yet.

The two of them were driving to the hospital the police had taken Mia to when they'd "found" her bruised and scared on the side of the road. Derek, having "run away" to find his sister, arrived there before either of their parents. It was all a mess. The Iravata had said they were going to deal with it, but Mia had a feeling they didn't know what they were doing here. They'd told her to pretend. Pretend like she was traumatized and she was terrified to be alone.

She hadn't had to.

Quietly, she and Derek waited for their parents while the doctors discussed what to do with her. Something about a psych consult, though they didn't have the resources. Mia knew that she was going to be put in therapy. That's what happened to kids who were kidnapped. But what could she say to a counselor?

What could she say to her parents?

Derek tugged on her arm. "I'm not going anywhere. I'm here. You can relax."

She did. She lay back down and rested her head against his shoulder, closing her eyes. She wanted to sleep. She wanted to do nothing but sleep.

But every time she tried, she was back in that room. She was back in Jae's mansion with all the kids who didn't deserve the fire that had destroyed their home. She couldn't sleep. She couldn't imagine a world where she ever could again.

"Derek?" she whispered.

"Yeah?"

"Can you help me sleep?" She hated Derek's power. She hadn't wanted him to use it on her for almost a year now. But she needed to sleep. She needed her anxiety to vanish. For the dreams to stay away.

Derek frowned. "Are you sure?"

Tears pricked her eyes and his frown deepened. She wiped them away. "I'm so tired."

Derek nodded and placed his hand on Mia's shoulder. A familiar warmth rushed through her. One she'd thought, all of her life, was her way of calming herself down. Now, she knew it was him. He was the one manipulating her emotions, keeping her calm. She hated him for it.

But as sleep claimed her, anxiety gone, she couldn't help but be grateful for his ability. For Cody's ability. For Blair's. For the magic that had saved her life. That had gotten her into this mess in the first place. The last thing she remembered before drifting off was Derek leaving her hospital bed to settle in a chair.

She wanted to reach out to him. Keep him next to her, but her arms turned to lead and her eyes slipped closed and she let herself fall into a blissfully dreamless sleep.

"Where is my daughter!"

Intira's voice echoed through the hospital wing, startling Derek awake. He blinked the sleep out of his eyes and glanced at his sister who didn't stir.

"Ma'am, please calm down. Our patients are sleeping."

"I will not!"

Derek slipped out of his chair and wandered out of Mia's room, glancing back at her every few seconds to make sure she was still asleep. It was late. A quick glance at his phone showed it to be almost midnight. His parents never stayed up this late.

"Mǎ?" Derek called out into the hallway. The yelling stopped and Intira appeared from around the corner with heavy breathing.

"Démíng?" Intira switched to Chinese and continued rambling, though in a quieter voice. "Where is she? Where's Méilián?"

Derek gestured to the room behind him, but before his mom could barrel into the room, he blocked the door with his body. She stepped back, confusion licking at his skin.

"She's asleep," Derek whispered. "She's been struggling to sleep. I think we should just leave her alone for a bit."

Intira must not have taken his words to heart, because she pushed past him. This time he let her, but he prepared to calm her down if she tried to wake up Mia. She didn't. Instead she stood in the doorway, hands over her mouth as she took in the sight of her sleeping, bruised daughter.

Derek had begged Mia to let Flora heal her, but she'd refused. Just like she'd refused his help. Just like she'd refused to let Eran erase her memories. Derek couldn't figure out if she was rejecting magic, or needed those parts of her to be broken so she could try and heal.

It didn't matter. He just wanted her to stop looking at him with such empty eyes.

"She's all right." Intira leaned against the doorframe, body shaking, emotions a swirl of relief and confused anger.

"She's a little shaken up, but physically she's fine."

Derek recognized the voice behind him and turned to find Mia's doctor holding a tablet, pushing his glasses up his nose.

Intira spun around and immediately bombarded him with questions. Derek, meanwhile, looked around for his dad, eventually finding him speaking to a police officer. The one who had "found" Mia.

Liang shook the man's hand and Derek rolled his eyes. The man had done nothing. It had all been part of the Iravata's plan to keep magic a secret.

Derek hadn't agreed with the plan. He'd argued with them for almost half an hour about how they couldn't just leave Mia alone. How Blair and Cody should get the credit for finding her. But that was unrealistic. And raised questions. And made the police look incompetent. Which they were, in so many ways. But the rest of the world didn't need to know that.

So, it'd been agreed. Blair and Cody would go get Cody's car and drive back to Colorado, pretending like nothing had happened. Mia would mysteriously appear on the side of the road, bruised and scared, but alive and safe. And Derek would wait for a call from the hospital and show up like the good brother he was.

Derek hated it.

He hated all of this.

Mia's emotions shifted, tickling his skin and he glanced back at her. From where he stood, he reached out and calmed them, wanting to give her a restful sleep for the first time since who knows when.

"When can we take her home?" Intira asked.

Derek glanced at her, then back at his dad who was walking toward them. When Derek and Liang made eye contact, Liang halted and his eyes narrowed. Uncertainty bled off of him. Derek swallowed thickly. He knew his parents had a million questions. But he also knew they had better sense than to ask those questions in public. Even in Chinese or Thai.

"As soon as she gets a psych consult," the doctor replied to Intira. "Someone should be here first thing in the morning, and then we can go from there. But your daughter is safe here. We have police officers stationed at every door. The people who took her won't ever get to her again."

Derek bit the inside of his lip to keep from snorting.

"Can we stay here tonight?" Intira glanced over her shoulder at Mia. "I don't want to let her out of my sight right now."

"Of course." The doctor touched Intira's arm gently. "We'll set up some cots for you."

"Thank you." Intira strode into Mia's room and settled by her side, brushing some of her hair out of her face. Derek watched from the doorway, tension releasing from his shoulders.

"Démíng." Liang appeared at Derek's side. Derek glanced up at him. "We have a lot to discuss."

"I know."

"She's all right?"

"Define 'all right'."

Liang didn't respond. Derek wasn't sure if he was in trouble or not. Maybe the relief of finding Mia alive and safe was enough to keep his parents from grounding him forever. But Derek wasn't sure. The anger seeping off his father was enough to make him shudder.

Liang joined Intira next to Mia's bed and Derek backed away, wanting to give them a moment with their daughter.

"I'm going to get some tea," he said. He wasn't really, but he wanted to give some excuse for why he was about to leave them. He knew they heard him because their emotions shifted, but they whispered to each other, probably about Mia.

He backed away, and then turned and hurried down the hallway of the small hospital. He needed air. He needed to get away from all of this for a moment. Mia would be fine for five minutes while he escaped from his parents' anger and frustration.

They were supposed to be happy. If Shubishi had never shown up, if Derek hadn't promised to tell them everything, if Mia had just appeared, would they be angry like this?

He didn't know, and he wasn't sure he wanted to know. Because as much as he hated their anger, he was also glad that he'd gotten some time with Mia. To calm her down. To make sure she got some good sleep.

The moment he burst outside into the night air, he let the events of the past few days wash over him.

Blair taking away his energy. Meeting Leo and Enya. His parents finding out about magic. Him learning about the Iravata. Breaking up with Blair. Rejecting Cody's apology.

It was so much and he didn't know how to handle it. He wanted to go back five days. Before Jae had taken Mia. When he was tired all the time but things were good and simple. He wasn't keeping a secret from Mia anymore, and he had his girlfriend and his best friend and....

IT'S NOT WORTH BEATING YOURSELF UP FOR WHAT YOU CAN'T CONTROL.

Lior's voice in his head made him jerk around, searching.

16

Where are you?

HIDDEN. IT'S BEST IF WE TALK LIKE THIS FOR NOW.

Derek grimaced. He hated communicating in his mind. It felt like such a violation.

MIA'S ALL RIGHT. THAT'S WHAT MATTERS.

I don't know about you, but she doesn't look all right to me. She's catatonic. A mess. She can't sleep on her own.

SHE'S STRONG. SHE'LL RECOVER.

She's scared out of her mind! Derek kicked the ground. *This is worse than last year. How is she supposed to recover from everything?*

WITH SUPPORT.

Derek grumbled. "I'm trying to support her."

YOU'RE DOING A GOOD JOB.

And all the rest? What about Cody and Blair? What am I supposed to do about them?

I CAN'T ANSWER THAT FOR YOU.

Snorting, Derek turned his back on the outside world and faced the front doors of the hospital. After three days of honesty, Derek was hoping for some kind of help from the Iravata, but they were, as always, distant. Not wanting to get involved in the drama of the kids.

CAN YOU BLAME US?

Get out of my head.

STOP THINKING SO LOUDLY.

Derek stormed back into the hospital, and Lior fell silent.

When Mia woke, the world seemed dull. It wasn't like last fall, when everything had turned gray. This was different. It was as though she'd walked into a room where everything was just a little bit dull. Not bright or vibrant.

The first thing she noticed, when she looked around, was that her brother and parents were asleep on cots. She watched them for a time, curling into a ball. The sun barely peeked into her room, so she didn't want to wake them, even though she was wide awake and thinking.

She didn't want to worry her parents. They'd already gone through enough, and from the bags under Intira's eyes, she'd barely slept for days.

Mia closed her eyes. She could still smell the smoke rising up around her. She could still feel the heat of the flames licking at her feet as Cody held her and the two of them wondered if they were going to get out of there alive.

Even though Lior had shown up and rescued them, sometimes Mia felt like she was back on that roof. That she was back in that room, unable to do anything to help herself. She'd been so weak and helpless. She'd relied entirely on Cody and Blair to save her from Jae. And that was a problem.

For the past few days, she'd wondered if there was a way to pretend like the magic world didn't exist. She'd decided, though not without some emotional consequence, that she needed to start separating herself from everything. She was a normal high school girl. She didn't need this in her life.

But that was going to be difficult. Her gaze landed on the passed out Derek. His phone next to him lit up. A text message from Cody. Curious, she reached over and picked it up, being careful to be quiet.

Jae still had her phone. Or, maybe it'd gotten destroyed in the fire. Either way, she didn't have one, and if Cody was texting Derek, that meant something had happened.

<<I know you don't want to hear from me, but Blair and I are back in Willow Creek. She rejected the clan. Her grandmother is a seer. Please let me know how Mia is.>>

Mia's fingers rested over the phone for a second as she debated texting him back to let him know she was awake and Derek was not. But in the end, she tossed the phone back on Derek's bed, which was a mistake because he jolted awake.

The two of them stared at each other for a moment, Mia unmoving, Derek unblinking, until he glanced at his phone.

"Oh. Morning," he said.

"Morning," she whispered.

And just like that, her peace shattered. A nurse came into the room, loud and bustling, to take Mia's vitals. Which woke her parents. Which led to a lot of tears and fussing.

And Mia let it happen. She let her parents fuss over her and ask her a million questions. She answered them as best as she could, avoiding any questions about what happened, and instead focusing on the now.

It took a while, but the psych consult showed up, asking Mia even more questions, though not pressing when Mia didn't answer. She didn't know how she appeared to her family. She didn't know how she appeared to the doctors. She tried to smile. She tried to answer with full sentences and show that she was fine. They didn't need to worry about her. She didn't need to see a therapist after this.

But the look on her parents' faces let her know that she wasn't succeeding. And when the psychiatrist suggested that they keep Mia for a few more days, she knew she'd flat out failed.

"No," she protested the moment the suggestion came up.

Everyone in the room looked at her.

"I don't want to stay in the hospital," she said. "Please, just let me go home."

She wanted nothing more than to go home. To see her real bed. Her real dresser. Her real clothes and books and pictures.

"Mia, I know that this is hard for you—"

"We'd like to take our daughter home with us now," Intira said. "You can't hold her here against her will, and she wants to go home.

We will find a therapist for her when we get there."

Mia wondered if they actually would.

The psychiatrist nodded. "I'll let the doctor know you'd like to be discharged."

"Thank you." Intira sat back on the edge of Mia's hospital bed and gripped her hands. "It's okay. We'll take you home and you never have to think about this again."

Except she did. They all had to think about it again, because this conversation wasn't over.

But she said nothing while the two of them helped her into the clothes they'd found her in. While her parents signed her out. While they wheeled her out of the hospital and to their car.

And then, when it was just the four of them behind closed doors, Intira turned around to face them, her mask gone.

"Explain," she said.

Liang took off. They had hours before they'd arrive home. Derek gripped Mia's hand and she looked at him. He looked at her.

"It's a long story," Derek said.

"We have time," Intira countered.

And so Derek told them his story. Their story. About the magic, and the fights, and the Iravata. Everything that had happened last winter. Everything that had happened since then. About Blair and Cody. Mrs. Arbour and her sons. And about Jae.

Together, somehow, the twins managed to spill all their secrets to their parents, and when they were done, Mia wanted to run into her mother's arms and have her make everything better.

Intira tapped her fingers on the arm rest next to her. Liang continued to drive.

Finally, Intira turned around and said, "Thank you for telling me."

Chapter Three

"You're what?" Blair sat up, staring at the walls of her room. Her beautiful, wonderful, amazing room. She pressed her phone against her ear.

"Grounded," Mia said. She was on Derek's phone. "We told my parents everything, and they're pissed. We're both grounded until further notice."

Great. Blair hated it when the twins got grounded. "Oh come on. It's not like any of this is your fault. How can they ground you? You were just kidnapped."

"Why do you think we *are* grounded? My mom says that we should have told them immediately. No secrets. No games. They think it's why I was kidnapped."

Blair groaned. That was ridiculous. Mia would have been taken whether her parents had known the truth or not. "Kay. So, they know. Should I warn my mom?"

"Definitely."

"They pissed at her?"

"Very."

"Shit."

"Sorry."

"Not your fault." Blair didn't want to blame Mia for anything right now. Even if Mia and Derek really shouldn't have told their parents the truth, it wasn't fair for Blair to put anything on Mia. She deserved a little leniency, and she wasn't getting it from her parents.

"Where are your parents now?" Blair asked.

"Getting food," Mia said. "They'll be back soon, but I thought I should warn you."

"Yeah, thanks." Blair didn't know what else to say. Mia sounded okay? Better than their few days in Shubishi's beach house. Still, there was an emptiness to her voice. Something was missing from her best friend, and Blair didn't know how to help her.

Blair didn't know how to help anyone right now.

She'd rejected her clan. She'd rejected her life's trajectory. She'd chosen to stay in Willow Creek, despite her promise to her grandmother. But her grandmother had lied to her all of their lives.

Her eyes flickered to the infamous paper. The woman had never admitted she was a seer, but Blair knew, without a doubt that she was. It was a calling in Blair's soul.

"Are you doing okay?" Mia asked.

"Me?" Blair laughed. "You're the one who's traumatized."

Mia went silent, and then said in a quiet voice, "Derek got a text from Cody about your grandmother."

Shit. She hadn't expected Cody to say anything, though through her silent cursing of him, she also thanked him. She wouldn't have to be the one to spill the beans. It wasn't her who'd let out the secret.

I'm technically still following the rul—holy shit I need help.

Blair shook her head. She'd rejected the rules of the clan. She didn't need to worry about spilling secrets anymore. What could her grandmother do to her? Kick her out?

"You love your grandmother," Mia said in a low voice. "You

love your clan. I just want to make sure that you're not freaking out."

Blair was freaking out. When she'd arrived home, she'd broken down in sobs that had threatened to rip apart her body. But she'd calmed down. Her mom had made her hot chocolate and her dad had heated up some chicken soup. Together, the three of them had sat in the living room while the boys peeked in now and then, and Blair let her parents comfort her while she told them everything.

"I've been better," Blair admitted. She curled into a ball and stared at the paper. There was so much on there. So much about seers and their powers. "But I'm okay. What about you?"

Mia was silent for a moment before saying, "I've been better too."

"Yeah." Blair sighed. "What about…Derek?"

"He's pouting in the car."

"Does he…."

"I don't know," Mia cut in before Blair could finish her sentence. "He hasn't talked about you at all. I think he's too afraid to tell me you broke up."

They didn't "break up." He'd dumped her ass because she'd tried to protect him. At first, she'd been devastated, but after having time to think about it, anger had taken over the sorrow.

"Yeah, well, whatever." Blair kicked her blankets, wanting to hurt something.

Mia sighed. "You two will figure this out. He's just angry, but he'll calm down."

Calm down? He'd said, very clearly, that he didn't trust her anymore. But she'd had no choice. He couldn't have come with them and she hadn't had time to argue with him about it. She'd done what she'd needed to do, and she wasn't going to try and get him to forgive her. If he couldn't accept that, then that was his problem.

She wasn't going to apologize, and neither would he.

"Shit, I gotta go." Mia muttered something in Chinese, then

back to English, "My parents are back. I'm not sure what they mean by 'grounded', but I don't think talking to you on the phone is included."

"Drive safe," Blair said.

"Thanks." The line went dead.

Blair sighed and lay back in her bed, closing her eyes. It felt good being back in her own bed. Sure, the beds in Shubishi's house were infinitely more comfortable, but something about the smell of her pillow, the weight of her blankets, comforted her in a way that she hadn't had in days.

She wanted to sleep. To try and process everything she'd learned. Everything she'd done.

But before she could rest, a knock sounded at her door. Light and simple.

Blair glanced at the door, debating whether or not she wanted to feign sleep, but when the knock sounded again, she groaned and sat up. "Yeah?"

The door creaked open, revealing her frowning father. "I heard you on the phone. Is everything all right?"

Benjamin Arbour was a simple man. A first grade teacher, he was responsible for shaping the lives of so many kids, and he took the job very seriously. Blair hadn't been in his class in first grade, but whenever the kids had talked about how much they loved him, she'd gotten jealous. So jealous, in fact, that it'd made her resent the other kids.

Looking back, she'd been absolutely ridiculous, but there was at least some kind of logic there. If her dad was a teacher who worked with kids her age, then he would find someone to replace her. This was right before the accident with Leo, when her parents had practically adopted Cody into their lives as their own son.

Blair hadn't wanted to be replaced.

"Mia called," Blair said.

"She's doing okay, then?" He stepped into the room and looked around at her mess. She hadn't cleaned her room in weeks, which was starting to get on her nerves. But she also found comfort in the mess. It was like someone actually lived there, unlike the rooms she'd stayed in the past week.

Blair shrugged. "I don't think she's ever going to be okay again."

Benjamin nodded before settling on the edge of Blair's bed. "I'm sure she will be."

But Blair shook her head. "Jae's still out there. He's still obsessed with her. You should have heard some of the things she's said about him. It's creepy. She was barely holding it together after what happened last fall. Now this?"

"I know." Benjamin gripped Blair's hand. "Mom is going to put a protection spell on her the moment she's back in Willow Creek. As long as she stays here, no one can take her again."

Could her mom do something like that? Blair knew that Esther was powerful, but this seemed a little out of her league. She mostly did small charms for people. Nothing like keeping a freaking Vilaim from taking Mia again.

Blair shuddered at the thought. She hadn't known about the Vilaim. As far as she knew, they didn't exist in the legends of her people. Or maybe they did and, like everything else, it was a secret.

"Mom can't protect us," Blair eventually muttered. "I know she wants to try, but she's just a mage. We need the Gray Spirits to protect us."

"Are they going to?"

"Yeah."

Benjamin kissed Blair on the forehead before standing. "Then I say get some rest. I know you're tired."

Blair curled into a ball and watched her father head for the door. Before he could get far, though, she called out, "Why aren't you and Mom mad at me?"

He paused and faced her. "Why would we be angry?"

"Because I risked my life and pissed off my clan to save Mia. I didn't call Mom when things were getting rough. I lied to my boyfriend."

"Do you want us to be angry with you?" he asked.

"No." She knew she'd done the right thing. If she hadn't gone, there was no saying what would have happened to her best friend. If Cody hadn't been there to save her on the roof....

"Did your friends get in trouble?" he asked.

Blair nodded. "Mia and Derek told their parents about the magical world. Now they're grounded."

"I could ground you too, if that would make you feel better."

Blair frowned and rolled her eyes. "Dad, I'm serious. Why aren't you guys furious with me?"

"Well, you didn't lie to us about what you were doing. We knew from the beginning that you were going to try and find Mia. Mom kept an eye on you the whole time."

"She did?"

"Of course." He chuckled. "You children really underestimate your mother's magic."

Blair wasn't sure why that statement hit her as hard as it did. She wasn't used to thinking of her mom as incredibly magical. It wasn't the same as her grandmother or her aunt. Her mom...well, she was a mom. She used magic like it was nothing to her, but she never did anything intense with it. It was always small things. Things that Blair took for granted, like cooking dinner, or cleaning around the house.

But when she thought about it, it made sense. The necklace had chosen Esther to replace Enola. The necklace only chose the strongest mages. Blair hadn't put two and two together, focusing mostly on getting Mia out of Jae's grasp. But her mom must have been dangerously powerful.

"We're glad you're home safe," Benjamin said with a small smile.

"When things have calmed down, and when you feel like talking, we'll discuss everything. Mom knows a thing or two about rejecting a clan. She can help you through this."

Blair merely nodded and then her father left the room, leaving her with a million thoughts.

She lay back on her bed and stared at the ceiling. For the first time since meeting the twins, Blair felt like she didn't belong in their lives. Mia, not a mage. Derek, hating her. She found herself connecting more with Cody. He understood what she was going through. He'd known about her magic for longer than anyone outside of her family. About her gift.

She sat up and grabbed her phone, staring at it like she wanted to send him a text. Asking him how he was faring with his parents. Because as loose as her parents were with disciplining her, Cody's were the exact opposite. At least, his mom was the exact opposite.

He hadn't talked about his parents recently. At least, not with her around. Maybe he'd said something to Derek. Or Mia. Blair didn't know where he stood with either of them at the moment. Mia was clearly attached to him, but who knew how long that was going to last.

With a sigh, she tossed her phone aside. She didn't want to talk to Cody. She didn't want to talk to anyone but Derek, and he'd made that impossible. Actually, no. She didn't want to talk to Derek. Derek didn't understand what she was going through. He didn't understand what it meant to reject a clan, to be a seer.

Only one person understood what she was going through.

Tears pricked her eyes. She wanted to talk to her grandmother.

Cody stood in the kitchen, washing dishes. The water flowed

over his hands, soap bubbling up with an apple fresh scent. Cody wrinkled his nose, but kept scrubbing. He needed to do something to keep his mind off of the past few days. He needed a moment to feel like a normal teenager doing chores. It's why he'd cleaned most of the house. It's why he'd put in headphones and let the music drown out his life.

He'd gotten a text from Mia on Derek's phone telling him they were grounded and she would see him at school.

School.

After everything they'd gone through, they still had to attend school. They had one more year left, and then it was time for college. In one year Mia would probably attend some university far away. Cody would move to Denver or Boulder or Fort Collins. Somewhere in-state. Somewhere close to home. He was going to apply to all those universities, wishing for scholarships to help him along.

It was all so normal. Thinking about college. Thinking about high school.

"Dammit." Cody wanted to throw the plate in his hands.

Nothing was normal anymore. Nothing would ever be normal again.

The front door opened and closed. Cody ignored it, turning up his music. He didn't want to talk to his dad. He didn't want to have a conversation about where he'd been or what he'd been doing. As far as Cody was aware, his dad was oblivious to the magical world. Cody hadn't told him about it, and he'd made no indication of knowing what was going on in Cody's life.

But then again, there were so many things Cody didn't know about his family.

He didn't know his mom's parents.

He didn't know why his dad was always so calm and patient.

He didn't know how his parents had met.

He didn't know why his mom had broken down so quickly. So suddenly.

And more than all of that, he didn't know why she'd treated him so negatively all of his life.

He was used to it by now. But as a child he'd wanted nothing more than to run into his mother's arms and have her make all of the bullying at school go away. Maybe that's why he'd clung to Mrs. Arbour. Even after the incident with Leo, even after Blair had decided to hate him, he'd still kept in touch with Mrs. Arbour. And then with Dr. Sòng. Any motherly figure who would pay him attention. He'd coped the best way he knew how.

"Cody?" His dad's voice was barely audible. Cody ignored him at first, but when his dad placed a hand on his shoulder, he knew that this was going to be a conversation he couldn't avoid.

With a deep breath, he turned off the water, dried his hands, and turned off his music.

He turned, but didn't look into his dad's eyes. Instead, he kept his gaze to the floor and waited for his dad to ask the questions he'd been avoiding.

"How's Mia?"

Cody shrugged. He wanted to try and contact Derek, but he also didn't want to push it. He was going to give Derek some space, and hopefully he'd get his friend back.

"How are you?" his dad asked.

Again, Cody shrugged.

His dad sighed. "Can you give me anything? Life is chaotic right now, I know, but I want to make sure you're doing okay."

He wasn't doing okay. He wasn't certain of anything in his life. His best friend was traumatized. Again. Derek wasn't speaking to him. His relationship with Blair had changed almost completely overnight. All of the stable things he'd had in his life were gone. Changed. Never to go back to the way they were.

29

Cody couldn't believe that this was happening to him.

"I'm all right," Cody muttered.

His dad was silent for a moment, and then placed a hand on Cody's shoulder. "Everything will be all right. I know that Mom being in the hospital–"

"I don't want to talk about Mom," Cody said.

His dad frowned. "I know it's not easy to talk about her, but she needs our support right now. It's not her fault that…that…."

"That she had a mental break and tried to kill herself?" Cody snapped. He flinched at the tone of his own voice and bowed his head again. He had been trying not to think of his mom. He'd been trying his best to put out of his mind finding her. Looking for Mia had been an excellent distraction from it. From his own life.

But now he had to go back to his life. With everything all messed up. No normalcy. Except school.

"Mom will be all right," his dad said in a low tone. "Mia will be all right. Things will…they will be all right."

Cody wasn't sure he could believe his dad. He pressed play on the music again, turned on the water, and went back to the dishes. The conversation was over. Cody's dad waited for a moment, then his footsteps disappeared out of the kitchen.

Meanwhile, Cody scrubbed the same plate, gripping it so tightly that a voice in the back of his mind told him not to break it.

Chapter Four

Mia stood in the doorway to her room. Her gaze darted around the familiar aspects. Her books. Her bed. Her stuffed animals. Her desk. She'd thought—she'd hoped—that when she saw her real room, she would fall back in love. But it was a reminder of the room back at the mansion. The same sheets. The same curtains. The same everything.

She shuddered, unable to step inside.

Behind her, in the kitchen, her parents and brother argued about something she couldn't quite make out. She didn't focus on them. Maybe that would have helped, but she didn't know if she could listen to their arguments again.

For much of the car ride, Derek had fought with them about the grounding. He said it wasn't fair. That he and Mia were just trying to protect their parents.

Mia hadn't added anything. She'd remained staring out the window the entire time, watching the Wyoming wilderness, and then the Colorado mountains, rush by. The thing was, even if she didn't want to be grounded, she didn't agree with Derek's arguments. He'd used the same ones back when Mia had learned about the magical world. It'd been an excuse back then, and it was an excuse now.

Mia didn't know if Derek was angry that she hadn't backed him up. The two of them hadn't said much to each other since getting in the car. She'd asked to use his phone. He'd given it to her. It was like he was afraid to say anything. That the wrong sentence would break her.

And, honestly, it probably would.

"Méilián?"

She didn't turn at the sound of her mother's voice. She continued to stare into the room, eyes darting over every little detail. The things that Jae had gotten right.

The things he'd made wrong.

"Do you want to sleep in Derek's room tonight?" Intira asked, placing a hand on Mia's shoulder.

She didn't. She wanted to sleep in her own room. With her own things. With freedom. But the more she stared at everything, the more she knew she couldn't go in. Not until they changed everything.

Nodding, she closed the door with hints of tears in her eyes.

"I'll set it up," Intira said. Her voice was calm and gentle. A stark contrast from earlier. "Tomorrow we can fix your room."

Fix it. Change it. Make it so it didn't remind Mia of Jae or the mansion.

"Thank you," Mia muttered. She followed Intira away from the room. Every few seconds, she glanced over her shoulder at it and tried to imagine it different. Tried to imagine what they'd have to do to make her feel comfortable in there again.

This was supposed to be a happy moment. She was supposed to have been here five days ago. Exhausted, but happy. Refreshed. Ready for her last year of school. Derek and Blair would still be together. She and Cody would be awkward around each other, but they would have figured it out. Together they would have eaten cake and celebrated the fact that Mia was back. A welcome home party.

Now, as she looked around, all she saw was sadness and trauma. Derek stood with his back to her in the kitchen, looking out the small window over the sink. Night had settled over the world, and Mia watched Derek watch the outdoors. Like he was looking at someone.

She recalled how terrified she'd been the first time she'd seen Kathleen out that window. The first hint that something was going wrong for all of them. A sign she'd more or less ignored, thinking she'd just imagined it.

Maybe he sensed her lingering fear, because Derek flinched and faced her.

She hated his empathy. She hated how reactive he was to everything she felt inside. Her emotions were supposed to be private. They were supposed to be hers and hers alone. All of her life she'd thought the emotions she buried deep down were safe.

They weren't. Derek could feel them. Every single one.

"What's wrong?" Derek asked.

Mia shrugged. "Just thinking about Kathleen."

He frowned and glanced out the window again. "I'm sorry."

"It's fine." It wasn't, and they both knew it. They fell into silence while footsteps up the stairs let them know that Liang was heading to bed, while Intira fussed in Derek's room.

"You sleeping in my room tonight?" Derek asked.

Mia nodded.

"Do you want to switch rooms?"

Mia shook her head.

"Are you scared to be alone?"

Mia hesitated, then nodded.

Derek breathed out heavily and then nodded as well. "Right. I don't think Jae would be stupid enough to come after you here, but I get it."

Did he? Did he really? Or was he just trying to be nice? A flash of anger boiled in Mia's stomach. She took a deep breath, trying to calm herself down so Derek wouldn't notice. But the anger continued to grow. It grew, and grew, and grew, until it was a tangled mess of roots settling in her gut.

She turned away, knowing full well that he was watching her. Neither of them liked when she was angry with him. Neither of them liked when he was angry with her.

Without a word, she hurried into Derek's room, wanting to push this anger aside. He didn't understand what she'd gone through, but that didn't mean he couldn't try and be helpful. It didn't mean she had to be angry at him whenever he offered his sympathies. After all, what else could he do?

Derek didn't move when Mia ran off. Even though her emotions fluctuated as she tried to control them, he could still feel the anger burning his skin. He wanted to calm her with his words. To apologize for whatever he'd said that had upset her. But he also wanted to give her space. Whatever she wanted, she got.

It was the only way that he could cope with the situation. He couldn't have saved her. He couldn't have helped Blair and Cody, but he could do this. He could give her space. He could make sure she felt safe. However long she wanted to sleep in his room, he'd deal.

He gripped his hands into fists, feeling the nails dig into his skin. Behind him, in the window, he knew that Niran's reflection waited for him. He'd seen it every time he'd looked into a window or a mirror. Sometimes for only a second before the reflection turned back to Derek's face. But still, the man was there.

He hated this. It hadn't been like this before he'd run into Enya.

Before meeting Leo. It was like something had changed inside of him. He no longer felt the exhaustion, but as a tradeoff, he saw Niran.

Despite having learned so much about the Iravata, he'd found that he hadn't learned much about his condition. Niran had killed himself. Niran had betrayed Enya and Lady Shion. He'd traveled the world, or at least a small part of it, and had been one of the most powerful mages in history.

And Derek was his reincarnation. A mage who'd grown up in a small town in Colorado. Who knew so much about the world, and yet nothing at all.

Intira exited his room, closing the door behind her before she leaned against it, staring at the ceiling. Her lips moved. A prayer, maybe? Derek had never known his mom to pray about anything. She was a stark atheist, believing only in what she could feel and touch. But the past few days must have challenged that. Her emotions were a conflicting mix of relief, confusion, and anger. Frustration. The different textures danced on the hairs on Derek's arms and he closed his eyes, wondering if he should calm her down.

Mia was safe. That's all that mattered. That's all that anyone should be concerned about. Not about magic. Not about how Liang and Intira's entire world had changed in less than a week.

Still, in that moment, seeing his mother look so small and fragile, Derek couldn't help but wonder if *she* would ever be all right.

"Mā," Derek called out. Intira looked at him and forced a smile.

"How are you doing?" she asked.

Derek didn't know how to answer. He was freaking out about the reflection. About Mia. About Blair and Cody. School was supposed to start in a few days and he wasn't sure what he was going to do with any of it. As far as he knew, none of the other students had heard what had happened to Mia. Willow Creek wasn't exactly in tune with the rest of the world. He hadn't gotten any texts from classmates about her. Hadn't seen anything on social media about it.

He wanted to keep it that way.

"I'm managing," Derek decided to say. "All of this…it's a lot."

"Yes." Intira moved into the kitchen. "This is all so much for us. You have to understand that."

"I do," Derek said. "Trust me. When I found out that I could use magic–"

"Why didn't you tell us?" Intira asked. "Did we ever make you feel like you couldn't tell us things? That you had to keep this a secret? I know you had Mrs. Arbour, and I understand that she is bound by…what is it, clan laws?"

"Yeah."

Intira nodded. "I understand all of that. I really do. But you should have *told* us. We've always known you were a little different, but this?"

Derek shrugged. "I didn't know how to tell you. I didn't even know how to tell Mia. She only found out last year."

Intira watched him, eyes scanning his every move. "From now on, I want to know everything. I want to meet these Iravata. I want to make sure that they aren't going to hurt you."

"Well, you've already met some of them," Derek said.

"I need to meet them as they really are, not as the fake neighbors they pretended to be for the past seven years."

That was fair, and Derek couldn't argue about it. When he'd told his mom that Mr. and Mrs. Smith were actually immortal, her emotions had gone from curious to absolutely flaming anger. It'd been difficult to stay focused enough to continue the explanation.

"I'll ask them about it," Derek said, though he wasn't sure he could keep that promise. Ever since they'd left the hospital, the Iravata had gone radio silent. Normally, Derek could feel them hiding around in the woods, but now they were gone. No emotions, no magic. He couldn't sense them no matter how hard he tried.

"Don't ask," Intira said. "Tell them."

"You don't really tell the Iravata anything."

"Make an exception." Her tone was sharp and Derek flinched. Her emotions fluctuated from irritation to regret. "I'm sorry. I know you've been through a lot."

Didn't stop her from grounding them. "It's fine."

"It's not." She sighed. "I should have noticed something. You're my children. I should have *been* here to notice. The fact that you were so sick should have taken precedence over the Thai government. I knew that something was going on with you. With the bookshelf and you not sleeping, and then sleeping so much–"

"Mom, it's fine." Derek walked over to her and brushed a hand against her arm, trying to calm her down a little bit. He didn't push much. Just enough to take away the increasing number of anxiety ants running up and down his skin. "We dealt with it."

Intira pulled away from him and went to the kitchen. "Yes. You dealt with it. And now Mia is traumatized. The man who took her is still out there and I don't think he's going to just let her go without a fight."

"We have the Iravata watching her all the time," Derek tried to say, but it wouldn't work. His mom knew nothing about the Iravata other than they'd lied to her for seven years.

The look on her face told him everything he needed to know, even without her disapproving emotions tingling his skin.

"Nothing is going to happen to her again," Derek vowed. "I promise."

"And what about you?" Intira tilted her head, staring up at her son. "What if something happens to you again?"

Derek wanted to promise her that he would be fine too. That it was all over now. But he couldn't. Because he knew too much about the Iravata's story. He'd seen too much in his dreams. He'd met too many interesting people.

He didn't have to be a seer to know that something was coming.

"I have magic," Derek said after a while. "I'm not like Mia. She's strong, but she can't fight against people with magic the way I can."

"I don't want you fighting at all."

"It's either that or I die." He remembered, all too clearly, the moment in the forest. When it was him or Steven. When Shubishi had given him the ultimatum. He'd had no choice but to give in. It was why he ran with Mia every morning. It was why he'd let her kick his ass in hand-to-hand combat while she taught him everything she knew. It was why he'd trained with the Iravata all summer, trained with Blair, trained with Cody.

He was involved in this in a way that Mia never would be. Enya wanted him for something. He didn't know what, but he had a feeling it had to do with the knife.

Intira closed her eyes and tilted her head back, lips moving. A prayer.

"Just...." She sighed. "Just keep me updated with what's going on in your lives. Even the bad things. I want to know. I *need* to know. I'm your mother, and if I can do anything to protect you, I will do it."

She couldn't protect him from this. "I'll tell you everything."

A small smile, and a hint of relief, spread across her face. She looked Derek in the eye and placed both hands on his cheeks.

"I love you, Démíng," she said. "Be safe. Be careful."

"I will."

She tilted his head down and kissed him on the forehead before disappearing up the stairs to her room.

Derek, meanwhile, stayed in the kitchen and tried to build up the courage to go into his room. Mia's emotions were all over the place. Dancing. She was awake and scared and he didn't want to leave her alone. But he also knew that she didn't want *him* to comfort her.

It was Cody she trusted. Cody, of all people. Despite knowing that Cody was half the reason that Derek wasn't able to save her, she trusted him. But Cody couldn't be here. So it was up to Derek.

With a deep breath, he headed to his room. He knocked on the door to let Mia know he was coming in, and then he entered, not sure what was going to happen next. Mia lay on a blow up mattress on his floor. She didn't look up when he entered.

She'll get over this eventually. She'll open up again. It's just like last winter. It took a while, but she got back to herself. We got back to ourselves.

And without a word, he climbed into bed and lay down, wishing that he could go back a week and make everything better for everyone.

Chapter Five

Cody stared up at the brick building. The warm morning breeze rustled his clothes and hair, seeming to draw him into the school and away from summer vacation. It was such a normal thing. Such a simple action that he'd done so many times before. And yet, this time was different. It was his last first day of high school. Something he'd been looking forward to, and also something he'd never wanted to happen.

He hadn't let himself think about this day too much. Just like he wasn't letting himself think about graduating. Everything would change when he graduated. Everyone would go their separate ways. Everyone would move on with their lives.

It was all so simple to think about, though. It was easy, when he lay awake at night, to drift off to the normal idea of friends breaking apart after high school. Because the reality of their situation was much worse.

Derek still wouldn't speak to Cody. Blair was still hesitant around him. And Mia....

Cody sighed and looked at the ground.

When they were little, Cody and Mia had clung to each other. Two outcasts finding comfort in each other's company. They'd had little in common, and yet they'd been everything to each other. It wasn't until Mia started to make other friends, until the girls stopped bullying her and the guys started *noticing* her, that they'd broken apart.

Recently, they'd gone back to those moments. Mia wanted him at her house. As far as Cody knew, only he was allowed to see her. Blair was off limits, something Blair complained about daily. Derek avoided them, but Cody would sit with Mia. They didn't speak much. Sometimes they played board games. Sometimes they watched movies.

Mostly they sat and read together.

He didn't want to push her. Even though he was desperate to understand what was going through her head, he also knew that she wasn't going to open up to someone who pushed her too hard.

Word had gotten out, slowly, about what had happened to Mia. Kidnapped from DIA. Missing for days. Found in Wyoming.

No one had confronted him about it, but he'd heard gossip as he'd walked through the streets. He knew that today was going to be difficult for Mia. She loved being wanted and needed. She hated being the center of gossip.

He'd offered to walk her to school today, to maybe head off some of the mass of people who wanted to ask her if she was okay, but she'd told him she would be fine.

He'd left it at that.

Still, he pulled out his phone and checked for any text from Mia's new number.

Nothing.

He glanced over his shoulder, wondering if maybe she and Derek would be coming up the walk anytime soon. When he only saw other students, he hurried into the school.

As he walked through the halls, head down, he listened for

the gossip about Mia. What they might say about Derek and Blair breaking up, if they knew about that. Mostly, he heard low rumblings asking if Mia was going to show up to school today.

Cody sighed when he got to his locker. Mia deserved better than a group of high schoolers gossiping about her. He hoped that, however her day went, it was better than the day he'd played in his head over and over last night.

The students asking her a million questions.

Her teammates trying to reassure her that she was all right.

Everyone treating her like a fragile doll who needed to be protected.

He hesitated at his locker for a moment. He was treating her like a fragile doll. He didn't ask her anything. He gave her whatever she wanted and didn't push.

He was scared she would break.

He was terrified that she would end up like his mother, stuck in a hospital because she couldn't take the weight of the world anymore.

Honestly, he didn't know what else to do.

It was a mess.

All of it was a giant mess.

"Cody."

Blair's voice brought him out of his thoughts. He glanced at her. She stood with her hair down, wearing her normal t-shirt and jeans, but not the bracelet her mother had made for her last year. He hadn't seen her since getting back from Wyoming, though they had spoken over text.

"Morning," Cody said.

"Have you seen Mia?" Blair asked.

Cody shook his head. "We'll probably see her at lunch."

Blair frowned and leaned against the lockers, arms crossed. "I haven't heard from her in a while. I know you two talk every day. Is she doing all right?"

"She seems…fine." Cody didn't know how else to put it. Mia was clearly traumatized, but she seemed to be recovering. "Why?"

Blair's eyes trailed to the ground. "I had a vision about her."

Cody froze. "What happened?"

"It was…." Blair waved her hands around her head. "It wasn't bad. It was just concerning. I kept seeing her walking away from us. Like she was drifting off in a different direction."

"I thought your visions were more concrete than that."

"They can be." Blair rubbed her eyes. There were dark circles under them. "Ever since I bonded with the necklace, my visions have been…." She waved her hands again.

Cody remembered, not too fondly, how constant and violent her visions had been when they were searching for Mia. "Have you had a lot of them?"

"No. But they're weird. More abstract. I keep seeing Mia, and fire, and the woods, and none of it makes sense."

Cody crossed his arms and closed his eyes, searching for Mia's mist. He wasn't amazing at finding people from far away, but Mia's mist had always been so bright and warm that sometimes, when he focused, he could reach out to her if she was close by.

But he couldn't find her.

"I haven't seen or heard from her today," Cody said. "I don't feel her mist. Maybe she stayed home?"

Blair whipped out her phone and stared at it. "Can you text her?"

"Why don't you?"

Blair shrugged. "She trusts you more than anyone right now. I don't want to bug her while she's healing."

Cody had a feeling it was more than that, but he didn't push. Instead, he sent Mia a quick text.

<<Are you at school?>>

"I'll let you know when she answers," Cody said, watching the little "delivered" message at the bottom of the screen. He waited a moment for it to turn to "read," but when it didn't, he slipped his phone in his pocket.

"Thanks." Blair nodded at him as the two minute bell rang. "Guess I should go. See you at lunch?"

Cody nodded. Something was off about today. Something was off about Blair. About Mia. Who knew about Derek, but Cody had a feeling something was off about him as well.

Still, he headed to class and tried to put all of it out of his mind.

Mia never texted Cody back.

He barely paid attention in class—not that there was much *to* pay attention to on the first day—and instead focused on his phone. If his teachers noticed, they didn't say anything. They wouldn't care. Cody was the top student. He could miss every single day allotted to students and still get one hundred percent on all of his exams.

But Mia not texting him back wasn't the only thing driving him mad. The other half of the dynamic duo, Derek, was in two of Cody's three morning classes, and through all of them, Derek hadn't said a word to Cody. Normally, in the rare occasion that the two of them had class together, Derek and Cody would sit next to each other. Work together on projects. Talk when the teacher wasn't paying attention.

Today, it was like Cody didn't exist. He'd thought that after a week of Mia being home, Mia being safe, Derek would forgive him. Or would at least forgive Blair.

But nope. By the time lunch rolled around, Cody realized that Derek was not one to let go of a grudge. Cody was the first to the normal table, and the moment Derek saw him sitting there, he turned and sat at a table with some of his other friends.

That, added to the fact that Mia still hadn't read his message, forced Cody to wonder if his life was going to go back to the way it'd been before he'd befriended Mia. Before she'd saved him from loneliness and pain.

He was about to get up and go to the library, having no food, when Blair appeared in the cafeteria. Her mist was blue, but it was different. It was lighter than when they'd met at the locker. Thicker. More consuming.

Cody shuddered.

"So, Derek's still pouting?" Blair asked when she sat next to Cody.

Normally, when the twins weren't there, Cody went to the library and Blair sought out other people to eat lunch with. The two of them didn't sit together, no matter how lonely they were.

Cody shrugged. "I guess. Did something happen?"

Blair frowned. "What?"

She pulled out her food, then looked at the empty space in front of Cody, then at the empty seat that Mia normally took up, and sighed before throwing Cody her sandwich. He caught it, and didn't argue.

His stomach growled, eager for the idea of food. It wasn't that he'd forgotten. Or that his father was starving him. It was more he'd lost his job and money was tight. One skipped meal never hurt anyone. At least, that's what he'd been trying to convince himself.

"Your mist...." Cody lowered his voice and glanced around them. "It's changed."

Blair took a loud bite of a carrot, staring at the table. "Like I said, I keep having visions."

Cody's eyes widened. "You had one here?"

"Yup." She took another bite of carrot. "It wasn't as strong as the one I had about Mia, but it still took me away from class for a bit. I got called on and had to pretend like I wasn't paying attention on purpose."

"Why didn't you just say you had a seizure?"

Blair frowned. "You know I've never liked that excuse. It's weird and kinda messed up."

"Right."

He unwrapped the sandwich, staring at it in case Blair decided she wanted it back. When she made no move to take it, he bit into it.

"Do you think anything will ever go back to normal?" Blair asked.

After last winter, things had gone back to normal to an extent. Their friendship had been strong. Blair and Derek had been closer than ever. Mia had even smiled and laughed sometimes.

But this fracture felt different than the one that had broken them last winter. There was no one manipulating Mia from behind the scenes. They weren't keeping deep dark secrets from one another. At least, not life changing ones.

"I don't know," Cody said after a time.

Blair grabbed another carrot, but didn't take a bite. Instead her gaze fell on Derek. Cody followed her eyes, and together the two of them watched him talk to a group of students who had spent years picking on Cody and Mia. Whose mists were a mixture of colors, ranging from bright pink to mustard yellow.

"Guess it's just us now," Blair said. "Like before."

But it had never just been them. Leo had been a part of the crew. And now that was a mess.

Just like everything Cody touched.

"Guess it is." Cody turned back to the sandwich and took a bite before pulling out his phone to check if Mia had read his message yet. She hadn't, and his worry grew. She wasn't at school. Had something happened?

Was she okay?

Mia watched the woods behind her house. The porch swing she sat on moved freely, shifting back and forth with a slight creak. She didn't pay attention to it. All she could do was stare at the trees rising into the sky. The familiar sight of home bringing her comfort that she'd sought for almost a week now.

Mia didn't spend much time in her backyard anymore, focusing instead on homework and her friends. They didn't come back here to play tag. They didn't get out the badminton net and exhaust themselves in the summer evenings anymore. Mostly they stayed inside. Mostly they hung out in the living room and talked or played games.

Mostly….

There was no mostly anymore.

Inside, Intira bustled about the kitchen. She'd said she was going to get Mia a nice cup of jasmine tea. Something to soothe her. Something to calm her soul and bring about peace so she could go to school tomorrow.

Mia didn't know why she hadn't left the house. Well, that wasn't true. She knew *exactly* why she hadn't left the house. She didn't feel safe. She didn't know when Jae would try and grab her again. No one had noticed her disappear from baggage claim. No one would notice if she disappeared in the school halls. Lior had taken his position as a teacher again, just to make sure she was safe, but she didn't trust him.

She didn't trust anyone.

So, she stayed home. She'd picked out new sheets and a new duvet cover for her bedroom. She and her mom had pulled everything off the walls and painted over the eggshell with a light blue hue. Her new desk would arrive in a few days.

It was a new room. Her bed was in a new position. Her dresser—one of the only things not in *that* room—was in a new position. She'd gone through all of her clothes and gotten rid of the ones that she'd seen in the other room. Then she'd gone online and ordered an entirely new style. One that she hated. One that didn't suit her.

One that didn't remind her of Jae.

She did all of these things and didn't leave the house once. Intira didn't try and get her to. Liang did, at times. He asked her if she wanted to go on a walk to the store with him. If she wanted to take a trip down to Denver and look at clothes in person. But every time he asked, she told him she was fine staying home, and he didn't fight her.

This morning, when she'd woken up, she'd planned to go to school. But getting ready, putting on her new clothes and staring at herself in the bathroom mirror, at the fading bruises, she'd found she couldn't leave.

The sliding door opened, startling Mia out of her thoughts. She jumped up, heart racing, swing creaking louder.

"Here's your tea," Intira said, appearing on the back porch. She held in her hands a wooden tray table with tea and a plate of food. Lunch. She'd been force feeding Mia at every meal, making her take "just another bite" when she could only finish half of her dinner.

Mia relaxed.

It was her mom.

It was just her mom.

A look crossed Intira's face. One of frustrated sorrow that Mia hated to see. She didn't want to be like this. She didn't want everyone and their mother—and her mother—worrying about her. She didn't want people to give her whatever she asked for without question. She wanted to be told no. She wanted people to treat her like normal.

Except she knew they wouldn't. Hell, if this had happened to

Derek, she'd treat *him* like glass. It was natural for them to worry about her. She recalled her mother's conversation with a therapist friend.

"Give Mia whatever she wants. She'll come out of it eventually, but she's been through a trauma."

This was supposed to help her heal. Except the therapist didn't know what had really happened, so maybe the logic didn't apply.

"Thanks." Mia settled back on the swing. Intira joined her, still frowning, and handed Mia the tray. She took it, but didn't drink or eat. Her throat closed at the sight the tea and food, and she wanted to throw it all away.

"Will you want to go to school tomorrow?" Intira asked.

"I wanted to go to school today," Mia muttered.

"You could have."

"I tried."

"I know." Intira brushed a lock of Mia's hair out of her face, fingers so gentle Mia barely registered them. "I know you're trying. I've talked to the school and they're okay sending home all of your work with Derek for a while. It's the first week of school. Mostly, it's nothing important."

She didn't want her work to be sent home with Derek.

"Or, I could try home schooling you," Intira continued. "It would just be for a year and then you could go to university. Or maybe take a year off from school and go see Yeye and Nainai. This man didn't take you while you were in Asia. He waited until you were back in America. Maybe...."

"Mā, I'll go to school," Mia said. She didn't want to talk about Jae or why he hadn't taken her when she was abroad. That's where they'd met. It would have been even more difficult to find her. Easier to make it seem like she'd just been kidnapped.

Intira fell silent.

Mia swallowed thickly and then picked up her tea, taking a

painful sip. Anything to make her mom worry less.

"It's okay if you can't," Intira said.

"I want to." She took another sip. This one was easier. But the food…her stomach turned and she found she didn't want to eat. "I'll try again tomorrow."

Intira nodded. "All right. But if you can't by the end of the week, let's try homeschooling. At least for a little bit. I think it would be good for you to have some structure."

Mia rolled her eyes. "Okay, Mā."

A normal response. Or, so Mia hoped. When Intira smiled, she smiled back and the two women sat there, staring at the woods in silence while Mia did her best to drink her tea and not think about how dangerous it was to leave her home.

Chapter Six

"You're really going to ignore me for the rest of the school year?"

Derek didn't want to face the owner of the voice behind his locker door. He didn't want to feel the frustration biting at his arms. He didn't want to close his locker door and find Cody standing there. He still couldn't look at Cody. He'd thought, after some time, he would be able to forgive Cody for helping Blair, but he couldn't yet.

Derek didn't reply. He closed his locker and headed down the hallway. Away from Cody. But Cody followed him.

"Look, we don't have to be friends anymore," Cody said. "I'm used to everyone ditching me anyway."

Derek rolled his eyes. The guilt trip wasn't going to work. This wasn't about Cody being smart or weird or whatever. This was about a conscious decision that Cody had made.

"I'm just worried about Mia."

At the sound of his sister's name, Derek froze. The emotions of the students around him fluctuated into curiosity, but he waited for them to continue on before he glanced at Cody.

Cody snorted. "So, that gets your attention."

"Mia's fine," Derek said.

"Then why didn't she come to school today?"

"Why don't you ask her?"

"I did."

And she hadn't answered. That pleased Derek in a way he didn't know how to explain. For the past few days, Mia had clung to Cody like he was a safety blanket. Ever since he'd saved her from Jae, the two of them had existed with this bond that no one could break. But today, she'd ignored him. Derek probably shouldn't have been as happy as he was, but dammit he was supposed to be the one who she felt safe with. *He* was her twin. *He* was the one who could help her sleep.

"If she didn't tell you, then I don't know if I should," Derek said. The truth was, Derek didn't know why Mia hadn't come to school. She'd gotten up. She'd skipped breakfast, but she'd gotten ready to go. And then she hadn't been able to step foot outside the house. She hadn't said anything. She'd taken off her shoes and retreated back into the kitchen.

But she'd been terrified.

"Come on, Derek, this is ridiculous."

Derek shrugged and kept walking. He needed to get home and give Mia all of her syllabi. He needed to check on her, because she'd ignored his texts all day too.

Unfortunately, Cody followed. In silence, they walked side-by-side until they were outside in the warm summer air and Derek stopped again.

"What do you want?"

Cody grimaced, then looked away. "Nothing."

Derek scowled. "Fine. I'm going home. You're not welcome."

And then he turned heel and headed off again, this time pushing satisfaction onto Cody to quell his curiosity.

In the past, it would have been difficult to push an emotion onto Cody, especially without physical contact. But with Derek's growing energy, it was simple enough. Without a word, Cody stopped following him. Derek smiled. He was getting stronger.

But then, as he walked through downtown, he caught his reflection in one of the windows.

No, not his reflection.

Niran's.

He paused and stared at the man staring back at him. He was young. Derek's age. The reflection wasn't twenty-three. Derek reached up and touched the glass, his fingers touching Niran's, and then he backed away.

He didn't know what it meant. He didn't want to know what it meant. All he wanted to do was pretend like it wasn't a thing. Like he wasn't looking into the eyes of the past. The dreams were enough. He'd gotten used to the dreams.

He didn't need anything more.

He took off, running to get home before he saw Niran again.

There were no cars in the driveway. At first, he thought his mom had managed to get Mia to leave the house, but her emotions were there. Strong and bright as always. He hesitated outside the front door, hand on the handle as he tried to understand why Mia wasn't terrified, being alone.

Who said she's alone?

Derek shuddered before opening the door. He couldn't feel them. Any of the Iravata. But that wasn't anything new. When they didn't want him to feel their emotions, he didn't, and when they did, he *really* did.

"Mia?" Derek called out.

"We're in the living room," Lior said.

Derek grimaced, but followed the voice into the living room where Mia sat curled up on a chair with a book, and Lior stretched out on the couch.

"I thought you had classes," Derek said to Lior.

Lior smirked. "I did. I came here after. Turns out your parents don't like babysitting their catatonic daughter."

Derek flinched and braced himself for annoyance from Mia, but she smiled over the edge of her book, emotions a mixture of comfort and amusement. Derek stared at her. This was the first time since they'd gotten back from Wyoming that Mia's emotions hadn't included some kind of fear. He relaxed.

"Where are Mā and Bà," Derek asked Mia, switching to Mandarin. He knew that Lior spoke it well enough, but the immortal didn't speak it in front of them.

"Bà's in Denver," Mia said. "He left this morning for a few days. Mā's out getting groceries, I think. She said she had errands to run."

Derek observed her. She looked better. She felt better. It was as though she was relaxing.

"Why are you staring at me?" Mia asked.

"I'm not," Derek said.

She raised a brow, then returned to her book. "Mā should be home in a couple of hours. She said you were bringing me stuff from school?"

"Oh. Yeah." Derek slipped his backpack off his shoulders and glanced at Lior, who grinned at him, but said nothing. "Cody asked about you. You didn't tell him why you didn't come to school?"

Mia shrugged. "I wasn't in the mood to talk. What did you tell him?"

"Nothing."

Mia frowned. "You're still mad at him?"

"I don't want to talk about it." Derek snatched Mia's folder from his backpack and handed it to her. Then he faced Lior. "I'm here now. You can leave."

The moment he said these words, Mia's smooth content turned to harsh panic. She sat up, eyes wide, and her knuckles turned white she was gripping her book so tightly. The onslaught of negative emotions so close and so unexpected took Derek's breath away and he struggled to get it back.

"I'm not leaving," Lior said. "Don't worry."

Mia's eyes flickered from Derek to Lior and then down to her book. She relaxed back into the couch, but Derek knew that her moment of relief was over. Her emotions fluctuated between anxiety and fear.

"Right." Derek ran a hand through his hair. "I'm going to do homework."

"You don't want to join us here?" Lior asked, though the smile on his face was anything but welcoming.

"I'm good." Derek watched his sister for a moment longer before disappearing toward his room.

"You should trust your brother more," Lior said, stopping Derek in his tracks.

He glanced over his shoulder. This wasn't a conversation for him, and yet he was curious to hear Mia's response.

"I do trust him," she said. "But he can't protect me from Jae."

"Cody can?"

"Cody has."

"Do you think Derek wouldn't have been able to if Blair and Cody had let him come with?"

There was a moment of silence, and then, "I think he would have tried."

Derek's grip tightened on his doorknob. He wouldn't have tried, he would have succeeded. Blair and Cody hadn't even given him a chance to be useful. They'd just taken off on their own.

But why did it matter to him so much that he hadn't been there? He knew, logically, the best thing for him had been to stay behind. His parents hadn't worried as much. He hadn't been able to stay awake. He'd been a mess.

"Jae wanted to kill him," Mia said. "I think he still does. If he'd been there, he would probably be dead right now. If he tries to protect me in the future, he might die."

The fear returned. Derek gasped and tried to remain quiet.

"Why don't you tell him this?"

"You've met Derek," Mia said. "He's stubborn. Even if I tell him, it won't change anything. He'll still blame Cody and Blair for not being there. He'll still try and be the hero of this story. But if he acts like the hero, then he's going to die, and I can't lose my brother."

"So it's easier to push him away?"

"Yeah."

Derek opened his door as quietly as he could and closed it behind him, blinking away tears. He knew that Lior had meant for him to hear the conversation. Lior knew he'd listened in. How could he not, with his power?

Don't take her distance to heart, Derek. Trust that she'll come to you when she's ready.

But he didn't trust it. He didn't trust anything anymore. All he knew is that his sister was afraid for herself, and afraid for him. She lived in a world of fear, and it was all because of Jae.

Derek's eyes narrowed. From what he understood, he wasn't strong enough to take on Jae by himself. He needed to get stronger. He needed to understand more about his magic and about Niran so he could become the person that Jae feared he could be.

He crossed his room to the place where he'd hidden the knife from his parents. They'd asked for it, and he'd lied and told them that the Iravata had confiscated it, all the while hiding it with his magic. He opened the drawer and stared at the bamboo handle. Killing Steven had haunted his nightmares for almost a year now, and he wasn't sure he would be able to do anything about Jae, but he wanted to.

He needed to.

To protect Mia. To protect himself. And to make sure that no one ever harmed his sister again.

When she was little, Blair used to play at the park with Cody and Leo. It was small. Unassuming. Two slides, a jungle gym, and some swings. She hadn't been here since she'd decided she was too old to play at the playground. Normally, when she got sick of her little brothers being loud and annoying, she took refuge with Mia and Derek either downtown or at their house.

She couldn't do that anymore.

So, instead, she sat on the swing, staring out at the sandy playground with emerald green grass stretching out until it hit the houses near where Mia and Derek lived. She wanted to go see them. To make sure that Mia was okay after skipping the first day of school. There were rumors floating around that she wouldn't be coming back. That she was too messed up in the head.

Blair had shut those down as quickly as she could, but she still had in her head the vision of Mia walking away. She didn't want Mia to walk away. She didn't want to lose her best friend. Hell, she'd chosen her Mia over her *family*, she was that desperate to keep ahold of her. Of course, her grandmother lying about everything helped, but it was still frustrating.

She had to do something. She had to help Mia feel comfortable. Safe. She had to get her friend back. And maybe if she helped Mia,

Derek would calm down. He would forgive her.

She pulled out the piece of paper she'd stolen from Jae's basement. It said a lot of things about seers, but it also said a lot of things about the other artifacts. Well, maybe not a lot, but more than Blair had originally known about. The knife had become legend in the Sixiang clan thanks to Niran, and the necklace was well known for its power with seers, but there were others.

She'd known this, growing up. She'd heard stories of the Staff of Storms protected in the hands of the Mauvais clan in Europe. Of the Stone of Language heralded by the Kyeema Clan in Australia. And finally, of the Bowl of Transportation that the Inyoni Clan in Southern Africa kept hidden away. But, in her childhood, she hadn't learned much about their powers, or what their powers could do together. The five artifacts of magical lore.

The paper, however, explained unspeakable power if the five artifacts came together.

Blair looked at her hand, which still burned from the last moment she'd held the necklace. She'd given it up to prove a point to her grandmother—she was no one's pawn—but she regretted it. If she could get all of the artifacts together, then maybe she could be powerful enough to protect her friends. Her family.

Herself.

She shuddered, thinking back to Jae controlling her body. If Cody hadn't saved her, she might have become a murderer. She might be dead herself. Mia might have never escaped from the mansion, and Derek would be even more of a wreck.

Her brow furrowed. She didn't want to think about Derek or how much of a mess he might be if they'd all disappeared from his life.

A tickle at the back of her mind brought her attention away from the paper. She knew who it was without having to look. His magic had grown even stronger over the past week, since he was finally using his powers for something other than passive observation.

"Haven't been here in a long time," Cody said, coming to stand next to her.

"Nope." She shoved the paper back in her coat pocket and stared out over the playground. "Figured no one would be here."

"Ah."

"You find out where Mia was?"

"No. Derek wouldn't tell me anything." Cody looked at his hands. "Pretty sure he used his power on me."

Blair balked. Ever since last winter, Derek had been so hesitant to use his empathy to manipulate other people without their permission. The two of them had talked about it one day when they were lying together.

"Would you ever use your power against me?"

"Never."

"You used it against Mia."

"And look where that got me? It's not worth it. Even if it would make some things much easier. Besides, even if I did want to, you're too stubborn to have your emotions controlled."

He'd kissed her and they'd stopped talking.

She missed him. Even if she was angry at him, she missed him.

"I think we should give him some space," Cody said.

"Whatever," Blair muttered. She was tired of having this conversation over and over. She was tired of thinking about Derek. She was tired of feeling stuck in limbo. She needed to *do* something. She needed to get out of her rut and focus on doing something other than waiting for Jae to come back.

"Look at this," Blair said. She grabbed the paper from her pocket and handed it to Cody, who took it without a word. "It has a lot of information about the artifacts."

Cody's eyes scanned the page. "Why did Jae have this?"

"No idea." Blair had been wondering that since she'd found it.

"But it is what it is. The rest of his little vault is ash, and this is all we have."

"We have the journals that Mia stole."

That was true. Except the Iravata had taken them under the pretense of learning more about Jae. Blair wanted to call bullshit. They just wanted the journals so Mia didn't obsess over them.

"Screw the journals," Blair muttered. Then she shook her head. "Anyway, I'm thinking if we want to be stronger, we need these artifacts."

Cody raised a brow. "Excuse me?"

"I can easily get the necklace. I'm bonded with it still." She could feel it, even if she'd rejected her place as clan leader, the necklace had not rejected *her*. "Plus we already have the knife–"

"No, Derek has the knife," Cody pointed out. "And he's not speaking to either of us."

"Leave that to me," Blair said with a wave of her hand. "That leaves three more. I know where the staff is. The Mauvais clan keeps it at that school I got expelled from. Shouldn't be too difficult to get. And if I use my powers, I can figure out where the other two are."

Cody frowned. "This is a bad idea. What if the clans find out what you're doing? They won't be happy."

"We'll have to do this quietly."

"We?" Cody laughed. "Blair, come on. I barely made it out of Colorado. You expect me to travel the world with you?"

"It's for Mia," Blair said.

Cody fell silent, staring at the crumpled piece of paper. Blair bit her lip, hoping, not for the first time, that excuse would get Cody to go along with her plans. He'd braved the outside world for Mia once. He could do it again. And again. And again.

"Give me some time to think," Cody said. "I don't think it's a good idea, but maybe it's the only thing we can do to give her some peace of mind."

"It *is* the only thing we can do," Blair insisted.

But Cody didn't seem to believe her.

She slid off the swing and stretched toward the sky. "Fine. Let me know when you're ready. Until then, keep a close eye on Mia."

Blair took a step, then another, but not a third as the world twisted around her, tilting and contracting. She halted, blinked, and then collapsed to the ground.

It was Mia, hesitating to knock on Derek's door. She took a deep breath. She reached out. She knocked. Once. Twice. A deep voice, Derek's deep voice, told her it was okay to enter, and she did, leaning her back against the door.

"You okay?" Derek asked.

Mia nodded. "I think I need your help going to school tomorrow."

Derek put his phone down. "What do you mean?"

"I just…every time I try to leave the house, I'm so scared. But you can help with that. You can take away my fear."

"You want me to manipulate your emotions?"

"Just to calm me down. So I can see that I'm safe."

Derek hesitated. "What if it only makes things worse?"

"It can't be worse than it is now."

There was a moment of silence, and then he nodded. "Okay. I can help you out tomorrow."

Mia smiled and turned to exit the room. But once she had her hand on the doorknob, she paused. "I know you were listening to my conversation with Lior."

"Sorry."

"It's fine. Just know that I'm glad Blair and Cody made you stay in Colorado. I know you hate them for it, but I'm glad you were home and safe and away from Jae."

Derek rubbed a hand through his hair. "Yeah. I guess."

"Are you ever going to forgive them?"

"Maybe."

"You should."

"I guess."

"I'm going to go," Mia said. "I'll see you tomorrow morning."

"Yeah."

And then she left, and the vision faded into darkness.

Like most of Blair's visions recently, she didn't know what to make of the private conversation she'd witnessed. In fact, she wasn't even sure it had even happened. All she knew was, when she woke up with Cody crouched next to her, her powers were growing stronger. Because though the twins hadn't been speaking in English, she'd understood them. Because she'd seen everything in clear detail. Derek's room. The panic in Mia's eyes. The concern in Derek's. All of those things wouldn't have been as clear in the past.

Her heart pounded. Her forehead burned.

And she wondered, as Cody helped her to her feet, asking what she'd seen, if there was some reason she'd witnessed that moment, and if her desperation to make sure Mia was all right had led her to have the vision she wished she'd never seen.

Part Two

Chapter Seven

Mia clenched the straps of her backpack, staring up at the school building.

Derek stood next to her, hand on her shoulder. Every time her breath tightened, every time her mind raced, a warmth spread through her shoulder and down into her gut, calming her. Training her mind to see the outside world as safe.

She hadn't made it the second day of school. Or the third. Or the fourth. But today was Friday, and she was determined to do it. Each day she'd made it a little further down the road.

"You can go home," Derek said to her. The same thing he'd said to her every day, when he knew her fear was spiking. "I've heard homeschooling is actually pretty cool. It'd make Mā happy."

Mia rolled her eyes and Derek chuckled.

"I'd rather not spend all day learning from Mā," Mia said. "She's...."

"Yeah, I know."

Derek removed his hand from her shoulder, and the fear trickled back in. But Mia swallowed it down. She could do this. She could go to school. She didn't need Derek to keep her calm. She was perfectly capable of doing this on her own.

"Okay." Mia stepped forward. There were only a few students here this early. She'd decided to come as soon as the school opened so that she could acclimate to it without everyone bombarding her. Derek had promised to keep people away, but he couldn't be with her all day. They had no classes together.

Of course, there was also Blair and Cody. Mia had talked to them a little over the week. Trying to make things normal again. But they were being so gentle with her, and she didn't want people to treat her like she was fragile anymore. She had to prove to them all that she was going to be fine.

Before she knew it, she'd entered school, Derek by her side, but not manipulating her emotions. The fear was still there. It was a growing devil deep in her gut waiting to destroy her from the inside. But she ignored it.

Jae wasn't here. Lior was. Derek was. Cody was. Blair was. The rest of the Iravata were on the outskirts, protecting her. Blair had said that Mrs. Arbour had placed a protection spell on Mia.

Jae couldn't harm her. He couldn't take her again.

School was exactly as Mia remembered it. It hadn't changed. The winding brick halls. The windows hanging high enough that no one could break through them. The lockers lining the walls. Mia breathed in the musty smell of the first floor. She could do this.

"Want me to stay with you until the bell rings?" Derek asked.

Mia shook her head. "No. I'm okay. I'll text you if something goes wrong."

"Sounds good." He clapped a hand on her shoulder, but this time there was no warmth. He didn't push away the fear. It was just a gesture of comfort. "You got this."

Mia nodded and Derek headed off toward his locker. Mia, however, remained still for a moment longer, taking in the place she'd spent so much of her time here in Willow Creek. First middle school, and then high school. The same building. Different teachers, but the same vibe. The same students.

She smiled. This place was safe. She was safe here.

The moment Cody felt Mia's mist in the building, he relaxed. She was here.

She was going to be okay.

He sought her out. He knew where she was. At her locker, probably contemplating whether or not this was a good idea. And he didn't blame her. The longer she'd been gone from school, the more the rumors had spread. Mia was, after all, one of the most popular girls in school. People had even braved coming up to Cody to ask him if she was doing all right. To give her a card from the basketball team.

Cody hadn't known how to handle the attention. He'd told them to give it to Derek and then took off, not used to people talking to him.

In retrospect, that probably hadn't helped with the rumors, but now Mia was back. Already, the mood of the school was different. The mists were lighter. The gossip was less about Mia. Things were finally going back to normal.

"Mia." He hadn't seen her since school had started, but she looked different. Her mist was a little brighter. Her cheeks a little fuller. The dark circles under her eyes were gone, though the dark side of Cody's brain reminded him that she could cover those up with makeup.

Still, she looked better. Healthier. Like a week of hiding away had been good for her.

She smiled at him and his stomach fluttered. He loved when she smiled.

"Hey," she said. "I made it."

"I can see that."

He stopped next to her locker, wracking his brain for a normal conversation starter. He didn't want to ask her how she was doing, in part because he was afraid he would scare her away. But he also didn't want her to feel like he was focusing on her absence. He also didn't want to bring up all of the gossip.

This was supposed to be a normal day. The only text Cody had gotten from Derek in the past couple of weeks was him, very sternly, telling both Cody and Blair that they needed to be careful with Mia. Not to mess this up for her. Cody didn't want to mess this up for her.

"Derek had to help me here," Mia said. "I feel kinda pathetic."

"You don't need to," Cody said too quickly. "We're all here to help."

Her smile turned sad, mist shifting. Cody wanted to take back his words, but they were already out there.

"I know," she said, voice quiet, "but it's weird, you know? I didn't used to need help."

"Yeah." He didn't know what to say. He was glad she was opening up. And glad that she seemed to be somewhat back to normal. But at the same time, it was weird. He kept thinking back to Derek's text. How Mia needed to be protected. And he wished that he knew how to act.

"I'm excited to be here, though," she said.

"That's good."

"Yeah." She closed her locker and smiled at him. "Thank you for all your help."

Cody opened his mouth to respond, to tell her that it was no problem. That he was happy to help her. That he would always help her, when a different voice called out her name. Cody froze. It was a voice he recognized. It was hard not to recognize every student in their class. But it was also a voice he hadn't heard in a long time.

Chad Rogers. The most stereotypical masculine male of all time. Cody had done his best to avoid Chad all of these years, as Chad was one of the kids who had bullied Cody when they were in elementary school.

A shudder ran up his spine. Mia's eyes widened and she looked at the young man standing next to them.

With bright blue eyes, sandy blond hair, and a six-foot well-built frame, Chad was easily one of the most popular boys in school. And, much to Cody's frustration, he had always had a thing for Mia. Even when she'd first moved here. Even when all the girls picked on her. He was kind to her throughout it all. They weren't that close, but he'd stayed on the periphery.

"Chad." Mia glanced at Cody. "Hi."

"Hey," he said. His eyes lingered on Cody. "Velt, how're you doing?"

Cody swallowed thickly. Chad had this thing about never calling guys by their first name. "I'm good."

"That's good." He focused on Mia again. "Heard you had a crazy summer. Sorry you had to go through all of that."

Mia's mist shifted. Chad's, a deep forest green, like the main school color, was perfectly still, but through it Cody could sense a hint of hesitation. Nothing strong. Just enough that Cody wondered what the hell he was doing there.

"I…it's…." Mia glanced at Cody, clearly looking for someone to save her, but Cody's words were caught in the back of his throat.

He *wanted* to tell Chad to leave Mia alone and not to harass her on her first day back.

He *wanted* to explain that it wasn't okay to just bring up someone's trauma like that.

He *really wanted* to tell Chad off in any way, shape, or form, but he couldn't.

"Oh." Chad glanced between the two of them. "Sorry. Wasn't thinking. Of course you don't want to talk about it. I just wanted to come say hi. See how you were doing. But I can head off." He jerked a thumb over his shoulder, turning to leave.

Cody had to hold back his smile.

"Wait," Mia said. "You don't have to go. We have first period together, right?"

Cody blinked. Mia was telling him to wait? She wasn't normally like that. His eyes lingered on her, trying to figure out what was going on in her head. And when they made eye contact, when she shrugged, he was even more confused.

"Yeah." Chad grinned, mist brightening. "Wanna walk together? You wanna come with, Velt?"

Cody knew Mia's schedule like the back of his hand, and he knew that their classes were on the other side of school from one another. Even though he wanted, more than anything, to join the two of them and act like the most annoying third wheel in the world, he couldn't.

"My class is near here," he regretfully admitted.

"Shame." Chad seemed sincere enough, but Cody knew he wasn't really upset about being alone with Mia. "Well, guess we should go. You coming, Mia?"

She nodded. Then faced Cody. "I'll see you at lunch?"

Lunch. Cody was used to only seeing Mia at lunch during the school day. His fists clenched as he recalled when they'd been alone. Holding her while she slept in Shubishi's house. That night with a bottle of wine. He didn't want to just see her at lunch.

"Yeah," he said. "See you at lunch."

He watched them walk away. He watched Mia's face remain gentle and calm. He watched Chad look at Mia with soft eyes.

And more than ever, he wished he could go back in time to when things were normal.

Mia wasn't sure why Chad Rogers walked to class with her. She liked him well enough. He'd always been kind to her, even if he was the one who had made Cody's life miserable for years. He seemed to have grown out of that, at least. He was even kind to Cody now, though Cody wanted nothing to do with him.

It was odd, but also kind of relieving that Mia was talking to someone *other* than the people who knew about Jae.

"You went to Asia this summer, right?" Chad asked. "I heard Kaylee and some other girls talking about it. How was that?"

Asia. Mia had completely forgotten about her trip with her aunt. "It was fun. I went all over with my aunt. We had a great time." And then it'd all fallen apart.

"That's good." Chad laughed. "I've always wanted to travel, you know? But it's hard with Mom as a school teacher. We're hoping I get a good scholarship so I can play at a good university and make something of myself."

Mia recalled when Chad's dad had left Willow Creek. It had been a big deal. All the adults had gossiped about it. Why he'd left. If he would ever talk to or see his son again. Mia's parents had tried to stay out of the gossip, having experienced quite a bit of it themselves, but even they'd stayed up talking about what would happen if the two of them ever got divorced.

"I hope you get a scholarship," Mia said with a smile. "When are the scouts coming?"

"Not till later in the season. But I'm ready for them." He grinned at her. "What about you? You gonna continue with basketball in college?"

Mia hadn't really thought about it. Well, she had before everything fell to hell last year, but now it was getting even more important. She had to start applying to colleges soon if she wanted to get admitted early and figure out where she was going.

A pang of panic struck her throat. Her breath caught and she clenched her fist.

Leaving.

Where she was going.

University.

She wasn't going to be safe there. She wasn't going to be safe outside of Willow Creek.

A warmth filled the outlines of her body and the panic subdued. She breathed out. Derek. He'd gotten stronger.

"You okay?" Chad asked.

She realized she'd stopped in the middle of the hall. She told herself she was being stupid. She could still apply to college. She could still be safe in other places. The Iravata would follow her wherever she went. She couldn't be afraid to live her life just because Jae thought she was some kind of angel.

"I'm fine," Mia said. "Just thinking."

"Can I ask about what?"

Mia shook her head. There was too much personal stuff going on in her head, and while she liked Chad well enough, she didn't trust him to open up about any of this. Not about her kidnapping. Not about the magic. Not about her fears.

"Okay." He smiled as the two minute bell rang. "We should get going."

"Yeah."

She fell into step beside him and the two headed to class in silence. Then, as they reached the room, Chad stopped her with a light touch to her arm.

"Hey, I have a question for you," he said. Mia tensed, ready for questions about what had happened to her this summer, but instead he asked, "Are you and Velt…a thing?"

Her and Cody?

She shook her head, even with the memories of how gentle he'd been with her at Shubishi's house. Even with the memories of kissing him, and him kissing her, back when she was drunk on wine. How warm and safe he was. How kind he'd always been, and how honest he'd always been with her.

"Really?" Chad ran a hand through his hair. "That's…I mean… cool. That's cool."

Mia's brow furrowed, but the bell rang before she could ask him why he'd been interested in her relationship status.

"See you later," Chad said, cheeks slightly pink. He rushed into the classroom, and Mia followed at a much slower pace, more than confused.

But she found she didn't have time to be confused about Chad's question, because the moment she entered the classroom, she was bombarded with people asking her *other* questions about her life. Even the teacher couldn't calm them down, and Mia spent her morning the way she'd hoped she wouldn't have to: fielding questions from fellow students without a buffer.

The entire time, she glanced at Chad across the room. He didn't ask her questions about what had happened. He didn't try and bombard her. He'd kept his distance and for some reason, Mia really, *really*, liked that.

By the time lunch rolled around, Mia wanted to go home and sleep. She wanted to escape her friends and teammates. She wanted to run away from school and not have to deal with this anymore.

Instead, she made her way through the halls, keeping her head down and hood up so no one knew it was her, and ended up at the cafeteria without being stopped once. She hurried to her normal table and sat at it, shaking from exhaustion. Needing food. Desperate for conversation that wasn't about her.

In her mind, things would be normal. In her mind, her friends and her brother would come sit with her, and they would complain about school. She could sit there, quietly, and listen to Cody and Blair bicker about whatever topic they were on about that day. She could ignore the rest of the school and have her safety net back.

But that's not what happened. She sat down, joined a few moments later by a downcast Cody. And then a few moments later by a quiet Blair. And then not at all by her brother.

She glanced between her two friends, and then around the cafeteria, eventually spotting Derek sitting at another table.

Were they all still that angry at each other?

"Um–" Mia said.

"Hey," Blair interrupted. "It's been a while. How're you doing?"

How was she doing? She looked at Cody, desperate for him to say something, but he focused on his books instead.

"I…uh…why isn't Derek sitting with us?" Mia decided to just go for it. Ask the question she knew neither Cody nor Blair wanted to answer.

Blair scowled. "He's being a baby."

"Oh." Mia wasn't used to Blair being angry at Derek. "Um, okay."

"So, how are you doing? How's your first day back?" Blair asked as if Mia hadn't just brought up her ex-boyfriend.

Mia shrugged. "Everyone has questions."

"I bet." Blair pulled out her lunch and threw a sandwich at Cody. He caught it, dropping his book in the process. He didn't say anything, but Mia stared between the two of them.

Blair was pissed at Derek, but she and Cody were friends now? Mia knew that they'd had some sort of breakthrough on their road trip, but she'd figured it wouldn't last long.

So much had changed.

"So…the two of you are…friends?" Mia asked, not sure how she would feel about the answer?

"Yup." Blair took a bite of her food and grinned at Mia. "Weird, isn't it?"

"A little."

"Better than the opposite, right?"

Mia wasn't so sure about that. Yes, all of their friendship, she'd hoped that Cody and Blair would eventually get along, but for it to happen while Derek was on the outside…it felt wrong. It felt like Cody and Blair had replaced Derek with each other, and Mia didn't like that. What she wanted was for things to go back to normal. For her family to get along.

"Maybe we should invite Derek to sit with us–" Mia started to say, but Blair waved her off.

"Don't bother. If he wants to pout, let him."

Cody looked up from his book. "Agreed. He's been an ass this past week. There's no reason to try and get him to change his mind about us now."

Still, it felt wrong not having Derek with them. It reminded her of last year, when he was sick, when he'd gotten suspended.

She didn't fight Cody and Blair on it. She knew that Derek would walk her home from school. She could talk to him then. Try and get him to stop being ridiculous and at least sit with them at lunch. He didn't need to take Blair back, and he didn't need to forgive Cody, but he at least needed to act like an adult.

Or maybe Mia just wanted to feel secure.

She couldn't tell the difference.

Regardless, she settled into her seat and got out her food so she could eat and be ready for another half day of people bombarding her with questions.

Chapter Eight

For the next two weeks, Blair plotted. She researched. She stayed in her room after school. She didn't try to hang out with Mia. She focused on figuring out the best way to obtain the artifacts from their respective clans.

She'd decided she'd get the necklace last. Even though she'd told Cody it would be easy to get back, she knew that wasn't true. When she lay down to sleep at night, she sometimes dreamed of the necklace. It was back in the cave, calling to her. But magic and elders guarded the cave. They didn't want her getting it. She couldn't get there by herself.

Cody hadn't given her an answer on whether or not he'd help. She waited, patiently, for him to decide, but he was driving her insane taking his sweet time.

So, she plotted. She plotted out what she wanted to do versus what she could do realistically. In all honesty, she needed Cody. She needed his intelligence and his powers to help her get in and get out without being noticed. If Jae could disappear Mia, then Cody could disappear Blair. Right?

But if Cody didn't want to help her, she would figure out another way. Which is why she pored over her brother's textbooks. Which is why she stayed up late at night with a flashlight and the piece of paper she'd stolen from Jae, translating as much as she could with the help of the internet and her own knowledge.

So far, she'd come up with a frustrating amount of nothing.

Which is why, two weeks after Mia returned to school, Blair found herself in the park, needing fresh air and perspective. The Friday afternoon sun beat down on her neck but she didn't care. She breathed in the thin mountain air and closed her eyes, trying her best to think of a way to do this. To get the artifacts and get out of there.

But she couldn't think of anything.

And before she realized what was going on, the air shifted. The mood around her darkened and a familiar sensation appeared in her gut. Her eyes snapped open as her grandmother appear out of thin air. Blair's eyes narrowed.

She hopped off the swing and tensed, prepared for anything her grandmother might do to her.

But Enola Demini didn't say anything. She didn't do anything but stare at Blair from the outskirts of the playground.

Blair took a chance. "What do you want?"

"To talk," Enola said.

Blair snorted. "You've had years to talk."

Enola took a step forward, and then hesitated, staring at the ground. Blair didn't understand why she didn't come forward.

Enola looked up from the ground. "Blair, I know you hate me, but we need to talk about your plan."

Blair gritted her teeth. "Don't know what you're talking about."

"Let's not pretend like your accusations were false, Blair." Enola tried to step forward again, and Blair realized she couldn't. It wasn't that she didn't want to, it's that something was stopping her.

Blair was stopping her. It took her a moment to recognize

her magic draining. The shimmer of blue surrounding the park. Somehow, subconsciously, Blair had created a shield around herself.

She grinned.

"Oh, so you're admitting it?" Blair asked.

Enola scowled. "Yes. I'm admitting it. I'm a seer. I have been my entire life and I've hidden it from everyone. Will you talk to me now?"

"No," Blair snapped. She turned her back to her grandmother. "Go away. I want nothing to do with you."

"We're family, Blair."

"Family doesn't keep secrets from one another."

"You kept the fact that you're a seer secret from me."

Blair flinched. That was to protect Blair from her grandmother. Mostly so she wouldn't have this conversation. Blair didn't want to be the new clan leader. She wanted to go to college. She wanted to travel the world. She wanted to live *her* life, not the life that her grandmother designed for her.

"Go away," Blair repeated. "I don't want to talk to you."

"You're going to make the clan leaders very angry with you if you try to steal their artifacts."

"They won't know what hit them," Blair said. "Unless you're planning on making my life difficult."

"I don't want to make your life difficult, Blair. Despite what you think, I love you and I care about your wellbeing."

Blair's fists clenched. "Just go, okay? I don't want to hear it."

The feeling in Blair's gut, the one that connected her to her grandmother, disappeared. She breathed out, relieved to be free of her grandmother's meddling, but also concerned. If Enola knew what she was up to....

She was going to have to be a lot more secretive if she wanted to pull this off. She was going to have to find a way to keep Enola from *seeing* her, but without her grandmother's help, without her knowledge, she had no way of doing that.

She cursed and kicked up sand before storming home, hands in her pockets.

It was all a mess. She needed to do *something*, but couldn't figure out what that something was. She had no idea how to help Mia. She couldn't get Derek to forgive her. She couldn't even get Cody to help her with her plan.

But she had to figure out a way to get this done, even if it meant hurting herself. Because being useful was more important than anything else. She couldn't save Mia from Jae, but she could do everything in her power to make sure that Mia was safe. Mia had come to school for over a week. A good sign. But that might not last. Nothing was certain. But if she could find all the artifacts—if she could make it so Jae could never get near Mia again....

That would be enough.

Cody felt them before he saw them. Colorful mists drifting into his dim room. They tugged at his attention. He tried to focus on his book. Week two of school and already he was drowning in homework. If he didn't have so much reading, he might not have minded it all, but he did. So, he ignored the mists trying to draw his attention away from normalcy.

He managed this for maybe five minutes before the mists got distracting. Living where he did, near the edge of town, he didn't have many neighbors or guests who got close enough to the house. His father was still at work, even this late at night. Not that either of the mists belonged to him.

Still, he recognized them. He knew who the mists belonged to. He'd only met them once, but they were like him. Their mists were different. They had a tinge to them. One that he knew from Steven and Kathleen.

He put his book down and hurried over to the window. With sly fingers, he peeled back the curtains to peek outside.

Two figures stood in his front yard, staring up at the house. In the dim light, Cody could see their mouths moving. Having a conversation. Why had they come here? What did they want from him? Were they here on orders from Jae?

He let the curtain fall closed and hurried to the front door, throwing on a coat and his shoes in a hurry. He wanted to ignore them. To go back to his book and pretend like they weren't there. But if he ignored them, would they seek out Mia? The last thing she needed was for two of Jae's people to show up.

The moment he was out the front door, tensed and ready for some kind of altercation, Heba and Parker looked at him with wide eyes.

Both parties froze for a moment, staring at each other. Cody examined them, watching their mists entwine with one another. Mocking him. Reminding him that even if he was trying to live a normal life, he never could. Because he was like them. The only difference was that he had a father who loved him and took care of him. It easily could have ended up that he was thrown out of the house, or lived through even worse abuse. He could be homeless. He could be angry at the world for every shitty thing he'd been through.

According to Mia, from what she'd learned staying in Jae's mansion, most Natara children didn't have parents who loved them. That's why they'd ended up with Jae. He'd taken them in when no one else would.

Would that have happened to Cody?

"Cody," Heba said, a grin spreading across her face. "What's wrong? Not happy to see us?"

"Not really," Cody said.

Heba's grin faded, and she glanced at Parker, who shrugged.

"We saved your life," she said. "Surely you'd at least be okay with us visiting you briefly."

Cody scowled. "Look, I have nothing against you, but for all I know, you're working with Jae again. He did save *your* lives."

Parker shook his head. "No. Look, we didn't come here to fight. We also didn't come here to harass Mia. She's struggling to get back to normal, and we don't want to add to that."

Cody hesitated. "How do you know she's been struggling?"

Heba and Parker exchanged another look before Parker said, "Can we come in? We have a lot to tell you and not much time. Plus it's not really safe out here."

Cody didn't want to let them in, but he also wanted to know if they were spying on Mia. Mrs. Arbour and the Iravata had done their best to protect Mia from Jae, but if Jae was using his lackeys to get information on her, they had a problem.

He stepped aside and gestured for them to enter. His father wouldn't be home anytime soon, so it was safe for them to spend some time here. But they didn't have forever.

Once the three of them were settled inside, sitting at the kitchen table, Cody with his arms crossed and Heba and Parker looking like they wanted something to drink, Cody demanded, "What are you doing here?"

Heba cleared her throat. "Well, you see...a lot has happened since I burned down the mansion."

Cody snorted. He couldn't help it. She'd said it with such a simple tone. No remorse or regret. He had to imagine that having the gift of fire would make life a little different, but at the same time, he couldn't understand it. She'd destroyed her home. Her life. The place where she'd felt most safe.

Heba scowled, but continued. "Anyway, everyone survived. A

few minor burns. But we didn't know what to do with the little ones after that. They didn't have homes and it's dangerous for them to go into the system. Us older kids know how to control our powers, but they don't. And the mages don't want us, so it's not like we could beg them for help."

"So, what did you do?" Cody asked, guilt gnawing at his stomach. It was because of them, because of Mia, that they'd lost their home.

"We found some of the older Natara who had left Jae's mansion. We'd thought something bad happened to them, but turns out they were just living their lives. When they'd left, Jae disowned them, but they agreed to let the kids stay with them while us older kids either went into the system, or started living on the streets."

Cody's eyes flickered around his house. It wasn't always a good time, living here, but it was better than being homeless.

"The kids are safe?" Cody asked. He hated Jae. He didn't hate the kids.

"They're safe enough."

Safe enough…was that going to be okay with Mia? She'd seemed to have bonded with some of them. Maybe he just wouldn't tell her about this conversation at all. That seemed like the safest bet.

"And what do you want with me?" Cody asked.

Heba and Parker exchanged yet another glance. Parker cleared his throat. "Well…we were hoping you would help us out."

"Why would I do that?"

"Because you're one of us," Parker said. "Because you know that we did nothing wrong. Because Jae has gone AWOL and none of us know what to do. Because you're his brother and the kids would trust that you can protect them."

"Protect them?" Cody laughed. "I'm a high school student who barely has enough money to eat lunch every day. What do you expect me to do?"

Heba shrugged. "No idea, but we could use some help."

"I'm the reason their home is destroyed," Cody said. "They're not going to trust me, even if I am related to Jae. Besides, it's not like Jae and I grew up together. Plus I hate him. Plus—"

"Okay, okay," Parker said, holding up his hands. "I get it. You don't want to help us."

"It's not that I don't want to." Cody wasn't sure what he wanted to do. "It's more like I don't know *how* I *could*. I'm barely surviving myself, plus I have Mia to worry about. And school."

"We get it," Heba snapped. "You have your own life. Ours isn't important to you."

"I barely know you." Cody was done defending himself. "We've met exactly once before this, and no one asked you to help us save Mia. You betrayed Jae all on your own. I don't owe you anything, and you don't owe me anything."

He stood. "Look, I wish I could help. I really do. None of the kids deserve what happened to them. But I can't. So just leave, all right?"

A pang of guilt ran through him. He was like them. He wasn't like Mia. Or Derek. Or Blair. He had more in common with the two Natara sitting in front of him than he ever had with anyone else. Being an outsider. Not understanding his powers. Not knowing where he came from or why he was always so different.

But he couldn't help them.

"Can we at least keep in touch?" Heba asked. "Even if there's nothing you can do now, there might be something you can do later. Or something we can do for you."

Cody hesitated. They had helped him. Would keeping in touch be a bad idea? They'd said that they weren't in touch with Jae, and that he'd abandoned them. Maybe that meant he could trust them.

At least a little bit.

"I'll stay in touch with you," Cody said. "But don't talk to Mia, and don't ask about her."

"Deal." Parker's voice was filled with sorrow. "We won't talk to her."

"Okay." Cody breathed out, and then sat down again. This wasn't that big of a secret, right? He was allowed to have a life outside of Mia, Blair, and Derek. They all had people they spoke to outside of the group. Still, he felt guilty doing this. All he was doing was keeping in touch with them. He wasn't helping them. He wasn't giving them anything.

Heba pulled out a notebook and Cody gave her his number, warning her that he couldn't talk much but he would make time when he could. And then, as quickly as they had appeared, they were gone, walking out of his house and down the street.

He remained in the doorway, staring after them, while he tried his best to keep his stomach from turning. If anything, he'd figured out that people could still keep an eye on Mia. If Heba and Parker could watch over her from far away, what was stopping Jae from doing the same? What was keeping Mia safe?

He pulled out his phone and stared at the lock screen for a moment before pulling up Blair's name.

<<Let's do it>>

<<Seriously?>>

<<Seriously>>

<<Let's talk tomorrow>>

Cody put his phone away and stared at the darkening sky. Stars littered the violet atmosphere, blinking down at him with their approval. He didn't know how things were going to go. He knew that Blair was about to get him in a heap of trouble. But he didn't care anymore. Because Blair was right.

This was for Mia.

He would do anything to make sure she was all right.

Chapter Nine

Mia knew Blair and Cody were planning something. The two of them kept disappearing, leaving her to sit with Derek and his friends at lunch. This pleased Derek, but worried Mia. She wanted Cody and Blair to at least tell her what they were plotting, but the two of them were tight lipped about it.

For a week, Mia tried her best to live her normal life. She went to school, she did her homework, she'd even participated in tryouts for basketball. All the while, Chad kept meeting her at her locker in the morning, coming up with conversations. Mia wasn't sure what his endgame was, but it was nice to talk to someone who wasn't part of the magical world. So, she didn't question his attention too much. Instead, she relished in it. It made her feel safe.

But there was something tugging at the back of her mind. The magical world, as much as she wanted to run from it, was always there. And with Cody and Blair hiding something, she knew that something had changed. Blair had had a vision. Cody had felt a mist. Jae's, maybe?

At night, she dreamed of Jae. Of the way he'd been so gentle with her, up until he'd lost his temper. How he'd insisted that he would protect her, up until he tried to kill her. The very idea that Cody and Blair had discovered something about him only made the nightmares worse, but she refused to ask Derek for help. She didn't want him to know that she was having nightmares. Instead she sucked it up. She went to school. She did her homework. She went to practice.

Until one day, it got to be too much. When she realized how lonely she was.

She pulled out her phone, ignoring the joke Derek had made, and sent a text to Blair asking what was going on with her and Cody. Blair never responded, which only frustrated Mia more. And through the rest of the day, she fumed about it. Her frustration with the magical situation turned to anger. Even when she had class with Blair, they didn't talk. Mia tried, but Blair told her she wanted to pay attention. Blair never wanted to pay attention in class.

What were they hiding from her? How could she make them understand that this wasn't okay? They'd been there before. They'd promised each other that they wouldn't keep secrets. But there the two of them were.

Frustrated, she couldn't focus during practice. Frustrated, she made an idiot of herself in front of her new coach. Frustrated, she excused herself early, saying that she wasn't feeling well. Her teammates all questioned her, but she ignored them. Because she knew that she had to find her friends.

The warm fall air greeted her when she left the school. She breathed it in, closing her eyes and trying to focus. Where were Cody and Blair? Where had they been running off to all week?

She tried to call them, but both calls went to voicemail. Frustrated, she shoved her phone in her pocket and decided to check downtown. But the longer she wandered around, the more she realized that they were nowhere to be found.

Exhausted, she went to their favorite place to get tea and ordered something cold to drink. It might not have been the best idea, and she knew that there were so many other places the two of them might be, but she was about ready to give up. Maybe she could ask Derek to track them down, though she doubted he would.

Groaning, she rested her head on the table, hand chilled from holding her iced tea. This was all ridiculous. All of—

A chill ran down her spine. Her eyes shot open and her head jerked up. Instinct told her to run. Fear kept her nailed to her chair.

Sitting across from her with a blank expression was the man she'd been having nightmares about for weeks. The man who had kidnapped her. Held her against her will. And then thrown her off a roof because she hadn't given him what he'd wanted.

Jae.

He looked the same. The same dark skin and hair. The same blue eyes. The same button up t-shirt and slacks. The same blank expression on his face, making it impossible to read him.

At first she thought she was hallucinating. She stared at him, palms sweating, and he stared at her. But why would she be hallucinating? It had never happened before. Even last year, that had all been Kathleen messing with her head. And Kathleen was dead.

Jae. Jae was….

Mia wanted to stand, but her legs turned to jelly. He was there. Staring at her.

"You don't need to be afraid," Jae said in a soft voice.

Mia's voice caught in her throat. She could scream. The people walking past her would react if she told them that this was the man who had taken her. The police would show up. Jae would get away, but they would know that she wasn't safe.

"I'm not really here," Jae said. He reached out and touched Mia's hand. She jerked it back, only to realize that he hadn't touched her. His hand had gone through hers. "I'm projecting myself here so we can speak."

Mia said nothing. She couldn't say anything.

"You took something of mine," Jae continued. "My journals. I'd like them back."

When Mia didn't say anything, Jae sighed. "Mia, I promise, you don't have to be afraid of me. I know I messed up when I took you. I'm not going to touch you again. Not that I can. This was the only way I could get in touch with you."

Not afraid of him? He'd made a mistake? Rage replaced Mia's fear. He spoke like he'd borrowed a book and never returned it, not like he hadn't traumatized her and made everything in her life so much worse.

"Please." Mia's voice was barely above a whisper. "Leave me alone."

Jae tilted his head. "I'm not sure I can do that. I need to protect you. But I can do that from afar. The thing I'm concerned about right now is my journals. They're very personal. I would like them back."

Mia shook her head. "I don't have them."

"You gave them to the Iravata?" His tone turned harsh and she flinched, recalling the way he'd shoved her against the wall. He took a deep breath. "I understand why you did that, but I wish you hadn't."

"I don't care what you wish." Her hand shook as she reached for her phone.

"That's harsh, Mia." Jae stood. "I know that I went about things the wrong way, but we have a connection. You cannot deny that."

She absolutely could. He was delusional.

She snatched her phone off the table and called Blair's number, but Jae was gone, leaving her alone with her iced tea and a pounding heart.

This time, Blair answered.

"Aren't you supposed to be at practice?" Blair asked.

Mia stared at the place where Jae had been only moments before. He'd shown up. A projection of himself. At least some of the protection was working. He hadn't been able to take her. He said he wouldn't do that again. Could she trust him? He'd said some delusional things, but he'd never actually lied to her before.

"Mia?"

"Whatever you and Cody are doing, I want in," Mia said.

The other line went silent for a moment. "It's not a good idea."

"I don't care." She needed to do something. To test Jae's words. "Tell me, what are you two planning?"

There were low voices. An argument? And then Blair came back on.

"We're going to France."

"France?" Perfect. Mia needed to leave Willow Creek. Mrs. Arbour's spell didn't work outside of Willow Creek. "Why are you going to France?"

"It's a long story."

Mia stood, leaving her tea behind, and said, "Take me through it."

Derek sat on his bed, staring at his math textbook, contemplating whether or not any of this was going to be useful to him in the near future. Or the far future. Or any future at all. He really didn't need to know calculus to be successful in life. Especially not if he wanted to follow his parents' footsteps into anthropology.

Still, he read through the passages explaining how to calculate the derivative of a slope, mind wandering all over the place. Mia was suspiciously late. Derek checked his phone to see if she'd texted him, but she hadn't. He sent her a text warning her to be home soon or face the wrath of their mother.

She didn't respond.

He sighed and tossed his phone to the side, staring at it still. Waiting for it to light up. It never did, so he returned to his textbook, but it was too late. He was unfocused and uncertain. So, he closed his textbook and lay down on his bed, staring at the ceiling.

He tried to put on a good face for Mia every day. Make her feel more comfortable. Safer. But really, he was dying slowly inside. Every day, when he sat with the idiots he called his other friends, he missed his normal table. He missed sitting next to Blair. He missed getting tea with Cody. He missed having his sister not stuck between her friends and her brother.

He longed to go back to last year. During the brief moment when Mia was doing better and they had no secrets. When he and Blair were a couple. When he and Cody were best friends.

He missed those days. He missed the summer when he could spend as much time with Blair as he'd wanted. Hell, he even missed being with his family in Beijing, as much as having to constantly hide his powers was more annoying than not.

Nothing was right, now.

His eyes slipped closed. He'd been so good about staying awake that he hadn't realized that it could hit him again. The exhaustion. The need to take a nap at all times and wherever he sat. School, doing homework, hanging with friends…it had taken over his life for a few months, but he'd thought he'd gotten over it.

He tried to fight the exhaustion, but it wormed its way through all of his being.

And before he knew it, he was back in his dreams. Not on the edge of the Mekong River, but in the darkness with the pond. With the pedestal. Where he'd set the lotus free.

He stared around him. He stared at his hands. *His* hands. Not

Niran's. His own. That was different. He looked around, trying to understand why he was here. Had the lotus called him back? He'd freed her. He'd freed Shion, the aster, and set off everything that had happened the past year.

But the lotus was nowhere. It was him, alone, standing on a glowing pool of deep black liquid.

Or…he started out alone.

Niran stepped out of the shadows without much warning. Derek barely had time to be surprised. Niran stood in front of him, matching his stance, wearing the same t-shirt and jeans as Derek.

Derek tilted his head.

Niran tilted his head.

Derek reached out with one hand.

Niran reached out and their fingers touched.

"What are you doing here?" Derek asked, voice echoing through the emptiness.

Niran smiled. "I want to talk to you."

Derek didn't like that. He didn't like how confident Niran sounded. The man always sounded confident in Derek's head, but there was something different, something eerie, about looking him in the eye—green on green—and hearing his voice.

"About what?" Derek asked.

"About us."

"What about us?"

Niran pulled his hand away, and Derek found that his hand moved without his permission, falling to his side. Just like Niran's. They were matched. Two halves of a coin. When one side flipped, so must the other.

"You're my reincarnation."

"I know."

"Has anyone explained what that means?"

Derek rolled his eyes. Niran did the same. "Of course. It means

I have all of your magic. I have your soul. Not that difficult of a concept."

Niran shook his head. Derek did the same. "It's more than that, Déming. It's more than just the two of us being one and the same. It's a cycle. A cycle that never gets broken. One that always ends the same way."

Derek's brow furrowed. Niran's did the same. "What are you talking about?"

"Us, Déming."

"What about us?"

"I was twenty-three when I died," Niran said, waving a hand. "So was the man I was reincarnated from."

Ice took over Derek's face. "What?"

Niran grinned. "You think you're special? You're not. I was a reincarnation, just like you are."

Derek couldn't respond.

"The Iravata don't know this about me," Niran said. He circled Derek. Derek circled him. Two sides. The same coin. A reflection in the mirror. "I'm actually pretty certain they don't know much about reincarnation. It's not fun, Derek. It's a curse. The man we are reincarnated from was cursed. His soul is to forever wander the world. Never settling. Always running from Death."

Derek stopped them from circling, holding out a hand. His palm ended up flat against Niran's. "Hang on. You're telling me that I'm cursed?"

"Not you. Your soul."

"Same thing."

Niran let out a boisterous laugh. "If only that were true."

Derek grumbled. "What does that mean?"

They shrugged. "It's something you'll have to figure out on your own, just like I had to. But let me tell you something, Derek. The longer you live, the more I will want to come alive. The stronger I'll become. You're already seeing it. By the time you're twenty-three, you'll have two choices: die or be consumed."

Derek's eyes widened. "Is that why you killed yourself?" The story had made it sound like Niran had killed himself to protect the Iravata from Enya.

Niran shrugged. "Maybe. Maybe it's the reason Shion thinks it is. Maybe it was for a reason you'll never truly understand. Regardless, fear your purpose in life. Fear your existence. Because it won't be yours forever."

Derek's eyes snapped open, breath heavy. He sat up, head pounding. The image of Niran mirroring his every move stuck in his mind, a heavy reminder of the conversation. He looked around him, trying to understand what he'd just heard. Trying to comprehend what it could mean.

He reached for his phone, needing to tell someone about the dream, only to discover it was three in the morning. He'd been out for hours. He'd missed dinner. He'd missed Mia coming home.

Any heat left in his face drained completely and he lay back down, staring at the ceiling once more.

He would either die or be consumed. But that didn't make sense. It seemed so unlikely....

Derek groaned and slipped out of bed. The house was silent, and he snuck through it, heading to Mia's room. He knew that she was sleeping, but he....

No. Wait. Derek stopped outside of her door and felt out for her emotions. To see if she was having another nightmare, only to find there was nothing. Quietly, he opened the door. There was a lump in her bed. But there were no emotions. And when he pulled back the blankets, he found that it wasn't his sister, but a pile of pillows in the shape of a missing body.

Chapter Ten

Cody had been clear when he'd said this was a bad idea. Very clear. Beyond clear. He'd written it in big letters. He'd shouted it from the rooftops. He'd argued with Blair and Mia for almost an hour, trying to convince them that this was an absolutely terrible idea.

And yet, there they were. At the park in the middle of the night with a spell book Blair had produced from nowhere, and some weird artifacts that she'd collected from her mom's house.

"These will help us get to Paris," she'd explained. But she hadn't explained how. And she hadn't explained why she thought it was a good idea for Mia to come with them.

It was supposed to just be the two of them. Blair to distract the headmistress while Cody snuck in and stole the staff. He'd been practicing his abilities. For the past week, he'd worked his ass off trying to figure out how to hide his mist, and therefore himself, from the outside world. He'd managed it, but he couldn't hold it for long. Ten minutes, tops. Nothing like Jae. But Jae had years more experience, so Cody didn't hold it against himself. Much.

The three of them stood around a large black stone with their names engraved on it: Mia's in Chinese, Blair's in the language of Sangota, and Cody's in English. Their native languages, according to Blair.

"What exactly is this going to do?" Cody asked. He nudged the stone with his foot, which caused Blair to smack him in the arm.

"Stop that," she snapped. "This will anchor us here. Even if the three of us are separated, all we have to do is say, "Return home" in our native language and we'll arrive at the stone."

"Even me?" Mia asked.

"Even you." Blair flipped through the book. "The anchor has my magic in it. As long as your true name is written on the stone, then it'll be good."

Cody wasn't sure about this. It wasn't a good idea, having Mia with them, and he absolutely wasn't certain about this ritual. He may have had mage blood in him somewhere, but all of his training had been about using his own magic. Not using artifacts to channel the magic through something else. But Blair knew what she was doing. Otherwise she wouldn't sound so confident.

Right?

"Are you sure you want to come?" Cody asked Mia. His anxiety spiked, leaving his brain a whirring mess of confusion and questions. "It might be safest for you to stay here. Who knows what'll happen. What if…what if Jae…."

"I can't live my life in fear," Mia said. Her mist shifted. Was she keeping something from them? What had changed? Or was she just recovering?

Cody grimaced. "I know that, but–"

"I'm here," Mia said. "Let's go."

He didn't like this. He didn't like any of this. A niggling feeling in the back of his mind told him that everything was going to go wrong. That all of their planning was going to go to shit. It was almost seven in the morning in France, which meant that school was going to start soon for the kids there. There would be a ton of students, many of whom would know Blair and might find it suspicious that she was there. Cody wasn't certain that he could keep his mist hidden long enough to do what he needed to do.

"Does your mom know we're doing this?" Cody asked, suddenly thinking of how supportive Mrs. Arbour had been of them over the past year. Staying out, but also paying attention.

"Nope!" Blair reached out and grabbed Cody and Mia's hands.

Cody's eyes widened, but he didn't have time to say anything before the stone glowed a light blue. The same color as Blair's mist. Mia, who hadn't seen much magic, stared at the stone with wide eyes, and then at Blair.

Blair seemingly ignored her, muttering under her breath. The stone glowed brighter, and for a second Cody wondered what would happen if anyone saw them. But he didn't have time to think too much about it because his body contorted and twisted. He hated it.

It wasn't like when the Iravata transported them somewhere. That wasn't the most comfortable thing ever either, but at least it was smooth. This felt like his insides were being torn apart.

And then it was over. All around him, the world spun, but his insides went back to normal. And when his vision cleared, he had to blink a few times to adjust to the light of the French morning. He glanced around him, confuddled by the surroundings. They were no longer in a park. Instead they were in a courtyard with flowing fountains and blooming flowers. The green grass spread out around the three of them.

Cody stared around them, taking in the atmosphere. The electricity. It was obvious to anyone who stepped foot in this place that it was filled with magic. Beautiful, amazing, wonderful magic.

"Okay," Blair said, "we don't have much time. Cody, you know where to go. Mia, you'll come with me. We're about to attract a lot of attention."

Cody shook his head. He didn't have time to be in awe of this magical world. The school Blair had rejected in favor of a normal high school. They had to get in and out before the headmistress realized what was going on.

"Right," he said. "I'll see you back at the park."

"Excellent." Blair gave him a thumbs up, while Mia continued to stare around them, completely dazed.

It's going to be okay, he told himself. *Everything is going to be okay.*

He only wished, as he took off in the direction of the school, that he actually believed it.

Mia whipped her head around, trying to wrap her mind around the fact that they'd traveled across half the world in a few seconds. Well, it wasn't really that they'd traveled quickly. She was used to that. What she wasn't used to was Blair doing it. What had she missed over the past few weeks? How ingrained was magic into her life now? How much did she want that to change?

"Come on." Blair grabbed Mia's arm and dragged her in the opposite direction of Cody.

They'd explained the plan to her, but she wasn't sure exactly how well thought out it was. They were relying on a skill that Cody didn't have much control over and hoping that no one figured out why they were there. Mia wasn't certain that her being here was a good idea, but she needed to test out Jae's claim.

So far, so good.

She let Blair drag her through the magnificent front lawn and toward the towering building that stretched up into the sky: a castle mixed with a chapel. Its beautiful spires reached high above the ground, intimidating her. She couldn't imagine going to a school like this. Something so large. So grand. So old. At least, it looked old.

"Tell me more about this school," Mia said.

"There's not much to tell. It's a school for kids with magic. Mostly kids from the Mauvais Clan, but my brothers and I got special permission since Mom isn't part of a clan."

"Oh." They were underneath the large arches now. "What about kids from other clans?"

Blair shrugged. "I mean, in Sangota all the kids learn magic in normal school. I think other clans do something similar, but I've never looked into it. Maybe they have a big school like this too, but that would be complicated since a lot of the sectors hate each other."

"They do?"

"Yeah. You think regular world politics don't affect the mage world?"

"I mean, I've never really thought about it before."

"Right." Blair peeked around a corner, and then gestured for Mia to follow her into the building. "I dunno. Maybe I can ask Mom about it. She'd know."

"She knows a lot."

"Yeah. She was supposed to take over for my grandmother before she married my dad."

"Oh." Mia had heard something about that before Blair had disappeared with Cody to go confront her clan. Something about the necklace choosing the next leader. Something about Blair's mom having worn it for a few years.

Mia hadn't pried.

"Do you think she'd be okay with what we're doing?" Mia asked.

"Oh, absolutely not." Blair and Mia continued to sneak through the dusty halls of the empty school. "She may not be part of a clan anymore, but she's really particular about clan politics. She doesn't want to do anything to jeopardize my brothers' magical education. Which is why when I got expelled...."

"Yeah, what's the story there?" Mia asked. When they first entered high school, Blair said that her mom was making her go to this fancy boarding school in France, of all places. Then, less than a week later she was back at Willow Creek High, saying that it wasn't for her.

Blair shrugged. "I just...did a thing."

"What thing?"

"Blair Arbour?"

Both Blair and Mia flinched. A sharp French accent pierced through the air.

"Shit."

Blair spun around, a false smile slipping onto her face. "M-M-Madame Gaudreault."

Mia didn't quite understand what happened next. Derek had always been the one good with languages, not her. So when Blair started speaking in what sounded like very, very rough French—though really, how could Mia tell—Mia could only stare between her and the tall, hawk like woman staring down at them.

Madame Gaudreault responded to Blair with much smoother, much more fluent French, leaving Mia completely lost. Then, Madame Gaudreault sighed and flicked a hand.

"You've always been terrible with your French," the woman said in perfect English. Barely an accent.

Blair made a face, only for it to disappear when Madame Gaudreault glared at her.

"And who is this?" Madame Gaudreault asked, gesturing at Mia.

"Um...." Mia didn't know what Blair's plan was. They were supposed to get caught, though not for another ten minutes or so, to give Cody some time to get the staff and get home. But the original plan hadn't had Mia. So what was Blair going to say?

"This is Mia," Blair said. "My friend from school. She was curious about where my brother's go to school, so I figured I'd... show...her."

Mia could have sworn that Blair was better at lying than this. Mia knew how quickly she could spin a tale. Whoever this Madame Gaudreault was, she was clearly upsetting Blair.

"You brought a non-mage to the school?" Madame Gaudreault said. Her arms crossed and she glared at Blair, ignoring Mia.

Mia took a step back. This was not going well.

"Well, yes." Blair smiled innocently, but it wasn't working.

Madame Gaudreault scowled. "You have always had a disrespect for rules, Ms. Arbour, but this has gone too far. For one thing, you're not allowed on these premises, but to also tell a non-mage about our school—"

"I didn't tell her about magic. Someone else did that." Blair sounded desperate. Mia had no idea what to say.

Madame Gaudreault did not look amused.

"If you don't leave, I will have to report you."

"Report me to who?" Blair asked. "I'm not part of the Mauvais Clan."

"I'm sure we can work something out with Clan Leader Demini."

"Ooh, yeah, about that." Blair backed away from the tall woman, and the heat drained from Mia's face. "See, I kinda disowned my grandmother and left my clan. Which means she doesn't scare me either."

Madame Gaudreault's face colored. "You did what?"

"Yeah, you did what?"

It was a new voice. One that Mia recognized, but only barely. All three women spun around to find Blair's middle brothers, Kyro and Luka, standing with bags hanging open.

"Mr. and Mr. Arbour, what are you doing out of class?" Madame Gaudreault asked.

The older one, Kyro, responded in French, which caused Blair to snap something in French, which left Mia even more confused than ever.

"Can we speak in English, please?" she asked in a quiet voice, not unaware of how hypocritical she sounded.

Blair shot her a look, amusement in her eyes, before she focused on her brothers again. "It's a long story."

"You disowned Grandma?" Kyro asked.

"We can do that?" Luka asked.

"No," Blair snapped at the same time as Madame Gaudreault.

This was getting out of hand. Mia wasn't sure what Blair's brothers knew about the situation with their family, as they'd already been in France when Mia had been kidnapped, but this was not the time to try and explain it.

Please, Cody, hurry up.

Cody had two jobs: get the staff and alert Blair that he had the staff. He was failing miserably at both.

Blair had said that when she'd gone to school here for that one week, they'd shown her and her fellow classmates the staff as a way to introduce the power of mages. It was kept in a large room in the center of the school, supposedly to keep the weather a temperate sixty-five degrees all year round. Which, of course, made Cody feel guilty about taking it. He didn't want to cause problems for the students or teachers. Sure, Blair talked about it like it was the home of the devil, but that didn't mean it actually was. Besides, Blair was known to exaggerate. And even beyond that, there was the problem of someone noticing that the staff would be missing *immediately*.

Cody shook his head. This wasn't the time to think about that kind of stuff. He had two jobs. Two freaking jobs, and he couldn't seem to get either one of them completed. He was inside the school, yes, trying hard not to pay attention to the vastness of the place, nor the incredibly strong mists behind every door he passed, but he couldn't find the center of the school. Blair had explained it to him pretty clearly: go inside the back door, take two lefts, and then one right at the end of a large hall.

Well, the problem was he couldn't find the large hall.

They must have come when the students were either getting ready for class, or were already in class, because so far Cody hadn't seen a single person—though he had seen all of their souls. It was a good thing, but also made him uncomfortable. Did they know that he and Blair had planned this? Blair had mentioned that her grandmother knew what they were planning. Had she gone behind their back and warned the school? Cody knew little about Enola Demini, but he wouldn't put it past her to do something like that.

Stop thinking like that.

He pushed his anxiety aside, like he had been doing since they'd arrived. Sure, he was in another country for the first time in his life, and sure they were about to piss off a very powerful mage clan, but he had to do it. He had to find a way to protect Mia, and once they had all the artifacts, then none of the other mage clans could hurt them.

Jae couldn't hurt her anymore.

With a deep breath, he turned right at the end of a hall and, to his surprise, managed to find the large room.

Blair hadn't been kidding when she'd said it was going to be large. He stopped, jaw dropping, and stared up at the vaulted ceiling, one that could rival the pictures he'd seen of the Sistine Chapel. Hand-painted scenes of what Cody guessed were of mage history littered the ceiling and the walls, telling a story that Cody didn't understand. The room was filled with books upon books, just like Blair had said.

And just like Blair had said, sitting in the middle of the room, untouched and floating without glass surrounding it, was a simple wooden staff.

If Cody hadn't been able to sense magic, he would have guessed it was just a regular walking stick. It didn't look particularly powerful or unique. In fact, if it had been thrown into a pile of sticks one might find in a tourist trap in Estes Park, he doubted that anyone without power would be able to pick it out.

But Cody could sense magic. And this staff exuded it. The magic spread across the room, deadening Cody's arms and legs. Slowing his heart. Tightening his chest.

He placed a hand over his breastbone and breathed in as deeply as he could. This staff…it was just like Blair's necklace. It was just like the knife. It was unique. It was special. It held the power of the mage clans.

The power of the weather.

Cody stepped forward before realizing that they probably had cameras or spells to protect the staff. He couldn't just take it. Not like he was.

Taking another deep breath, he closed his eyes and focused on his mist. For all of his life, he'd never been able to see it, but ever since he'd saved Mia, he knew that it was a deep purple. He pictured it in his mind. The purple. The swirling deepness that held his soul, his magic, his life.

And then he imagined it vanishing. The color disappearing into a clear wind of nothingness. An icy chill ran down his arms. He recognized the feeling, having practiced this with Blair. He couldn't hold the ice over his body forever, or he would start shivering. And then the shivering would get worse. And then he'd lose control of it.

Ten minutes.

He had ten minutes to figure out how to get the staff.

He opened his eyes and stepped forward, aware of how invisible he was to the rest of the world. Unless someone could also see mists, they wouldn't be able to spot him. They'd see nothing. Because he'd made himself into nothing. He'd turned his soul invisible, and therefore himself invisible.

For ten minutes.

When he was close to the staff, he reached out, only to find it repelled him. He frowned and thought. The knife was an artifact, and it'd done something similar to Kathleen and Steven that night in the woods. No matter how hard they'd tried, they couldn't touch the knife without Mia's permission. It had protected her when Kathleen had tried to take her.

"Shit."

Blair had been so convinced that they could just take the staff, and Cody had a feeling it was because Blair had been able to so easily take the necklace. She hadn't thought about this part: they couldn't get the staff, or any of the other artifacts, unless the person who wielded it gave it to them.

That was when Cody heard the voices. Two hushed voices. Panic struck his slow heart and he spun around to find somewhere to hide, completely forgetting that he was invisible.

He spotted a couple of chairs in the corner and dashed behind them as the footsteps of two people entered the grand hall.

Cody couldn't see them from his hiding spot, but he could hear them talking plain as day.

He just hoped they couldn't hear him breathing heavily.

"Are the Gray Spirits really back?" It was a man with a British accent.

"They are," a woman with a French accent replied. Her voice was thick and heavy, while his a light flutter.

"What are we going to do?" the man asked.

"We have to protect ourselves," the woman said.

"How?"

"The same way our ancestors did." There was a brief pause, and then, "We have the power to control the weather, and our *personne spécial* is growing stronger every day. When she's able to use her powers to help us...."

"She's a teenager. It'll be years before I'd feel comfortable with her helping us fight the Gray Spirits."

Cody's chest tightened more than before. The mage clans were aware of the Iravata's return? They still thought that the Iravata were evil. That they were out to destroy the clans and their powers. Cody knew that the fear didn't come from nowhere, but he also knew that the mage clans didn't know everything. They didn't know about Enya.

"I know," the woman continued. "She's young, but we'll do what we can to protect her."

"And her father?"

"He's aware of what's going on."

"What of the children that the Gray Spirits have taken under their wing?"

The woman snorted. "They're probably lost to us. Who are they again?"

Cody's face drained of color.

"Mia and Derek Sòng."

No.

"Cody Velt."

They couldn't know....

"And Blair Arbour."

How did they know? How could they know about what was going on? Were they spying on them? Or maybe something else was going on?

"Blair Arbour?" The woman hummed. "We have her brothers here as students."

"Is that so?"

"Yes. She was expelled years ago for trying to break the staff. She has been banned from these grounds."

Cody's eyes widened. Blair had *not* told him that. She'd mentioned that they wouldn't be happy she was back, but that would only cause more distractions for them. She had not mentioned anything about *trying to destroy a freaking artifact.*

"Madame Duquette!"

Another voice, this time a young man, rushed into the room, bouncing off the ceilings and walls.

Cody chanced a peek over the chair at the three people standing in front of the staff. The British man was bald, wearing a suit and staring between the young man, a student perhaps, and Madame Duquette. She was as Cody had imagined: a short heavyset woman wearing a skirt and blouse, with her arms clasped behind her back.

"What is it?" Madame Duquette snapped.

"It's…we have a situation," the young man said.

Madame Duquette scowled. "Spill it, Mr. Thomas."

"It's…it's Blair Arbour."

Shit!

Cody knew then that this was a bust. He wasn't going to get the staff, and Blair and Mia's time had run out. He wasn't sure what had happened while he was gone, but he wasn't about to risk getting Mia in any sort of trouble because of him and Blair.

He grabbed the bracelet on his wrist, the one that Blair had given him as the signal, and focused his magic into it.

"Do you feel something?" the British man asked.

Shiiiit.

The bracelet warmed to his touch and he figured that was enough as Madame Duquette's footsteps neared him.

"Return home," he whispered, still focusing his magic on the bracelet. The world around him twisted, and then everything went black.

Blair's wrist warmed as Madame Gaudreault went on and on about how Blair was not allowed on the premises, and to bring a non-mage, and to disown her grandmother, and this and that. She had no interest in the lecture. All of this was for show, anyway. Just a distraction to help buy Cody some time.

She hoped that Madame Duquette, the headmistress of the school, wouldn't get involved in either of the situations, but she had a feeling Madame Duquette would, if only because she was a nosy bitch who had no respect for boundaries.

That was part of the reason Blair had decided to get expelled in the first place. Madame Duquette wanted to know everything about her pupils. Every tiny little thing. Blair had no idea how her brothers could stand the scrutiny of this place.

Speaking of, she hadn't expected to see her brothers. She didn't know why they'd slipped out of their classes. They'd said something about feeling Blair's magic and wanting to know why she was there, but that felt like an excuse for them to be out of class. They were good students, but they were not…the best.

Like Blair.

Blair glanced down at her wrist. It was too early for Cody to send the signal, but there it was.

"When Madame Duquette finds out you're here…," Madame Gaudreault said.

Next to Blair, Mia shook, probably with fear, and Blair knew that it was time to go. Cody must have the staff, and they didn't want to be here when the rest of the adults found out that the staff was gone.

"Madame Duquette doesn't scare me," Blair said, rolling her eyes.

She grabbed Mia's arm. "Sorry for dropping in. But we gotta *return home*." She said the words in the language of Sangota, gripping Mia so that the magic would work through her too. The world around them twisted, and Mia gasped.

The last thing Blair saw before the world went black was her brothers whispering to one another, and Madame Gaudreault's burning red face.

The darkness encased her for a long moment before the world twisted again and the playground returned. Blair's wrist still burned, her hand wrapped around Mia's arm, as day became night and Blair's energy diminished.

The first thing she saw was the playground.

The second thing she saw was Cody without the staff.

And the third thing she saw was her ex-boyfriend standing with crossed arms and narrowed eyes, staring at the three of them with fury expressed on every inch of his body.

Chapter Eleven

It wasn't difficult to track Mia. At first, Derek thought he was going crazy, feeling Mia's emotions without her in the house. But the longer he focused on them, the more he realized that she was in town.

Except she also wasn't in town.

He made sure his parents were still asleep before he slipped out of the house to follow the trail of Mia's emotions. They were faint, and before long, they mixed with the emotions of two other people Derek knew very well: Cody and Blair.

With each step toward the park, his anger grew. He knew that the three of them had planned something terrible. He should have seen it. The way that Cody and Blair kept disappearing during lunch. He'd thought that they were sending Mia to him because he could help her. He'd thought, probably stupidly, that Blair and Cody were pulling away from Mia to protect her.

No. They were just planning something. And they'd dragged Mia into it.

When he'd arrived at the park, the first thing he'd noticed was the magic. The second thing he'd noticed was the stone. The third thing he'd noticed was that Cody and Mia's names were written on the stone. Mia's was in Chinese. And there was a third name, probably Blair's, written in the language he'd come to recognize as the one Blair spoke with her mother. The language of Sangota.

He didn't know what the stone was for, but he wasn't about to try and move it. Whatever it was, it was anchoring Mia's emotions to the park, and that meant that Derek needed to protect it. He felt around, reaching out with his magic, to see if Blair had been smart enough to put a protection spell on the park.

She had not, and so he did. He focused, thinking of creating a barrier that would keep out anyone. Even those with magic. His own magic flowed out of his body and surrounded the park, creating a golden film around him and the playground. Then he leaned against a pole and he waited.

He waited.

And waited.

Until the stone glowed. He practiced what he would say to Blair and Cody. Maybe what he would say to Mia, if this had somehow been her idea.

Cody came first. He appeared out of nowhere, stumbling, holding his head with his hand. On his wrist was a bracelet, similar to the one that Blair had given Mia last year. Derek stared at it, wondering why there was so much of Cody's magic in it, and then he wondered why Cody was alone.

What the hell is going on?

It took a moment for Cody to regain his composure, but once he had, he looked around until his eyes landed on Derek. Derek raised a brow, and Cody's face paled.

"Derek," Cody said.

"Evening," Derek replied. "Where the fuck is my sister?"

He didn't care about anything else. But the fact that Mia wasn't there with Cody could only mean something bad.

"She's…." Cody gestured at the stone, which glowed again.

Cody stumbled away from it, but Derek stood there with crossed arms and stared at it, waiting for it to spit out his sister and Blair. Mia so he could take her home. Blair so that he could scream at her.

Just as Cody had, Blair and Mia appeared in the park, both looking like they were about to puke. Blair, breathing heavily, let go of Mia's arm and looked around the park. She opened her mouth to say something until she and Derek made eye contact.

Then, like with Cody, the color drained from her face.

"Shit," she muttered.

"Yeah, shit is right," Derek snapped. He pushed past Blair and grabbed Mia's hand, pulling her away from the stone and from her friends. "Where were you?"

"None of your business," Blair said. She had a tone to her voice that Derek used to find attractive, but in this moment, it infuriated him.

"None of my…." He threw his head back and laughed.

Mia touched his arm. "I'm fine, Derek. It was my idea to go with."

"Go with where?" he asked.

Mia glanced over his shoulder, then back at him, bowing her head. "We went to France."

France? What the hell were they doing in France? He rounded on Cody and Blair, who stared at each other.

"What the hell?" he asked.

"Like I said, it's none of your business," Blair snapped. "Take Mia home if you want, but what we're doing is none of your business."

"None of my business my ass." Derek hadn't felt this angry in months. Not since the night he'd almost died. "You two get my sister involved when she's so terrified she barely leaves the house and–"

"Derek!" It was Mia yelling at him. He fell silent and turned to her, trying to gauge her emotions. They were fluctuating between fear, confusion, and anger of her own. "I told you, it was my idea to go. They didn't want me to come, but I needed to test it out. I needed to see that I was safe to leave Willow Creek."

"Why?" Derek asked.

"Because…." The fear overtook all the rest of her emotions. "Because I need to make sure that the Iravata are there to protect me. I can't stay in Willow Creek forever. Just like I can't stay at home forever. But look." She held out her arms. "I'm fine. I'm not injured. Nothing bad happened to me. Blair and Cody were just trying to find a way to keep me safe. That's all."

Keep her safe? They'd dragged her across the world to France. That wasn't keeping her safe.

He faced Blair again. She crossed her arms, holding up her chin in the most defensive way she possibly could. Rage boiled in Derek's gut, but he pushed it down. Mia *was* safe. She wasn't injured and she hadn't been kidnapped again. It was possible that this had been a good thing.

Still, he was pissed. "Next time you want to disappear in the middle of the night," he hissed at Blair, "you tell me. *Especially* if you're taking my sister with you."

Blair snorted. "Nope. You've made it perfectly clear that you want nothing to do with me or Cody. You can't just demand that we do you a favor. If Mia doesn't want to tell you, then that's between the two of you."

Her defiance blistered his skin and he rubbed his chilled arm.

"Why are you even here?" Cody asked. "Mia said you were passed out."

Suddenly, the whole reason that he'd sought Mia out came back to him. The reason that he'd gone into her room in the first place hadn't been to check on her. It'd been because of his dream. The way that Niran had smirked at him in his reflection.

"That's none of *your* business," Derek snapped at Cody.

But it was clear that Cody wasn't going to let it drop. "Something happened, didn't it?"

"No."

"Tell me what happened, and I'll tell you why we went to France."

"Cody!" Blair exclaimed.

But Cody waved her off and stepped toward Derek. "I know you want to know our plan. So tell me what happened to you, and I'll tell you what happened to me."

He could have said no, but he knew how stubborn both Blair and Cody were. If Derek was going to get out of them why they'd dragged Mia to France, he was going to have to give them something.

He scowled. "Fine. I had a dream."

"You always have dreams," Blair said.

He glared at her. "I had a dream where I spoke to Niran. Like, really spoke to him."

The three other teens were quiet, and Derek gauged their emotions. The three of them mixed together, a combination of fear and curiosity. He couldn't tell who was feeling what the most, since they were all expelling powerful emotions, but he did know that they weren't going to want to hear what he had to say.

Still, he told them about the dream. Everything that Niran had said about him and his role as a reincarnation. How he wasn't the first. How Niran was a reincarnation. Something about his twenty-third year. Something about the Iravata not knowing the real reason Niran killed himself.

And when he was done, they stood there in stunned silence.

He didn't have to look at Mia to know that she was the most afraid of them all. Her fear had jolted out against his skin like knives. He wanted to quell it, to make her feel better about the fact that he might die or become Niran in six years, but he couldn't.

Because that's not what he'd promised.

"So…." Blair's face contorted.

"No questions," Derek interrupted. "I told you why I was awake, now it's your turn to tell me what you were doing in France."

Blair cursed Cody. Blair would talk to him about it later, when it was just the two of them and she could really grill him about why he *didn't have the staff.*

"Cody?" Derek asked, crossing his arms.

Cody glanced at Blair, who ignored him, staring instead at Mia. If Mia hadn't come, then none of this would be happening. Derek never would have known about their jaunt to France. She never would have known about his situation.

Her heart tore at the idea of losing him. Yes, she was angry with him. Yes, she wanted to scream at him until she was hoarse, but she still loved him.

There's no saying Niran is right.

Blair didn't know how Derek's dreams worked. They weren't like her own prophetic ones. For all she knew, Niran was trying to scare Derek. But why would he want to scare Derek? He lived through Derek. He only existed if Derek existed. He didn't want Derek to die.

Anything is possible when it comes to magic.

Blair hated that statement. It was useful with her magical abilities, but it also meant that it was possible the Niran in Derek's reflection was telling the truth, and who knew where that would lead?

"I have something else to tell you," Cody said, nudging Blair in the arm. She glanced at him. Derek looked absolutely pissed. Cody must have finished talking about their plans.

"Huh?" she asked.

"The clans know about us," Cody said. "I was going to tell you later, but the reason I didn't get the staff is because it's protected. Just like Derek's knife and your necklace. No one can touch it without permission from the wielder."

Blair smacked her forehead. Of course. She hadn't thought of that. Cody hadn't thought of that. Blair had no idea who the wielder was. She didn't know how it worked with the Mauvais Clan. All she did know was that they'd have to figure that out before they tried again.

"Also," Cody continued. "I overheard some woman named Madame Duquette and some British guy talking about *us*. They know that the Iravata have taken us under their wing and I don't think they're happy about it."

That was a major problem, one Blair hadn't foreseen. She didn't know why she hadn't foreseen it. She was a freaking seer. She should have known that this was going to happen, but her visions weren't cooperating with her.

Scowling, she wrung her hands together. "Right. I'll talk to my mom."

Her gaze landed on Mia who was oddly quiet.

"What does it even mean that they know about us?" Derek asked. "Who cares? They aren't going to hurt a group of children, are they?"

Blair wouldn't put it past them. "Maybe."

"Then stop your stupid plan," Derek said.

"No!"

Blair half expected herself to shout that, but Cody got it out before she could. She stared at him as next to her, Derek doubled over, hand on his chest. Without thinking, she went to his side and placed a hand on his back. But he batted her hand away and stumbled toward Mia, breath heavy.

Blair glanced at Cody, who was paler than normal.

"No," he said. "They can still see Mia. We can't let Jae have any access to her. If we get the artifacts, then we can protect her. The mage clans won't be able to do anything to us. We *have* to do this."

Now Blair was confused. Cody never had told her why he'd agreed to help her, and she'd been too happy to question him about it.

"Cody, what's going on?" Blair asked.

Cody's eyes flickered to Mia. "I...I...two of Jae's Natara came to visit me."

No.

Tonight was too much. Blair didn't want to hear more. She wanted to crawl into bed and let the exhaustion from using so much magic take over her. She wasn't used to transporting herself, much less two people. And then to anchor them here. It was all exhausting. So exhausting that she wasn't sure she wanted to use magic again for a month.

But she had to know. She had to know what the hell Cody had been keeping from her. Why he'd decided to go with her to France. To help her out.

In a quiet voice, Mia said, "Who?"

It was the only sound, and Blair wasn't sure she wanted to look at Mia. No one, as far as Blair knew, had brought up Jae's name around Mia in a long time, and she'd wanted to keep it that way.

But Cody had.

And it was too late to take it back.

"Heba and Parker," Cody said.

"They're...." Derek's brow furrowed.

"Dangerous," Blair finished for him. "You sent them away, right?"

Cody hesitated, and anger took over Blair's heart. "Seriously? You know they're working for Jae, right? They're here to spy on

Mia."

"They're good people," Mia said, voice a lot stronger than before. "They aren't working with Jae. They helped us escape."

Blair didn't believe Mia.

"I'm serious," Mia said. "I know it seems weird, but…what did they want?"

Cody hesitated, looking at the ground before he said, "They wanted me to help them with the kids."

Mia's breath was sharp. Blair watched her, trying to gauge how she was feeling, but she wasn't an empath. She had no idea, so she let Derek take over comforting Mia. He placed a hand on her shoulder and whispered something to her in Mandarin. She looked to the ground.

"It's late," Mia said. "Maybe we should all head home and regroup in the morning. We can talk more then."

But Blair knew that the peace they'd brokered with Derek wouldn't last until tomorrow. Tomorrow, they'd go back to the way things were. Derek ignoring Blair and Cody. Mia trying her best not to get in the middle of it all. They wouldn't talk tomorrow. Yet, she also wanted to head home. She wanted to crawl into bed and sleep.

Derek and Cody also seemed to agree with Mia. Or maybe they just didn't want to talk anymore. Maybe they didn't want to get into another fight. Because they both nodded and Derek wrapped an arm around Mia's shoulders, leading her away from the park without another word.

The glistening gold barrier around them shattered when Derek stepped through it, and Blair knew that they'd have to hurry home. She glanced at Cody before snatching the rock. Their names were no longer etched into the black side. The spell was complete. They hadn't gotten what they wanted, but they'd learned quite a bit.

"I'm sorry," Cody muttered.

"For what?"

"Not getting the staff."

Blair shrugged. "Not your fault. I didn't think it through. We'll know better for the next one."

Cody cocked his head. "We're going through with the next one?"

"Of course. I don't care what Mia says. We can't have anyone being able to track her. Not Jae, not Heba and Parker, not even the Iravata." She was going to protect her friend, no matter what it took. No matter what the consequences were. Blair was safe from the world of magic. Mia was not.

"So, what are we going to do about? We can't get the artifacts without permission."

Blair hesitated, then said in a low voice, "Guess we're going to have to get permission."

"How?"

She shrugged. "I'll figure that out. Let's get home before our parents realize we're gone."

"Okay." Cody walked away, waving at her over his shoulder, but she waited for a moment, stumbling to the swings where she sat, staring at the stone.

She hadn't asked Esther if she could take the stone. She hadn't told her mom about this at all. Even though her grandmother knew. Even though Esther had made Blair promise she'd keep her in the loop if anything came up. She couldn't involve her mother in this.

"I see it didn't go as planned."

Blair didn't even flinch. Her grandmother's magic filled the park and connected to Blair's.

"No," Blair said. "But that's none of your business."

Enola scoffed. "I tried to warn you. It's not going to be easy to get the artifacts."

Blair didn't need a lecture right now. "Why can't you just leave me alone?"

"Because you're my granddaughter. And you're the only other

seer I've ever met. We have a connection, whether you like it or not."

Blair scowled. "There are always two seers. You're telling me that you didn't know the other one?"

Enola shook her head. "I knew he existed. I could always feel him in the back of my mind. But he'd left the clan long before I was born. As far as I know, no one knew about his powers."

Blair didn't want to ask why her grandmother had kept it a secret all of those years. And yet she did. She asked in a low voice why. Why. Why. Why.

"Because I didn't want the clan to control me," Enola whispered as if sensing Blair's question.

"And yet you want to control me?"

"I want to protect you."

"Then protect me," Blair said, jumping off the swing. "But let me live my own life. You never let Mom do that, and you're not letting me do it either."

"Is that what Esther told you?" Enola asked.

Blair didn't respond.

"There's a lot you don't know. But never forget this: I care about you and I care about my daughter."

Blair was too exhausted to argue. Instead she walked away, holding the stone close to her heart as her grandmother disappeared into the night. She didn't turn around. She didn't stare at the swings. She kept walking home, wondering why her grandmother was opening up to her now. Why she hadn't just opened up her entire life. Why she'd never been this gentle with Blair before.

She kept walking and realized that she'd used up so much of her energy, put Cody and Mia at risk, and upset Derek even more, and all of it was for nothing. No staff, no protection, and possibly a clan that knew something was up.

The night consumed her as she walked, and as it consumed her, it put out the fire in her stomach that had let her take the risk tonight.

Next time she'd have to be better. More research. More information. She wouldn't mess up next time.

But first, she needed to sleep.

Chapter Twelve

Mia hadn't managed to focus all weekend, which meant that for the first time in a long time, she hadn't completed her homework. But she didn't care. There was so much going on in her personal life that school seemed far away.

Ever since the trip to France, Derek had been cold to her. All weekend, he'd stayed in his room, not speaking to her or their parents. Intira had asked Mia what was going on with him, but Mia honestly didn't know. Was he that angry that she hadn't told him about going to France? Was he that pissed at Blair and Cody that he couldn't move past them agreeing to take Mia? It wasn't like she'd given them much choice.

Not that she could explain that to Derek. He'd led her home and they'd snuck in, careful not to wake their parents, but the entire time, he wouldn't let her speak. She'd tried to explain to him that she'd needed to go, but he wouldn't listen to her.

And honestly, she was tired of it. She didn't need to be protected like this. Especially not by him.

So, she let him pout. He'd come around eventually, she told

herself. And when he did, they could talk about it. They could talk about the trip to France, and more about the dream he'd had.

Mia didn't believe it was true. Derek was a reincarnation, yes, but that didn't mean anything. She knew so little about reincarnations. She knew nothing about what would happen to her brother when he was the same age Niran had been when the priest had died.

Mia shuddered. She didn't want to lose her brother. Even if he annoyed the crap out of her, he was still her twin. Her other half. She just hoped he'd get over whatever was going on so she could have her life back the way it was.

Or, at least most of the way it was.

But that was why she hadn't done her homework. She'd been too busy focusing on Derek's pouting, and then on Blair and Cody being secretive again. They hadn't gotten the staff, but honestly Mia didn't care. She didn't need them to find all the artifacts. She'd wanted to prove that Jae was telling the truth. That the moment she'd left the safety of Willow Creek, he wouldn't come after her.

And he hadn't. Granted, she hadn't been away for long. Ten minutes, maybe, but ten minutes was all it had taken.

And now she was back in Willow Creek. Safe. Unharmed. Feeling just a little more confident in herself as she put her afternoon books into her locker.

"Hey."

She jumped at the sound of Chad's voice. He walked toward her, one hand in a pocket, the other raised and waving at her. He'd texted her over the weekend, but she'd been too distracted to think of a reply. Another person she'd let down.

"Hi." She closed her locker door and leaned against it. The other students rushed past, having grown bored with Mia's summer drama. They no longer bugged her about it. No one asked questions. They didn't tiptoe around her the way that Derek, Blair, and Cody did.

It was nice.

"Busy weekend?" he asked with a light smile.

"Yeah. Sorry." She didn't know how to talk to Chad. He was nice. He'd always been nice to her. But at the same time, he had no idea what she was going through. She couldn't tell him about her life. Not really. She couldn't explain that she'd taken a quick trip to freaking France to try and steal a magical artifact. She couldn't explain that her brother was having weird dreams about the man he used to be three thousand years ago. She couldn't explain that she kept looking over her shoulder in case Jae's apparition appeared again.

But Chad didn't seem to care that she was vague with all of her responses. Chad only seemed to want to be around her. To be near her.

The last person who had done that had been, well, Steven.

"It's totally fine," Chad said. "I was just...well I had a question for you."

Mia tilted her head.

Chad ran a hand through his hair and looked at the ground, kicking it. "Well...I was just...wondering if maybe you'd want to go out with me this weekend."

Mia blinked back her surprise. Any other year, she might have seen this coming. She might have realized he was interested in her *that* way. But she'd been so focused on the magical world that she hadn't stopped to think that maybe someone might want her.

Flashbacks of Steven entered her mind. Memories of studying with him. Of getting to know him. Of kissing him. Of him kissing her. That night she spent at his house, back when she'd thought that her brother and friends were pushing her away. Back in the days when she'd first learned magic was real and the knife had haunted her.

None of those things had been real, though. His feelings for her had been fake. A trick to get her to come with him to stay with Jae.

And her feelings for him…well, she didn't exactly know.

She'd known Chad for seven years. He'd always been around. She'd met his mom. Knew stories about his absent father. It wasn't the same as Steven. He wasn't part of the magical world—and Mia had asked Blair if there was anyone else with magic in town, just to be certain. He was just a normal boy.

A normal boy asking her out.

Her face heated and she bowed her head, letting her hair cover her face. This was the most normal thing that had happened to her in a year, and she didn't know how to react.

"I…."

"You don't have to," Chad said quickly. She glanced up at him, only to find him looking anywhere but her. "I mean, you're just so great and…but we're friends and…it's fine."

Mia watched him for a moment. Probably only a few seconds, but it felt like longer. She wasn't used to Chad being a bumbling, confused mess. He was taking a huge chance, and she found she wanted to say yes. Not because she had feelings for him, but because he was so normal. He was someone to talk to. Someone who didn't know about the magic. Who wasn't using her. Who wasn't treating her like a fragile doll because he knew the truth.

It was tempting.

"I'll have to talk to my parents," Mia admitted. "I'm kind of grounded."

Chad's gaze connected with hers and his eyes widened. "You're grounded? What for?"

For not telling them about the magic world. "Just for some family drama that happened this summer when I was in China."

The lie hurt, but she kept at it, wanting to preserve his innocence. Keep him out of what was really going on. There was no point, she'd decided, in dragging him into her mess. But that didn't mean she couldn't go out with him. And who knew? Maybe her parents would be okay with her having some normalcy in her life.

"I'll text you," she said as the two minute bell rang. She glanced at the ceiling. "We should get to class, though."

"Yeah." There was a light happiness to his tone. "Yeah. We should...class."

Mia smiled at him, and enjoyed the way his own smile broke out across his face. She giggled. It was all alluring. Tempting. Drawing her into its warm embrace.

Together, the two of them headed down the hall toward their first class, not speaking, but both smiling.

Cody was never late to school, but this morning was a special case. Technically he wasn't late. His dad had called him in for the first half of the day. Still, it was awkward not going. But he couldn't go. Not when his mom was getting out of the hospital today.

He stood in the kitchen, waiting for his dad to return from Denver with his mom. As far as he knew, she was better. He hadn't spoken to her in months, being too afraid to hear what she had to say, but his dad insisted that things were better. That his mom wasn't in that place anymore.

Still, Cody could remember coming home from work and finding an ambulance outside the house. Blood on the kitchen floor. He hadn't seen them take his mom away. They hadn't let him say goodbye to her. There was no time, they'd said. He could see her in the hospital.

But he hadn't wanted to go to the hospital. Maybe that made him a terrible son. He didn't care.

He'd pushed all of that aside for the rest of the time she'd been there. He went about his life, trying to pretend like his mother hadn't tried to kill herself.

And then Jae had kidnapped Mia. And then he'd learned about the Iravata. And then Blair had come up with this insane plot. And then Heba and Parker had shown up. He hadn't had much time to think about his mother.

He hadn't wanted to think about her.

But today, he had to think about her. He had to be here, sitting in his kitchen, waiting for his dad to come home. Because his mom wanted to see him.

Blair kept texting him.

<<Where are you?>>

<<Are you sick? You're never sick>>

<<I have something to talk to you about>>

<<At least tell me if you're coming at all>>

He hadn't replied, which he knew annoyed her. She didn't do well with people not responding to her texts, but what could he say? He hadn't told anyone about his mom, and the fact that Blair hadn't confronted him meant that she hadn't had a vision about it.

She hasn't.

Cody's head jerked around, searching for the source of the voice. *I'm not near. But I'm keeping an eye on your mother. Don't worry.*

He wasn't worried.

You can't lie to me, Cody.

Cody scowled. He hated it when Lior got into his mind. They all hated it, but that didn't stop him from invading their minds. Invading their space.

If your minds were a little quieter, I wouldn't be here.

Cody shook his head, knowing full well that that wouldn't actually help. Or maybe it did, because Lior went silent. Cody's mind, on the other hand, exploded with questions and confusion as he heard the key enter the lock.

He stood, trying to keep his mind silent. Any second now his mom would enter the room. His mother. The woman who had birthed him. The woman who had, at some point in her life, slept with a Vilaim, probably without knowing it. The woman who didn't know anything about her parents. Her grandparents. Who didn't know if she had siblings or not. Who had appeared in Willow Creek eighteen years ago with no memories of her life.

Cody had tried his best not to think about those things. He had his dad. He had his dad's family, even if they didn't visit often. But now, knowing things about himself, the fact that he was half-Vilaim, half-mage, had created more questions than answers.

Like, who was his real father? Like, was his mom actually a mage? Like, why didn't his mom remember anything? And why did she get worse over the years? Slipping into depression? Seeming to hate her own child more and more as time went on?

There were voices. Low voices speaking to one another. His father and his mother. Dylan and Ava Velt. He tensed, trying to get his legs to move. Trying to go see his mother for the first time in months. He had so much he wanted to ask her. So much he *couldn't* ask her.

She looked better. When she entered the kitchen. Her skin glowed a healthy olive, auburn hair clean and groomed. But more than that, she was smiling. Cody hadn't seen his mother smile in such a long time.

When she spotted him, his hands curled into fists. They stared at each other for a moment before she spread out her arms.

"Cody," she said with all the love in the world.

Cody blinked, but stepped toward her, allowing her to pull him into a hug. He glanced at his dad who shrugged, but had a smile on his face.

Ava pulled away from Cody, hands on his arms, and looked him up and down. "You look so good. Stronger. How are things?"

There was a strange lilt to Ava's voice. He didn't know how to feel. But it was good to see his mother smile.

"Things are...good," he said.

"School is going well?"

"Yeah."

"How are your friends? Mia and Derek?"

She remembered them. Sometimes Cody wondered if his mom saw the world in the way that he did. She often confused his friends. Sometimes she was convinced that he was still close to Blair. But not Leo. She didn't remember Leo. No one remembered Leo.

"They're good." He didn't know what else to say. He didn't know how to talk to his mother, and she seemed to sense this. Still, she smiled and placed a soft hand on Cody's cheek. Her eyes, shining, spoke of love and happiness to see him, but he still remembered the last time they'd spoken. The things she'd said to him.

He looked to the floor. "I should go to school now."

"Cody," Dylan said with a slight warning to his tone.

Ava, however, laughed and moved away from him. "Of course. You should be there now. It's good to see you, but school is important. We'll have dinner tonight, right?"

"Right." He didn't want to have dinner with her tonight. He wanted to meet up with Blair and plan their next excursion, this time to Australia where Blair insisted they would be able to get the artifact. He didn't believe her, or in her plan, but it was something to do.

"Have fun at school." She touched his cheek again, and then bustled into the kitchen, saying something about grocery shopping. It was like she was back to normal. Back to the way she'd been before the past few years. The mom that Cody remembered from his childhood.

"She's better," Dylan whispered to him. "I know that things were rough for a few years, but the hospital stay has really helped her. I don't think we have to worry about her anymore."

Cody said nothing. He merely glanced over his shoulder at his mom writing down things she needed from the market. She was back to normal, but he had a feeling it had nothing to do with the hospital. Lior had said he was looking out for Ava. Why had he said that? Why were the Iravata invested in the mental health of Cody's mother?

THINK ABOUT IT.

Leave my brain alone!

SERIOUSLY, CODY. THINK. FOR TWO SECONDS. WHY WOULD WE BE INVESTED IN THE WELL-BEING OF YOUR MOTHER?

Because they were invested in Cody's life? Because what impacted Cody impacted Mia and Derek?

THINK A LITTLE MORE CLOSE TO HOME.

You could just tell me.

ACTUALLY, I CAN'T.

Cody didn't know how to respond, so he grabbed his backpack, slipped on his shoes, and headed out of the house, breathing in the chilled fall air. It was almost time for lunch. Which meant he could have spent more time with Ava, but he couldn't bring himself to. He wasn't looking forward to her being home. He wasn't looking forward to having to talk to her every day.

And he really wasn't looking forward to whenever Ava spiraled back into her darkness. Because it wasn't like her to be happy all of the time. It wasn't like her to be this empty.

He was almost to the school when he felt her.

Lady Shion.

It'd been weeks since the last time he'd spoken to her, or seen her at all. He stopped in his tracks, looking around the deserted area. He eventually spotted her standing with her back to him, staring at the sky. Her hair billowed in the wind, as did her black dress.

Always in black.

He didn't understand why she always wore black.

"Lady Shion," he called out, crossing the street to greet her. She looked down. Faced him. "What are you doing here?"

She bowed her head. "Lior was worried about you."

Cody scoffed. "Why?"

"He worries about all of you children," Lady Shion continued, as if Cody hadn't spoken. "You and Mia in particular. He thinks you're too passive and she's too trusting."

Mia? Too trusting? "Mia doesn't trust anyone anymore."

"Hm...." Lady Shion brushed a lock of hair behind her ear. It was hard to look at her black hair and red eyes now, knowing that it was part of a curse. Her calm demeanor, the way she held herself, screamed that she was the queen Death and Shubishi had raised, but the red eyes broke through that. It was haunting, looking into her eyes.

"I have to go to school," Cody said. He didn't have time for her cryptic comments.

"Watch out for Mia," Lady Shion said as Cody turned to walk away. He halted in his tracks and faced her.

"What?"

"Mia. She's not part of this world, and yet she is one of the most important people in this war. Jae taking her...we think it was part of a larger plan on his part. And possibly on his mother's part."

Jae's mother. Enya. The woman who Derek had run into in Denver. The woman with fiery red hair and a jealous streak. Cody wasn't sure what Enya wanted with Mia. He wasn't even sure what Jae had wanted with Mia. Still wanted with Mia. None of it made sense, and Cody wasn't sure that he had the energy to try and figure it out right then.

"I'll do whatever I can to protect her," Cody said. "Don't worry about that."

Lady Shion showed him a rare smile. "All of you need to take care of each other."

"Derek and Blair can take care of themselves."

"I hope so." And then, without warning, Lady Shion vanished into nothingness, leaving Cody alone on a suddenly much busier street.

He bowed his head and headed toward the school with all intentions of telling Blair and Mia about his conversation with Shion, even if it was cryptic and all over the place.

But when he got to the school, he found himself pausing. Because he noticed Mia, but Mia wasn't alone. She wasn't with Derek or Blair. She was with Chad. Speaking to him in a low voice. She reached out and touched his arm, and he smiled and nodded.

Cody couldn't hear them, but his mind went everywhere at once. Mia had never wanted to be part of the magical world. She'd always resented it. And Chad had always shown interest in Mia. He'd talked about her with his friends when he'd thought no one was listening.

"She's beautiful. She's intelligent. She's athletic. She's kind. She's so perfect."

And while Cody agreed with him, he certainly didn't want *Chad Rogers* saying them about Mia.

Before Mia could see him, he dashed around to another door, heart racing. Had Chad asked Mia out? Had she said yes? She was grounded, so could she say yes even if she'd wanted to?

He didn't know how to feel about any of this and closed his eyes, trying to get a handle on his emotions.

It was too much today. All of it was too much.

Needing to think about something else, he pulled out his phone and texted Blair to meet him behind the school so they could talk about their excursion to Australia. Something. Anything. To take his mind off his mother and the fact that Mia might be dating someone else.

Chapter Thirteen

Blair was shocked her mother hadn't grounded her. She had, after all, caused a ruckus at the school in France. She had, after all, taken off in the middle of the night, stealing a priceless tool, and hadn't told anyone. She had, after all, accidentally revealed to her brothers that she'd disowned her grandmother.

It was all a mess, she'd decided.

But her mother hadn't gotten angry with her. It was like she was trying to let Blair figure out how to exist in the real world without her help. Which, on the one hand, Blair really liked. On the other, she couldn't help but wonder if Esther was being irresponsible. Mia's parents hadn't found out about the excursion, but if they had, Blair had a feeling both Derek and Mia would get pulled from school so that their mom could keep a watch on them at all times.

Two extremes.

Still, as Blair sat in the living room of her house, planning how to get the artifact from Australia, she wondered if she should be doing this.

The stone of language was known for impacting anyone who

stood around it. Even if they weren't the chosen wielder, the stone made it so they could understand any language, and that anyone else could understand them.

It was a fascinating concept. Blair didn't actually find languages fascinating, and she wasn't the best at them, but she thought a lot about Derek and his love of language. How he could speak Thai, Mandarin, and English with ease and didn't seem to struggle switching between them. How, if she'd let him, he could learn the language of Sangota with a snap of his fingers. He would love this stone. Or maybe he'd dislike it, because it would nullify his natural gift, but regardless, thoughts of him were tied to the stone.

Blair hated it.

She didn't want to think about him, much less about one of the most fascinating things about him. He had this gift, not because of magic, but because it was him.

She recalled, not too fondly, the way he'd snapped at her in the park. He never would have spoken to her that way in the past. He'd always been gentle with her, trying to understand her sarcasm and rough demeanor. He'd enjoyed her rough demeanor. Saw through the exterior shell and to the person she actually was.

And she missed him.

Which was making planning this so much harder. If she could convince *him* to go with, then maybe they'd stand a better chance. Yes, she'd told Cody that she had a plan that would go without a hitch, but she actually didn't. She just didn't want to appear weak or pathetic in front of Cody. Not right now.

She noticed her mother enter the room, carrying a tray of food and some hot chocolate. Blair looked up from her notes as Esther settled next to her daughter and placed the tray in one of the few empty spots on the ground.

"What are you doing?" Esther asked. Blair hadn't told her about the second excursion idea. All she'd said to her mom about the last trip was that they'd gone to France to look for something and overheard that the freaking leader of the Mauvais Clan knew about them. Esther hadn't known what to say to that.

"Just...." Blair sighed and closed the book she'd been poring over about the stone. "Trying to figure out a way to protect Mia."

Esther hummed. "You know, you could ask your grandmother for help."

Blair snorted. "Seriously? You think I'm going to ask Grandma for help after everything she put me through this summer?"

There was a moment of silence. Blair watched the steam rise off the hot chocolate and tried her best not to spill everything to her mother.

Finally, Esther sighed. "I know that my mother can be... difficult."

"That's putting it lightly."

"But she means well."

Blair snorted. "She meant well when she kicked you out of the clan because you married dad?"

"That's not exactly what happened."

"She meant well when she lied to *everyone* about being a seer?"

"Well–"

"She meant well when she tried to trick me into becoming the next clan leader when she'd promised me that she would help me find Mia?"

Esther didn't say anything.

"Seriously, Mom," Blair continued. "Even if I wanted Grandma's help, she wouldn't lift a finger to protect Mia. She could have helped me find her. She could have used the power of the clan to protect her. But she didn't. Instead she made it impossible for me to ever go back to Sangota."

"You can always go back to Sangota," Esther said. "It's your home."

"Willow Creek is my home."

"No." Esther placed a hand on Blair's shoulder. "Willow Creek is where you grew up. But you know as well as I do that Sangota is different for us. It calls to us in a way that nowhere else ever will. Even though I haven't been back in over twenty years, I still miss it every day. My *soul* misses it. The beautiful sky. The freedom to use magic. It's our home, and Grandma is, and always will be, family."

Blair couldn't help but roll her eyes before she picked up the mug and took a sip of the thick drink. "Yeah, well, I'm sick of her using family as an excuse to be a bitch to me."

"Blair!"

"What? It's true. Grandma has always treated me differently than the other kids. She knew for years that I was a seer. And for some reason that meant my life needed to be miserable."

Esther sighed. "I can't speak for my mother, but I think she was doing it to prepare you."

Blair took another sip. "Prepare me for what? If she wanted to prepare me, she should have told me what she was and helped me figure out how to control my visions."

Again, Esther fell silent. Together, the two sat without speaking for some time, Blair looking at her notes. Esther reached forward and grabbed one of the pieces of paper, holding it up to read it.

"Australia?" she asked. "Are you going on another trip?"

"Going to try and stop me?"

Esther shrugged. "I know that I can't stop you. Trying will only make you go quiet."

"True." Blair leaned against her mom's shoulder and closed her eyes, gripping the handle of the mug. "Mom, why is everything such a disaster?"

She wanted her mom to fix everything. To step in and make things better between Blair and her grandmother. Between Blair and Derek. Hell, even between Blair and Mia. The two of them hadn't been the same in over a year, and she was tired of it.

Esther wrapped an arm around Blair's body before kissing the top of her head. "Things aren't a disaster, my dear. They're just complicated. But everything will get figured out in time. I promise."

Blair wasn't sure she believed Esther. Still, the words were comforting, and Blair continued to lean against her mom, wishing that this moment could last forever. That she could go back to being seven, when it was acceptable to sit on her mom's lap and just be held. Back when Leo was still around. Before she'd met Derek and Mia. When she and Cody were friends, with Cody coming over every other night for dinner.

Things weren't complicated back then.

That was before she'd had her first vision.

That was before her grandmother had started "preparing" her for life as a seer.

It was before her magic had become a negative thing in her life. She looked at her younger brothers. At James, in particular. He was so young, and magic was such a fun part of his life. He knew not to use it at school, and Esther helped suppress it so he didn't have accidents, but when he was home, it was mystical. It was magical.

It wasn't magical to Blair anymore.

Derek lay on his bed, staring at the ceiling and wondering. He hadn't spoken to Mia in a couple of days, but he was tired of being angry. He was tired of snapping at Blair. Of not talking to Cody. Of punishing Mia for living a life he thought was dangerous.

It was all stupid, he told himself. He knew that the three of them were being idiots, but brave idiots. What bothered him the most was that he wasn't part of it. He was the outsider now. He no longer had his friends. He no longer had the trust of his sister. All he had was his dreams.

There was a knock at his door. He looked at it. He knew his father stood outside the door, and he wasn't sure he was ready to talk to his him. The two of them had barely spoken since the car ride back from Wyoming.

"Démíng?" The door creaked open and Derek rolled to his side. But his father didn't leave. Instead he entered the room and pulled Derek's chair across the wooden floor until he was sitting next to Derek's bed. "Can we talk?"

"About what?" Derek asked. He tried to gauge his father's emotions, but they were oddly subtle. Derek glanced over his shoulder, expecting to see his father, only to come face to face with Niran.

Derek gasped and scrambled away from Niran's face on his father's body. His back hit the wall and he rubbed his eyes.

"Démíng?"

It was his father's voice. And when Derek opened his eyes, it wasn't Niran's face, but his father's, concerned and confused. The emotions flooded out of him, tickling Derek's skin like gentle feathers brushing against him.

"What's wrong?" Liang asked.

Derek glanced around him, breathing heavily. He could have sworn it was Niran. That he was dreaming. He'd never…he'd never seen Niran other than in his own reflection.

"I…." Derek's breath calmed. "I thought I saw something."

"What?"

"Nothing." Derek shook his head. "What did you want to talk about?"

"Well, I've been busy and haven't been able to talk to you about the magic."

Derek sighed. He really didn't want to have this conversation.

"Bà, we don't have to do this."

"We do." He clenched his hands, resting them on his legs. "I'm trying to understand what I missed. How I missed that you had magic all of these years. If maybe I spent a little too much time on my job, and not enough time with my children."

Yes, was Derek's immediate answer, but he held his tongue. He didn't want to fight with his dad, especially not when he was already grounded for keeping secrets. It would be better to just let this conversation happen the way his dad wanted.

"I'm also worried about you and Mia," Liang continued. "The two of you were always close, but in the past year it's like something fractured. I know that you two had your issues last winter, but I'm worried that it will impact your relationship forever and I don't want that."

"We don't want that either," Derek said.

"So why haven't you two been talking? Did something happen?"

Derek bit his lip. If he told his dad what Mia had done, she would be in so much trouble.

"Is it because of this boy who asked Mia on a date?"

Derek blinked. "Huh?"

Liang cocked his head. "Don't you know? A boy at your school, Chad Rogers, asked Mia on a date. She came to us asking for permission."

Derek didn't know how to respond. He'd never imagined that Mia would want to go out with *Chad Rogers*. Star quarterback of the football team. Not the smartest in the world, but smart enough to keep up with all of his classes, at least. He wasn't a bad kid, but Derek always pictured Mia with Cody.

"What did you say?" Derek asked, too bewildered to be annoyed that she hadn't told him.

"We told her she could," Liang said.

"Aren't we grounded?"

"Yes, but we decided that this is a normal thing, and Mia needs normal right now."

"So, if I wanted to go on a date—"

"No."

Derek rolled his eyes. Of course he didn't need normalcy. He wasn't the one who had been kidnapped. He was also the one who'd kept his magic a secret for all of his life.

"Son, I just want to make sure you're okay." Liang had a serious look in his eye, and Derek found he couldn't lie to him anymore.

"I'm not okay," Derek said. "Everything is falling apart. Not a single one of us is happy right now. You can't imagine how it feels to know that all of your friends, and your sister, are constantly feeling negative emotions. I try to ignore it. I try to pretend like Cody and Blair don't matter, but they do, and because of it I'm more attuned to their emotions. To all their frustration and fear and it's exhausting."

He was absolutely exhausted. It wasn't like summer when he could barely stay awake. This was deeper than that. It was in the very depths of his soul. Just pure exhaustion, and he wanted to be done with it.

Liang didn't say anything at first. He stared at his hands, glasses slipping down his nose. Derek was starting to wonder if he'd said too much. If maybe he'd overstepped by trying to open up to his dad. He was just so sick of keeping all of this a secret. He was tired of being angry all the time. He was tired of wanting to hide from Blair and Cody. And he was very tired of feeling their emotions. Feeling Mia's emotions.

Then, without warning, Liang stood and gestured for Derek to follow him. Derek frowned, but followed. They headed out of his room and toward the stairs that led to the second floor. Derek hesitated. He'd only been up there a few times. It was for their parents. Their office. Their bedroom. It wasn't a place for either of the twins. But Liang headed up the stairs and Derek had no choice but to follow him.

Liang didn't lead Derek into his parent's bedroom, but instead in the opposite direction, toward the office. There was something strange about the way he walked, and Derek recalled the moment when he'd seen Niran's face. Maybe this was all a dream still. Maybe Derek was working through his problems in his sleep. What else would explain why Liang was leading him into the office?

But the office didn't look as Derek remembered it. His parents' desks were in different places. Instead of right next to each other, they were across the room from one another. The shelves had also changed. They were no longer disastrous black holes, but were neat and organized. Books and artifacts lined them. The floor, which used to be littered with maps, had a beautiful rug with a couch and two chairs.

Liang led him to the couches and gestured for him to sit. Derek did, back stiff. He kept glancing around the office, trying to make sense of why he was there, while his father grabbed a book off the shelf near his desk.

When he returned, he opened it, and Derek realized it was a photo album of them when they were children.

"I've always wondered about you," Liang admitted, gesturing to a photo of Derek and Mia wearing their kindergarten uniforms. White shirts with little red scarves and deep blue shorts. "You've always been so attuned to people's emotions. I remember when Mā and I were talking about divorce, you were the rock for everyone. I should have seen it coming. I should have known that you were blessed with a gift from the gods."

Derek watched his father. He hadn't known Liang to be spiritual at all. It was odd, hearing him talk about this.

"But I didn't know. I pushed it to the side, preferring to pay attention to science rather than religion. The mystical was always something my parents spoke of, but I never believed in. It wasn't until you disappeared with…what did you call him?"

"Shubishi," Derek said in a quiet voice.

"Yes." Liang sighed. "I also should have seen that coming. Shubishi was always a strange man. Never seeming to age or change. Always knowing things. Coming from a mysterious, wealthy family. Something was always off about him."

Derek didn't disagree.

"But even when you talked about how frustrating your powers are, and all of the issues that you've been through, I've always thought of your ability as a gift. You know—actually know—what someone is feeling at all times. You can help these people feel better. I can't imagine being able to do that."

"Well, it's only gotten me in trouble," Derek muttered.

"Didn't you help Mia feel safe enough to go to school?"

"Well, yeah, but she wouldn't let me help her for a year."

"But she still trusted you with her fears."

"What's your point?"

Liang shrugged. "Maybe I don't have one. All I do know is that you're hypersensitive to emotions, which must make everything so much more extreme. I can imagine why you're exhausted. But I do think that you shouldn't give up on your friends or your sister because they're unhappy. Be the sunshine in their lives."

But he was angry with them. They were being stupid. They weren't telling him things. Then again, would he want to talk to himself if he was angry like this?

He knew that he needed to talk to his sister. He needed to apologize for shutting her out, and ask her all about what was going on with Chad. Not because he thought it was a bad idea, but because he'd promised her that he wouldn't do this again. He wouldn't shut her out or keep things from her, and she'd promised the same to him.

"Thanks, Bà," Derek said. "I feel better."

The man smiled, eyes scrunching at the corners. "Maybe soon you can talk to your mother about being ungrounded. I'm sure she'll relent once she sees that things have calmed down."

Derek's eyes came alive. He hated having to come home right after school. He hated that he was under constant supervision. He hated feeling like he couldn't do whatever he wanted. "Really?"

Liang nodded. "Mia seems better, and you've both been good. I don't see why not."

Derek grimaced. They had not both been good. But he wasn't about to say anything to jeopardize his freedom. "Thanks."

Liang merely nodded and then stood. "I have some work to do. Would you like to sit with me and do some homework?"

That was a first. Normally Derek did his homework in the kitchen or at his desk. He nodded. "Sure."

And as he headed downstairs to get his textbooks, he smiled to himself. Because things were getting back to normal. Slowly but surely.

He paused, staring in front of him where Niran flickered in and out of sight. An apparition. A translucent body smiling back at him. His smile faded. Niran's smile faded, and then he disappeared.

Chapter Fourteen

Mia hadn't seen Cody in almost a week. As she walked to school, the autumn leaves around her glittered gold and orange, bringing with them a welcome relief from the warmth. Derek wasn't with her today. They hadn't spoken much, though it felt different than last winter. This was more they didn't know how to face each other, rather than either one of them being angry or hurt.

Granted, she didn't want Derek with her. After all, she was heading downtown to go on a date. With Chad Rogers. Of all people. She still couldn't believe that she was doing this, nor that her parents had said yes. She wanted to go on the date, make no mistake, but she wasn't sure that it was the right thing to do.

Still, she was on her way, walking down the sidewalk toward downtown. With a deep breath, she examined the world around her. She took in all the sights and relished in the gentle breeze rustling her hair. They were going to get coffee. A simple date. Nothing fancy. Just spending time together outside of school.

She'd never spent time with Chad out of school before.

The entire school had caught wind of their date, which only

seemed to make things more awkward for Mia. Her basketball friends cheered her on, but Cody hadn't spoken to her in almost a week.

She recalled that night. The one with the wine. The one with the crying. Had it meant more to him than it had to her? Was he angry that she had found someone? Or was he busy planning his next heist with Blair?

Mia didn't know the answer to any of those questions, and part of her really didn't want to care. Cody was a big boy. If he wanted to pout because she was going to on a date with a nice, normal, non-magical boy, then he could do that. She wasn't going to feel guilty for normalcy.

When she arrived downtown, she realized she was early. About ten minutes. Not bad, and maybe Chad would be there early too. She decided to go to the coffee shop where she usually spent her time with her brother and friends and ordered a cup of decaf coffee, before returning outside.

She sat and sipped her hot coffee, a small smile on her face. This was…normal.

She didn't notice him at first. At first she was so engrossed in her coffee, in her normality, that she didn't realize Jae was there. When she looked up from her coffee, she didn't flinch. She didn't scream or point or run away. Instead she stared at Jae. Or maybe it was an apparition of him?

"A date?" Jae asked.

Mia said nothing.

"You don't live in a normal world, Mia. You're part of the magic whether you like it or not. Trying to pretend otherwise is going to cause you more harm than good."

Mia sipped her coffee, debating whether or not to reply to him. She believed that he wouldn't do anything to her. He'd kept his word.

"Are you ignoring me?" Jae asked.

Mia placed her mug down and stared straight at Jae, wondering why he'd ever scared her. He himself looked frightened. Like a scared boy who'd never been hugged a day in his life. Yes, he was powerful. Yes, he'd disappeared her in seconds with no one the wiser. But that didn't mean he was always dangerous. He'd lost his temper, like a child. He'd thrown a tantrum when he hadn't gotten his way, like a child.

He was a dangerous child.

Did Mia need to fear him now? Now that she'd broken his expectations and taken away the angel persona that he'd put on her?

"Mia."

"What do you want me to say?" Mia asked.

Jae's eyes widened. She'd never spoken to him with that tone, and the fact that it caught him off guard made her smile.

When he didn't respond, she continued. "I've made it very clear that you aren't welcome in my life. I don't want you checking up on me. I don't want you trying to warn me about who I can and cannot date. In fact, why don't you stop spying on me altogether?"

She wasn't aware of where this boldness was coming from. Maybe the coffee was giving her courage. Or maybe Derek was spying on her, controlling her emotions. She checked her heart, placing a hand on her chest. Whenever Derek calmed her down, her heart slowed.

It wasn't slow.

Jae let out a heavy breath. "If I don't watch out for you, no one will."

"I have the entirety of the Iravata watching over me."

"They don't know what's coming," Jae said. "I do."

"And what is coming?"

Jae went silent. He crossed his arms and looked out to the street, watching the cars and people hurry by. It was oddly busy today, Mia noted. She wasn't used to seeing so many people downtown, but it

146

was also the time of year when they got tourists. Maybe this year they had more than usual? She didn't know, and she wasn't sure she wanted to know. What she did want to know, however, was whatever Jae was keeping from her.

"What's coming?" she asked again, this time with a bit of meat behind her voice.

Jae glanced at her, then back at the street. "I know that Blair and…Cody are planning to go to Australia. Don't go with them."

Mia blinked. She hadn't heard anything about them going to Australia. "Huh?"

"The more you leave Willow Creek, the more dangerous the world becomes for you."

"Because of you."

"Because of my mother."

"Enya?"

Jae flinched at the name, then glared at her. She shrunk back and found her coffee very interesting.

"How do you know that name?" Jae asked. "It wasn't in my journals."

"The Iravata told us about Enya," Mia muttered. "From when they were Vilaim. I put two and two together."

"And you know who my father is?"

"No." She had suspicions, but she hadn't wanted to confront him about it. For one thing, he terrified her. For another, she wasn't sure she *wanted* to know who Jae's father was. She didn't want to change her perception of the Iravata anymore than she already had. She'd found comfort in her knowledge. She didn't want to know more.

Not yet, anyway.

"Good," Jae said. "It's better if you don't know."

"Why?"

"There is no good reason I can give you."

147

"Then tell me."

Jae watched her. "You're not afraid of me today. Your soul is bright and curious."

Mia rubbed a hand on her arm, hoping to get rid of what Cody called a mist so Jae couldn't see it anymore. She wanted to brush it away and pretend like it didn't exist. The more she acknowledged all the strangeness of the magical world, the more involved she got with it and the more danger she was in.

"I'm not going to Australia," Mia said eventually, ignoring Jae's comment. "I don't know anything about it."

"Good."

She didn't like the way he spoke to her. Like a parent to a child. But she already had two parents, and she certainly didn't need another one.

She opened her mouth, but Jae had disappeared, leaving her alone with her coffee and her thoughts.

Just then, her phone vibrated. She ignored it at first, only for it to buzz again. And again. And again. Finally, she took a look, wondering if maybe Chad was late. But it wasn't Chad.

<<I had a vision about Jae. Are you okay?>>

Mia flushed.

<<I saw you two together. Did that happen? Has it happened?>>

<<Mia, answer me>>

Mia typed a quick response. <<It hasn't happened. I'm okay.>>

She wasn't quite sure why she'd lied to Blair. Twice. But she didn't want Blair to tell anyone, because they'd all try and bubble her up again. Jae wasn't hurting her. Jae wasn't trying to take her away.

<<So it's going to happen?>>

<<How would I know?>>

<<You haven't seen him at all?>>

Mia considered in that moment telling Blair the truth, but the moment faded when she heard her name and Chad appeared, grinning like a fool.

With a smile, Mia put her phone away, ignoring the buzzing, and focused her attention on her date.

"You're early," Chad said. "I thought I was going to be the first one here."

Mia shrugged. "You know how parents can be. I needed to get out of the house." Her mom, pleased with the fact that Mia was having a normal life, had fussed over her until Mia had all but yelled at her that she had to leave.

Derek had remained quiet the entire time, staying in his room. Mia didn't blame him. This was, after all, a weird thing for both of them. Her not telling him that she had a date, and him being angry at her for having a date. At least, that's what she guessed was the problem.

"I'll go get a drink and be back here in a few," Chad said, pointing over his shoulder at the door to the coffee shop. "You want anything else?"

She smiled and gripped her coffee. "No, I'm okay. Thanks though."

Chad disappeared into the shop and Mia let out a heavy breath, wondering if this was a good idea. If Jae hadn't appeared, if he hadn't spoken to her with such intense, caring tones, she wouldn't think twice about this. But this date was so normal, and Jae was so not. He was a mysterious being who belonged in a different dimension surrounded by people who weren't even human. Just like the Iravata.

She was so lost in her thoughts that she didn't notice Chad returning until he was waving his hand in front of her face.

She blinked and looked up at him.

"You okay?" Chad asked.

Mia looked around her, maybe looking for Jae, maybe looking for one of the Iravata who were lingering around. Maybe, she was looking for an escape from the disaster that was her life.

Then her eyes landed on Chad and she realized that he was an escape from the disaster that was her life.

She smiled. "I'm fine. Just thinking."

"What about?"

"Just what's been going on in my life."

Chad nodded. "It's been a lot, right? I try not to listen to the gossip at school, but sometimes…you know."

Mia did know. It was hard not to hear *everything* in that school. The kids were bored, living in a small town. There were no clubs in Willow Creek. Nothing to do after school. So they talked about what was going on in the lives of their fellow students. Sometimes what was going on with the adults in town, but that usually stemmed from their parents, who were also bored as hell.

"We don't have to talk about it," Chad said suddenly. "I know you've been avoiding the topic."

She sipped her coffee. She could talk to him about it, but not really. At least, she couldn't talk about the details of what had happened to her. But she could talk about other things. About what it was like to be back in a normal world after being kidnapped. Held hostage. Thrown off a roof. "I've been having trouble adjusting to real life again."

"I'd say I can imagine, but I really can't." Chad smiled at her. "All I can say is I'm sorry that happened to you and you should take your time returning to normal."

"Thanks." Mia didn't know what else to say, so she took another sip of her coffee and stared back out at the street. "Tell me something interesting."

"Something interesting?" Chad's voice lilted up, though not by much. He definitely had a deeper voice than either Cody or Derek, like he'd gone through a much stronger puberty. It made Mia smile. It was so different.

"Yeah, something interesting. We've been friends for a long time, but I feel like I barely know you."

Chad hummed. "I'm not really that interesting."

"I'm sure that's not true." She smiled at him and watched his face flush. "Come on. Tell me something."

"Okay…." He thought for a moment, eyes rolling up to look at the cloudy sky. "I guess…you know how we're graduating this year?"

"Of course," Mia said with a laugh. "It's all anyone can talk about."

"Well, I'm hoping to go to Harvard."

Mia blinked. "Harvard?"

"Yeah." His eyes lit up. "Mom's always been talking about how I should aim for the sky when I go to college, so I've set my sights on Harvard. I have some fall back schools, but I've been talking to a recruiter from there and they're going to come to some of my games and see if I have Harvard football material."

"What would you major in?" Mia asked.

He shrugged. "No idea yet. Something computer science related, I think."

"Really?"

"Yeah. I like math. I'm not as good at it as you are. Or Velt. But he's like some kinda super genius, right?"

There was no animosity in Chad's voice. A few years ago there might have been, and Mia would have called him out on it. But today was different.

"He's really smart, yeah," Mia said. "No one compares."

"So true." Chad sighed. "I used to hate him so much for being smarter than me. But I guess I was just jealous because I struggled a lot in school until I found a physical outlet. Mom thinks I might have ADHD but we don't have the money to get me tested. Or medicated."

"You should tell him that," Mia said. "He thinks you hate him."

"I don't hate him." His tone took on a defensive nature. "I never really did, you know?"

That's what all the girls had said about Mia when they started being nice to her. They didn't hate her, they just didn't know her. They just weren't sure who she was, and she was so different. They were sorry. They'd changed.

Mia eyed Chad, wondering if he was trying to convince her or himself.

He must have noticed the tension because he sighed. "Sorry. Bad topic."

"No, it's fine." Anything was better than talking about her summer. Or about magic. Or about Jae. "It's just hard to forgive people who made your life hell."

"Yeah, I know. Honestly, it's one of my biggest regrets that I was so awful to Velt in elementary school. I wish there was a way to make it up to him, but I'm not sure he wants me to make it up to him. Or, if he does, how to do it."

Mia wasn't sure what to say. Cody didn't like Chad, and probably never would. She knew that. Part of her felt guilty. Just a little bit. About going on a date with him. Because Cody was her friend. Cody was her rock. She cared about Cody. But she couldn't stop her life because of him. She couldn't judge people based on his opinions forever. People changed.

"I think it's good that you want to make it up to him," Mia eventually said with a small smile. "I don't know how you could either, but I think it's good."

"Yeah, I do too."

They fell silent, both staring out across the street at the busy people bustling by. After a while, conversation changed. It moved from talking about Cody and bullying to school and homework. To family. To friends. And through it all, Mia found herself smiling more. She found herself really enjoying Chad's company, and not just because when they talked, magic was never on the menu. He was kind of a dork. Kind of a nerd. When he talked about computer science, she was surprised to find he already knew how to code, though she didn't understand what he meant when he talked about the specifics.

They also spoke about sports. About Mia's basketball season, though she hadn't really had her head in the game and she'd been benched as a starter. She didn't mind. Basketball didn't hold her attention the way it used to. She honestly wanted the season to be over so she could focus on school.

Her parents wouldn't agree, but she didn't care.

It was time to move on.

They finished their coffee and agreed that it was time to head home. They walked together, toward their neighborhood, and talked about what colleges they were going to apply to. It was, by all means, the most normal conversation Mia had had in a long time. She was excited to have more conversations like this. And when they got to the split between his road and her own, they stopped.

"This was a lot of fun," Mia said, and she meant it.

"Yeah, I had fun," Chad said. "Wanna do it again sometime?"

Mia nodded. "I think that'd be...."

"Fun?"

She laughed. "Yeah. Fun."

They stared at each other for a minute before Chad ran a hand through his hair, letting out a heavy breath. "All right. Well, I'll see you at school on Monday?"

"Absolutely."

He reached out and squeezed her hand. For a moment, she thought he was going to lean in and kiss her, but then he let go of her hand and backed away, still grinning. It wasn't until he reached halfway down his street that he turned around and headed to his house. Mia giggled and turned toward her cul-de-sac, grinning the whole time.

Chad was so sweet. So kind. So honest.

The opposite of Steven.

She was about to take a step when she realized that Cody was standing there, watching her with wide eyes, and she froze.

He hadn't meant to intrude on her privacy. He'd planned to go to her house and explain why he'd been gone for so long, but she hadn't been there, and Derek hadn't been in the mood to deal with him. He'd been heading home. Honestly. He'd just wanted to go home when he saw them together. Mia and Chad, holding hands. Her mist bright and alive, and his mixing slightly with hers. A forest in the middle of a snow storm.

His mind had told him to run. To vanish. To disappear. But he couldn't move. He couldn't get his mist to turn into nothingness. And when she saw him, when she froze, he knew that he really should have gotten out of there.

"Cody?" she called out, walking toward him.

He panicked. He could run, but then that would hurt her. He could vanish, but then she'd be even more confused, and possibly a little traumatized. Or a lot traumatized.

Instead, he swallowed thickly and walked toward her, hoping his panic wasn't visible on his face.

"Are you okay?" she asked. He couldn't tell if she was annoyed or concerned. Part of his brain said concern. He must have been pale. He must have been shaking. He *was* shaking. He could feel his hands twitching. But the other part said annoyance. Because he had vanished on her for a week. After seeing her with Chad that day.

"I'm okay," he said.

"You don't look okay." She examined him up and down, blinking rapidly. Her mist dulled, and Cody cursed himself for trying to make things better between them.

He bit his lip. "I uh…just had a lot going on recently. I went to see if you were home but you were with…."

"Chad." Mia's voice was harsh. Cody flinched. "Yeah. We went on a date."

"Oh."

"I know you heard about it," she said, looking to the ground. "It was the only thing the school could talk about all week."

He had heard about it. And seen Mia with Chad. With the guy who had made his life hell for so many years. "Well, yeah."

"Is that why you were avoiding me?"

Straight to the point. Cody hadn't expected that. Mia was normally a lot more tactful. She'd jump around the topic and then bring it up lightly. But maybe she'd changed. All of them had changed over the past year.

Cody thought about lying to her. He could do it. He could easily tell her that he was angry she was on a date with Chad. No, he was angry that she was on a date with *anyone*. Wasn't she grounded? Wasn't she not supposed to hang out with people outside of school? What had happened to her relying on Cody for support? Why did she keep not seeing him the way he saw her?

The anger built up in him. He knew he was being ridiculous. They were friends, and just because he loved her didn't mean she had to love him back. Still, his anger built. Because it was Chad that she'd chosen to go on a date with. Chad who had caught her attention. He'd understood Steven. A new kid. Smart. Kind. She hadn't known he was manipulating her until it was too late. Until they'd already started seeing each other in that way.

But Chad Rogers?

"Why him?" Cody asked in a sharper tone than he'd meant.

Mia flinched, white mist darkening. "Excuse me?"

"Of all the people at school, why are you going out with him?"

"Because he's nice?"

Cody groaned. "Yeah. So nice."

"He's changed," Mia snapped. "He feels bad about the way he treated you."

Of course he would say that. He wanted her to like him the way he liked her. But Cody knew it wasn't true. Otherwise he would have apologized. Otherwise he wouldn't have done it in the first place.

"Just, why not stay away from him?" Cody said. "Come on. It's not like he can be part of your life. Not really."

"Why not?"

"Because he doesn't have magic." Cody knew he was overstepping. He wasn't supposed to have an opinion on who Mia did or did not date. And the look on Mia's face told him everything he already knew.

"Did it ever occur to you that I like him because he doesn't have magic?" Mia asked, voice ice. "Did it ever occur to you that I don't want to be part of this magical world? That I want to be able to have a normal life?"

"But magic is part of your life!"

"No," Mia hissed. "Magic is part of your life. I'm a normal girl who happens to be caught up in magic because of who I'm friends with. I'd love to just have a normal boyfriend who isn't some mage, or Natara, or a Vilaim, or anything like that. I want to be normal!"

"Well, I'm so glad you get to pretend the magic world doesn't exist."

Mia groaned. "Cody, what is this about?"

They'd never fought before. In all the years they'd been friends, the two of them had never gotten in a fight. Mia's question brought Cody back to that fact. What was this about? Was this about Mia going out with Chad? Was this about his lingering feelings for her? The fact that he kept missing his chance? The fact that she'd never want to be with him because of his magic?

Was he taking her passive rejection so harshly because of his mother?

"My mom isn't doing well," Cody said without warning.

Mia blinked. "Huh?"

"My mom." Cody crossed his arms and looked away from her. "You were in China, and we weren't really speaking, so you missed it, but she was in the hospital all summer. She got out a week ago but something isn't right with her."

She smiled too much. She doted on him. She acted too much like a mother and less like a ghost walking around the house, shrieking at anything that moved.

Mia's face softened and she placed a hand on Cody's arm. "Why didn't you say something?"

"What could I say?" he asked. "You were a mess. You could barely sleep without someone watching over you. I couldn't put my issues onto you too."

Mia's eyes lowered. "I'm sorry. I should have noticed something was wrong. It's just…so much has happened and…."

"I'm not angry at you," Cody said, stopping her. She looked up at him from beneath her lashes and he froze. She was so pretty. So sweet. So amazing in every way possible. He wanted to kiss her. To tell her that she shouldn't date Chad because he wanted her.

But he couldn't.

Because that's not what friends did.

"I'm always here for you," Mia said. "I know I haven't been that present, but I'm trying. You can talk to me about these things. I promise."

He couldn't, though. She'd made it clear that she wanted nothing to do with the magical world, and his mom was somehow connected to it. She had to be, if he was a half Natara half mage creature. Not really human, not really Vilaim. Just someone who belonged nowhere.

He stepped back from Mia. "I should go."

"Wait, Cody."

"It's fine," Cody said with his best smile. "Go out with Chad. You said he's changed? I believe you. I gotta get home. My parents want to do a family dinner." A complete lie. He hated lying to Mia.

She frowned but didn't stop him as he took off past her. Toward his side of town. Where his mother waited for him with a weird smile and fake reactions. Like she was a doll.

He couldn't believe that he'd told her. That he'd snapped at her like that. He knew she was watching him walk away. He could feel her mist twisting and turning. Maybe she contemplated coming after him?

OF COURSE SHE IS.

Get out of my head.

ALL YOU KIDS WANT ME OUT OF YOUR HEADS WHEN YOU DON'T REALIZE THAT I'M HERE TO HELP YOU.

Cody ignored him and continued on, shoving his hands in his pockets. Around him, fall continued to shift the world from the beautiful green to flaming orange. And he couldn't help but wonder if this was a symbol of the changes in his own life. Things weren't okay. And he knew that they'd never be okay again.

Even if his mother was home.

Even if his dad was finally making some money.

Even if Mia was healing.

Something had changed over the past few weeks, and Cody couldn't help but try and grasp for what he couldn't reach.

Part Three

Chapter Fifteen

Blair sat at the table, listening to her brothers chant the Hanukkah prayers while they lit candles. She didn't participate.

It was winter break. She hadn't realized how much time would pass, and how quickly it would pass, while she researched the artifact in Australia while also keeping up with school. Outside the window, light flecks of snow sprinkled down on the icy ground, reflecting the moonlight. She glanced at it, candles burning in the corner of her vision as the boys began to sing the traditional Arbour songs.

Kyro and Luka were super into it this year, which was abnormal, and James was jumping around, asking for gelt. Everyone around her was happy, and she couldn't figure out how to tell them all that she wasn't in the mood for this energy. She wanted to retreat into her room and continue her research, but this was "family time".

Blair mouthed along with the songs, trying not to let her father know that she didn't want to be here. He was so thrilled to celebrate Hanukkah with all of his children this year, since Kyro and Luka had come home for winter break. A first. Blair hadn't caught the reason for their return to Colorado, but she had a feeling it had to do with her trip to France. Kyro, the older one, had been messaging her about it for months.

Her little brothers knew close to nothing about Blair's life. They didn't know the reason Mia had been kidnapped. They didn't know about the Iravata. She and her mom had decided to keep it from them so they wouldn't be too scared to go back to school.

But that didn't mean that she wasn't tempted to tell them. Especially now, with all the questions they had about Blair and their grandmother.

Speaking of, she hadn't heard from her grandmother in quite a while. Not since she'd gotten back from France. She'd half expected Enola to show up and try to talk her out of her plans.

Blair wanted to spy on her, but she didn't know how. In fact, she hadn't had a vision recently. Not in the past few weeks, at least. The last time she'd had a vision, it had been about Australia. It had been about the person who had the artifact. How miserable they were with it. And Blair knew that was going to be their in.

The singing stopped and everyone moved into the kitchen, but Blair remained behind, looking at her phone. She hadn't really spoken to anyone since school ended. Mia was busy with freaking Chad Rogers, which had caught Blair off guard, Cody was basically MIA and had been since the last moment of school before break, and Derek still wouldn't look at her.

<<How's your break going?>> Blair asked Mia, hoping that Mia would respond. They hadn't spoken much, but Blair missed her. Missed her friend. The whole point of rescuing Mia from Jae, besides the obvious, had been so Blair didn't lose her best friend. But it seemed like that was happening anyway. Not that Blair would do anything differently, but it was still odd that Mia was pulling away so sharply.

Blair waited a few minutes for Mia to respond, and when she didn't, joined the family for dinner.

Her dad stood at the stove, frying latkes, while the boys hovered around him, sneaking the fresh ones the moment he put them down. Her mom, however, sat at the table, watching her children with a smile and soft eyes.

Blair's stomach turned. This was supposed to be a fun and peaceful night. Well, a peaceful and fun week. The festival of lights. It had always been Blair's favorite holiday, growing up. Her dad didn't give out massive presents, saying that it wasn't worth "competing" with Christmas, but the food was good, the songs were fun, and it was always bright and warm in the house. She loved being around her family and playing with the dreidel. It was one of the few times she actually felt Jewish. The rest of the year, her grandmother pulled her into the world of Sangota. Into the world of the mages.

Blair sat next to her mom and rested her head on her shoulder.

"Are you okay?" Esther asked.

Blair shook her head. Everything was such a mess. And she had a feeling it was because of her.

"The boys keep asking me why you rejected Grandma," Esther continued. "I don't know what to say to them. Do you think it's time to tell them about the Iravata?"

A burst of laughter sounded from the group surrounding the stove. Luka had made a joke about something, sending the other boys into a fit of laughter. Blair wished she could join them, but she was tired. So freaking tired.

"No," she said.

"Why not?"

"Because if they learn about it, they'll just be in danger." Sometimes, when Blair dreamed, she couldn't tell if they were prophetic or not, but they were haunting. Her brothers getting involved. Being part of the world of the Iravata and losing parts of themselves, the way that Leo had lost his magic.

Esther nodded. "That's a good point."

Blair's phone buzzed and she checked it. Her heart leapt when it was a message from Mia, saying, <<It's going okay. No longer grounded.>>

That was a relief. The twins had been grounded for so long that Blair had wondered if their parents would ever relent.

<<I'm glad.>>

<<Want to hang out sometime?>>

The invitation caught Blair off guard. Mia wanted to hang out? Mia, who had been rejecting anything magical, who had barely spoken to Blair or Cody at school, was inviting Blair to hang out?

She wasn't about to say no.

<<When and where?>>

<<Tomorrow at my place?>>

<<Will Derek be there?>>

<<Yes. Oh. Um…how about we go to your house?>>

Blair breathed out. She hated that she couldn't go to her friend's house and escape her family for a bit. All because Derek had decided he couldn't handle being friends with her again. Or stand being around her.

<<No, it's fine. We can just hang out in your room.>>

This was actually perfect. Blair needed someone to go to Australia with her. If Mia was opening up again, maybe she'd want to go with. Maybe she'd be willing to help protect her own future by helping Blair get the artifact.

<<Okay. See you tomorrow around noon?>>

<<Deal.>>

"Who are you talking to?" Esther asked.

"Mia."

"Oh?"

"Yeah. We're hanging out tomorrow."

"As long as you're home in time to light the candles."

Blair sighed. "I'm not in a very festive mood, Mom."

164

Esther wrapped an arm around Blair's shoulders. "I know, sweetheart. You've been through a lot. But this is important to Dad. And we never get Kyro and Luka around for this time of the year. Just try."

Blair sighed. "Okay. I'll try."

She got up and went to the stove, putting on a smile.

"You guys going to steal all the latkes?" Blair asked with a joking tone.

Kyro smirked at her. "Yes."

"What? No." Luka held out a paper towel with an oily, fresh latke for Blair.

She took it and bit into the savory mixture of onions and potatoes, letting the softness of the center wash over her tongue. A smile—a real smile—spread across her face. There was nothing quite like her father's latkes to raise her mood. "Delicious."

"Why thank you," her dad said with a fake bow. "Now all of you get your plates. There's more food than just latkes to eat."

"Okay, Dad," Luka said with a roll of his eyes. He scampered off, followed closely by Kyro and James. Blair, however, stayed next to her dad and watched the boys again. They were so innocent. So unaware of what was going on. Just like she'd been this time two years ago. She hadn't almost died more than once. She hadn't almost lost her best friend. She hadn't lost her boyfriend.

She hadn't lost anything.

Except Leo.

Her hands twitched. Sometimes, when she was focused, she could search for him. He didn't have his magic, and his body was withering away, getting closer and closer to death. She closed her eyes and felt out for him again. To have a vision about him. Like she knew her grandmother could do for her.

Like she wanted to be able to do for everyone.

She wanted to get stronger.

165

She wanted to be able to protect the people she loved.

She just didn't know how to make that happen, and there was no one around to teach her. Still, she focused on Leo. On his essence. Not his magic. Not his soul. Him. His being. And she found him sitting alone in his room staring out the window at the snowless winter of Denver.

Only for a second before she was back in the warm kitchen with her other brothers and her parents, as they all celebrated the holidays.

Derek was sitting on his bed, reading, when the door creaked open. He glanced over at it, knowing full well who was at his door. What he didn't know was why Mia hadn't knocked. She normally did, if they spoke at all. It wasn't that they hadn't spoken at all, but their conversations had been very basic.

"How are you?"

"Good, you?"

"I'm good. Doing homework?"

"Yeah, wanna join me?"

"Sure."

And then they'd sit in silence and work on their homework like everything was completely normal. Even though nothing was normal. Maybe that's why she hadn't knocked.

"Hey," he said. He closed his book and watched his sister close his door behind her. She leaned against it, looking anywhere but him. "Everything all right?"

Mia shrugged. "Blair's coming over tomorrow."

Her emotions grated at his skin, telling a story of anxiety and uncertainty.

"I offered to go to her house," Mia continued, "but she said here was fine. Just thought I'd warn you."

"Thanks for letting me know," Derek said, voice cool.

Mia pouted. "Oh come on. You're still pissed at her? Can't you just forgive her already?"

"No."

"You're being stubborn."

"So?"

Mia rolled her eyes before heading into his room and sitting on the edge of his bed. "We aren't grounded. I'm home and safe. Just give Blair a chance."

Derek sighed.

She didn't get it. None of them seemed to get it.

"How did you feel when Jae froze your mist?"

Mia tensed. Fear clawed at his skin and he shuddered.

"That's how it felt when Blair took away my energy," Derek said. "I was a mess. I couldn't do anything. I couldn't move, I could barely think. She did that to me because she'd thought I was a liability. How am I supposed to look her in the eye knowing that she took away my energy like that?"

Mia remained quiet.

"I know it's not the same thing as what happened to you," Derek said. "I know that you were kidnapped and put in danger and all of that. But to me, it *feels* the same. All that anger and fear you feel, that I feel coming off of you, is the same as my anger and fear. So please, stop asking me to make up with Blair."

"What about Cody?" Mia asked.

"That's…." Derek sighed. "Cody was part of it. I know he didn't know what Blair had planned, but he went along with it. I'm angry at him too."

"And you will be forever?"

"Eventually I'll go to college and forget about them."

"So…this is it?" Mia's eyes flickered to the book he was reading, and then back to his face. "You're just done with our group?"

"Not with you," Derek said. "You're my sister."

"But you're angry with me."

"I am not."

"Because of Chad."

Yeah. The whole Chad thing. Derek didn't understand it, and he didn't know why Mia hadn't just told him about it, but he wasn't angry.

"I can't be angry with you because you want something normal," Derek said. "My life is stuck in the magical world forever, but that doesn't mean yours has to be."

A wave of relief washed over his skin. Mia nodded, smiling. "Okay."

"And don't worry about tomorrow," he continued, picking up his book again. "I won't bother you about anything. Promise."

Mia nodded, and then scuttled further onto the bed until she was sitting next to Derek, back against the headboard. Without a word, Derek grabbed one of his pillows and offered it to her for her back. She took it. She leaned against it and closed her eyes.

And then the two fell silent. Derek returned to his book as Mia rested her head on his shoulder. He felt out for her emotions, keeping an eye on them as they settled into a low hum. Sleep.

Derek sighed and placed his book on the bed, staring out the window across the room. He didn't know exactly what was going on with his sister, but he was absolutely certain that things would eventually go back to normal between the two of them. Even if things wouldn't ever be normal between him and Blair, or him and Cody, again.

He had his sister, and as long as things continued on the way they were, with everyone staying peaceful and quiet, then that was all right with him.

There was laughter in the house. Cody didn't know how to respond to his mother laughing. It'd been a few months since she'd arrived home, but he still couldn't get used to her smile. The way she danced around the living room, decorating the pathetic looking tree for Christmas, unnerved him, even as it brought about warmth to his stomach.

They hadn't had a Christmas tree in years.

"Cody," she said in a sing-songy voice. She hurried over to him and reached out, grabbing his wrists to pull him to his feet. "Come on, help me decorate. Let's surprise Dad."

Cody let her pull him to his feet. He'd been watching her. Watching the way she cooked. The way she sang to herself when she thought no one was there. How she tried her best to make him feel loved. Something he'd never really experienced before. There was something wrong with her.

He kept waiting for the other shoe to drop. She held up ornaments he hadn't seen in years. Little trinkets he'd made in school. Beautiful ornaments that had been passed down his dad's family for years. He didn't know what to say, but he helped put them on the tree, watching his mother from the corner of his eye.

It wasn't just her actions that were off. It was her mist. A beautiful shade of maroon. Bright and alive, but just...off. Moving differently. Like whatever she'd gone through at the hospital had changed her soul. Had given her something to hold onto.

Cody glanced down at his hand. He still couldn't see his mist. He knew that it was purple, unlike his mother's, but he didn't know why he couldn't see it. Why could he only witness its color, its viscosity, when he was using his magic? Or when he'd mixed his mist with

Mia's, holding her steady up on the roof?

He clenched his fist. He didn't want to think about Mia.

"What's on your mind, sweetheart?"

His mom's voice brought him back to reality and he glanced into her eyes. She tilted her head, smiling, waiting for a response.

"I'm just thinking about...." She didn't seem to know about the magic that flowed through his veins. That must have flowed through her veins. He couldn't spoil the world for her. He needed her to remain happy, as unnerving as it was. Because if she was happy, that meant that he was safe here.

"Thinking about what?"

"My friend. Mia." He decided to give a partial truth.

"Oh?" His mom nudged his arm. "She's just a friend, still?"

Cody flushed. "She's always going to be just a friend."

"The way you talk about her, I thought you two would start dating." She sighed and held an ornament to her chest. "I would love to see you find someone who makes you happy."

Cody's eyes trained to the ground. Mia made him happy. But he didn't make her happy. Not in the way that Chad could. Freaking Chad Rogers. The most normal and average guy of all time made Mia happy in the way that Cody wished he could. But Cody had magic. But Cody was related to Jae. But Cody this and Cody that.

She'd never see him that way.

"You should tell her how you feel," his mom continued, placing more ornaments on the tree. "I'm sure she feels the same way."

Cody coughed. "Mom, come on."

"I'm serious!" She turned to him and pinched a cheek with a smile. She'd never done anything like that before. "You're an amazing young man. Smart, kind, handsome. She'd be a fool not to have feelings about you."

Cody watched her. The way she smiled. The way she floated on air, on the world, like she didn't actually belong. A year ago, she never would have complimented him. A year ago, she wouldn't have pinched his cheek, but slapped it. A year ago....

He turned away from her and continued placing ornaments on the tree. His dad was thrilled with the change in her, but Cody couldn't help but wonder if there was something else going on.

Something magical.

He looked out the window, half expecting Lady Shion to show up and tell him that he's right to be worried, but she wasn't there. In fact, he hadn't heard from any of the Iravata in weeks. It was like they were hiding from him. Even Lior, masquerading as Mr. Becker during the day, didn't speak to him or even acknowledge his existence in class.

It was odd.

But Cody didn't know how to prove his theory. He wasn't sure he wanted to prove his theory. Because for the first time in years, he wasn't afraid to go home after school. For the first time in years, he hadn't dreaded winter break. And he no longer dreaded not having Mia and Derek to visit. It was good, he'd decided.

It was all good.

For now.

Chapter Sixteen

Mia hadn't had a friend over in so long, she'd forgotten what it was like to hang out without the pressure of a date, the overhanging of her trauma, or the stressors of school. Just her and Blair sitting in the living room, chatting about their winter break and their schedules for next semester.

"It'll be nice to have classes together," Blair said.

"Seriously," Mia said. "I can't believe we've gone this long without having even one class together. It's not a big school."

"It's like fate didn't want us to be in the same room."

"It's too afraid of how dangerous the two of us are together."

They both laughed, but there was something off about it. Something not quite right. If Mia had made this joke over a year ago, then there wouldn't have been the undercurrent of magic there. She wouldn't have known exactly how powerful Blair was, and how weak Mia was in comparison.

Mia fell silent and Blair looked at the ground. It wasn't the first time that they'd fallen silent. In the past, they used to talk for hours without getting bored. They'd come up with some topic to keep things going. But now Mia wasn't sure what was going on, but there was a fracture there.

She glanced over her shoulder at Derek's bedroom door. They often had Derek joining in on their conversations. It was just all so abnormal.

"Hey, Mia?" Blair asked.

"Hm?"

"I…uh…wanted to ask you something."

"No, Derek doesn't want to talk to you," Mia responded, almost on reflex.

Blair's eyes narrowed and then she rolled them before saying, "No. That's not what I was going to ask."

"Oh. Sorry."

"I was going to ask if you'd be up for a trip."

"Stay away from Australia."

Mia blinked, looking around. The voice had sounded so real in her mind, but she pushed it to the side. The only person who could enter her mind was Lior, and he hadn't done that in a long time. It must have been a memory. Jae's warning making its way back into her mind.

"What kind of trip?" Mia asked.

"Well…." Blair, who had dropped her backpack to the floor, grabbed it and pulled out the stone from when they'd gone to France.

"Oh no," Mia said. "I'm not going to go somewhere dangerous."

"It's not dangerous," Blair said.

"You're trying to get another artifact?" Mia's voice rose in volume and Blair shushed her, looking at Derek's door.

Mia clamped her mouth shut and Blair sighed.

"Look, I know that last time went weird, but I've done more research. We can't just take the artifact. We have to convince the person it's bonded with to give it up. I think I know how to do that this time."

Mia frowned. She remembered the conversation about the artifacts, about the knife, and recalled very vividly how impossible it'd been for anyone to take the knife from her. It'd protected her. It'd chosen her.

Why had it chosen her?

Derek had it now. She knew that he kept it hidden from their parents, who would never understand why he kept it. They would want to study it, and then put it away somewhere safe where Derek couldn't hurt anyone again.

Mia shuddered. During the first few weeks after the incident with Steven, Derek would wake up with nightmares. Not wanting to concern their parents, Mia and Derek had kept it hidden from them, but she'd stay in his room until he fell asleep, wanting to make sure that he was all right. But he wasn't all right.

None of them were all right.

"Why me?" Mia asked. "What about Cody?"

"Cody's been MIA, I guess." Blair shrugged. "Haven't you noticed that he hasn't been around much?"

Yes, but Mia had guessed that was because of their last conversation. "Well, he got mad at me for going on a date with Chad and we haven't really spoken since."

Blair raised her brow. "Seriously? He's pouting because you're dating Rogers?"

"We aren't...." Mia groaned. She didn't know how to explain what was going on with Chad. They'd gone on a couple of dates, but they weren't dating. They weren't boyfriend and girlfriend. They hadn't even kissed yet. And she wanted to keep it that way. She'd jumped into it with Steven, and that hadn't ended well at all. Of course, that wasn't her fault, but she still felt like taking it slow was the best idea.

And Chad had, strangely enough, agreed. He'd told her that he'd never dated before and he was okay taking it slow. He hadn't tried to kiss her. He hadn't tried to hold her hand. He didn't even push her to go on dates with him. If she said no, he said okay and maybe next time. And there always was a next time.

"Look," Mia said, "I don't think it's a good idea to go after these artifacts. You're going to get yourself in a lot of trouble with a lot of very powerful mages. That's not what I want."

"But if we don't do this, then Jae will be able to find you," Blair whispered.

Mia fell silent. There had only been the two meetings with Jae, but they felt like a huge part of her life. He could see her. He could see the others. He could appear before her, though he was nothing but an apparition.

"What do you mean?" Mia asked.

Blair placed the stone on the floor. Their names weren't written on the stone anymore, but Mia could imagine them there, and her eyes traced the lines of her name. Not Mia, but Méilián. The characters she'd known since she was little.

"I keep having visions of him," Blair admitted. "They're mostly when I sleep, but he's there. Watching you. Watching *me*. I think that even though everyone is trying to protect us, he's too powerful, and who knows if he's going to try and take you again. Or worse."

Mia knew he wouldn't. He'd told her he wouldn't. But she couldn't tell Blair. Because then she'd have to admit that she'd spoken to Jae.

"If we get the artifacts, we'll be more powerful." Blair reached out and grabbed Mia's hand. "We could protect you from him for good. Please, I need your help."

Mia grimaced. She didn't want to go. She wanted to spend time with her best friend and hang out. But things were awkward. They weren't back to normal, and Mia knew that she couldn't go back to normal. As much as she tried to pretend with Chad, it was all a mess and the more she pulled away from magic, the more she pulled away from her old normal. Her friends. Her brother.

Everything was changing.

Mia touched the stone, tracing her imaginary name with her finger. "You're sure it's going to work this time?"

Blair nodded. "I've been researching so much. Knowing the language of every person to ever exist, to know how to speak any language, is exhausting. You never have a break. You never misunderstand. You know too much."

Mia frowned. "We want this why?"

"We don't want to use its powers," Blair said. "We just want to keep it with us."

"And you're *sure* the wielder is going to want to give it up?"

Blair nodded.

Mia hesitated, but in her mind she knew that she'd have to go. As long as Jae could visit her, she'd never be free of him. As long as Blair was worried about her safety, she'd never be able to relax. And maybe if Mia was completely safe, things *could* go back the way they were.

Maybe....

Just....

Maybe.

"Fine," Mia said. "I'll go with you. But this is the last time."

Blair grinned. "Of course. I won't ask you to come with me again. Hopefully Cody will be out of whatever funk he's in for the last artifact."

Mia doubted that. The way he'd spoken of his mother had physically hurt her. She didn't know how to handle his frustration, nor the way he'd pushed her away.

"Yeah, hopefully."

Blair breathed in, then wrote her name in chalk. Mia did the same, before Blair held out her hands for Mia to take. "We gotta do this quick. Who knows if Derek will decide to check in on us when he notices our emotions are gone."

Mia took Blair's hands and nodded, but secretly, she hoped that Derek would notice. That Derek would come out and see they were gone, see the stone, and know. That he would be forced to talk to Blair and would get over his anger at her. He'd compared what happened to him to what happened to her, but they weren't the same thing. Blair had been protecting him. Jae had tried to uproot all of Mia's life because he was delusional.

Derek was ridiculous.

Blair muttered something under her breath and Mia closed her eyes, letting the warmth of magic wrap around her arms and body as the two disappeared to Australia.

Cody felt the moment Blair and Mia disappeared. He hadn't meant to be searching for them. He hadn't meant to be watching over their mists, but he'd been dozing and not thinking. Really, it wasn't Blair that he'd been watching, but Mia.

The minute they disappeared, his eyes snapped open, heart racing. He slipped off his bed and ran to the door, but as soon as he opened it, he nearly crashed into his mother. He'd been so focused on where Blair and Mia had gone, he hadn't felt her maroon mist.

"Cody?" Ava asked. "Are you okay?"

No. No he was not okay. He'd been so focused on himself, so obsessed with being angry at Mia, that he hadn't even thought that Blair was still focused on getting the artifacts. He'd planned to tell her to stop. To leave Mia alone and let her be happy with her normal life. But now....

If he'd been there to go with her, would she have taken Mia?

"I...." He didn't know what to say to his mom. He couldn't tell her that he was unintentionally spying on Mia's soul to make sure she was all right and then without warning she was gone. There was no easy explanation for his panic. For his racing heart. His heavy breathing.

"Come, have a cup of tea," his mom said. She slipped her arm in his and pulled him toward the kitchen, smiling. He watched her, then glanced in the direction of Mia's house. Through all of the mists, he found Derek's gold one and sighed in relief. It was a good thing that Derek was still there. He could give Blair an earful when the girls got back.

He let Ava drag him all the way into the kitchen before he pulled his arm out of her grasp. She didn't fight him, but she did look up at him with wide, brown eyes. Cody hadn't gotten her eyes.

He had so many questions. Questions about her. Questions about her past. About where her magic went. About who his real father was, though he had strong suspicions about who. But she didn't seem to know any of those answers, and he wasn't sure if he should break through the unnerving happiness that had taken over.

Instead of asking questions, he sat at the table and stared at his mother as she prepared the tea, humming to herself.

In the back of his mind, he searched for Mia and Blair's mists, but they were long gone. If he hadn't known what Blair's plan was, he would have no idea where they were, but he recalled that she had set her sights on Australia next. He cursed himself for pulling away. For not going with her. It wasn't safe for Mia to leave Willow Creek, and he wondered how the Iravata were handling this.

He hated how quiet they'd been recently. He'd hated it when they were loud and always around, but this felt more ominous. Like they were expecting something to happen and it wasn't anything good. Or maybe they were embarrassed? They had just revealed the entirety of their history to the teens, and it wasn't exactly a pretty story.

Death.

Slavery.

Murder.

Betrayal.

Lies.

Secrets.

It was a lot to take in.

Cody bit his lip. This wasn't the time to think about the Iravata. Not with his mom standing in the kitchen. Not with her humming and making tea.

He breathed out, giving up his search for Mia and Blair. He wasn't going to find them because he knew where they were. They were on the other side of the world—in every sense—and they were probably getting into so much trouble.

He just hoped Blair knew what she was doing this time.

"How are you enjoying your break?" his mom asked. "Are you excited for Christmas?"

Cody shrugged. Christmas had lost its childhood sparkle a long time ago.

She returned to the table with two steaming mugs of tea. Cody wrapped his hands around his, staring at the dark brown liquid.

"You've been really quiet since I came back," his mom said without warning.

Cody looked up at her. "Have I?"

"You've always been quiet, but this seems different. Are you upset about what I did?"

Cody blinked. "What do you mean?"

A soft, sad smile crossed her face. "When I tried to kill myself."

Cody shifted and looked away from her. From the tea. It warmed his hands, but to an extreme. Burning them. Still, he didn't let go, wanting the physical pain to numb the emotional one.

"We don't have to talk about it," he said.

"I think we do." She reached out and nudged one of his hands.

He let go of the mug, staring down at it as she gripped his fingers. "I went through a lot of therapy while I was in the hospital. I was having these memories that weren't real. Memories of a life I didn't have. I thought they were real. You know I don't know much of anything about my childhood."

Cody didn't want to hear this. He didn't want to know the reason his mom tried to end her life.

"But the memories weren't real," she said. "I've never left the country, and I certainly wasn't born abroad. In a different time. It was just my mind getting the better of me. But the doctors, they helped me so much. Did you know that the Sòng's old neighbor is a doctor?"

Cody's head perked up. "What?"

"Mr. Smith. He was one of the doctors who helped me. He did some kind of hypnotherapy and those memories have faded. I feel so much better."

Cody wanted to scream. He wanted to shout. He wanted to stand up and storm out of the house, demanding that the Iravata explain themselves. This was their influence. Her strange happiness was their influence. He wanted to yell at them. To tell them to put his mom back to normal because he hated all of this. He felt safe at home, but barely more than before.

"Mom…." The words were lost on his tongue. He couldn't tell her that Mr. Smith's real name was Eran and that he had control over memories. He didn't know how to tell her that the memories the doctors had convinced her were fake were probably real. He couldn't take away her happiness.

Instead, he gripped her hand back, blinking back frustrated tears.

"I'm glad you're feeling better," he said. "I'm glad the doctors helped you."

Her smile was still soft, but no longer sad. "Me too. I've always been a bad mother to you, but I want to be better. I want to help you in whatever way that I can. I don't want you to be scared of me anymore."

A tear streaked down his face. This is what he'd wanted all of his life. A stable, happy, normal mom.

"You did the best you could," Cody whispered.

She shook her head. "I didn't. And that's not okay. I'll do my best from now on. I'll be a better mom and a better wife to the two most amazing people in the world." She lifted his hand and kissed the back of it before smiling at him. "Promise."

Cody didn't know what to say. And before he could think of anything, a familiar mist appeared outside of his house. A mist as black as night and as cold as the dead of winter.

Lady Shion.

Cody pulled his hand from his mom's grasp and stood. "I'll be right back."

And then he rushed from the kitchen, out into the cold of winter with his shoes and coat half on.

Chapter Seventeen

Derek had known the moment Mia and Blair had disappeared from the living room. He'd been, as promised, minding his own business and playing video games. But when they'd disappeared, their emotions and Blair's magic, Derek had known that they were pulling some stupid stunt again.

He'd thought about going to the living room. He'd thought about trying to figure out how to get them back, but instead he'd left the house. He wasn't sure why. It made the least sense, considering it was in the negatives and he was freezing, but he couldn't stand to be in the house anymore.

Not with Blair dragging Mia into more danger. Not without knowing where they'd gone or why. It wasn't like Blair had told him about her plans. Why she didn't take Cody was beyond him, but he decided not to care.

Or, he *tried* not to care.

Because he did care. As he shivered his way down main street, he cared very much that Blair was *still* not thinking about the consequences of her actions. She was only doing. For a seer, she certainly lived very much in the present.

Or maybe that was because she was a seer. Maybe she didn't want to think about the consequences because if things went the right way—or wrong way, he supposed—then she didn't have to assume the consequences: she saw them for what they were.

Either way, he cared very deeply about all of it and couldn't get the feeling of Mia and Blair's emotions vanishing into nothing out of his head.

He tried. He looked at the scenery. He paid attention to where the plows had shoveled the snow. He reached out to the emotions of the people in the shops, trying to escape the cold. They were all gentle emotions. No one was in distress today.

And then he felt it. Not an emotion, but magic.

He blinked and looked around, trying to figure out whose magic it was. It was familiar, but not one he'd met before. Or maybe he had? Maybe it was Enya. No, it was different. Just different.

He didn't see the man until he turned the corner and almost smacked into him. Almost, not because Derek noticed and stopped, but because he walked straight through him.

A cold shudder ran up Derek's spin and he spun around, tensing as he expected to find Niran stalking him again. But it wasn't Niran. It was someone else. A man, half turned toward Derek with a familiar smile. Not one he'd seen on an Iravata or Enya. But one he'd seen on Cody.

This man, though his skin was darker and his eyes were more blue than gray, could have been Cody's twin.

Jae.

Immediately, Derek called out to the Iravata, but there was no response.

"What are you doing here?" Derek asked. Jae tilted his head and said nothing. Derek gritted his teeth. "You stay away from my sister. I wasn't there to help her, but I will stop at nothing to make sure you can't hurt her again."

Still, Jae said nothing. He looked Derek up and down, making Derek feel both vulnerable and like a piece of meat. And then, in a low voice that didn't sound anything like Cody, Jae said, "So, this is the mighty Niran and his reincarnation."

Derek all but snarled. "What do you want from me?"

"Nothing," Jae said. "I would find you better dead, but it's clear that Mia would be far too upset if I killed her brother."

"Since when do you care what Mia thinks?"

"I've always cared what Mia thinks."

Derek clenched his fists as it warmed, allowing the magic to make sparks between his fingers. It would take nothing to shoot a bolt of lightning at Jae. But it wouldn't do any good. Even from this distance, Derek could tell that Jae was not really there. The Iravata and Mrs. Arbour's magic was doing its job. Kind of.

"Smart boy," Jae said. "Your magic wouldn't work, even if we were in the real world."

Derek started back. "Excuse me?"

Jae waved his hand around. "You think I'd risk coming to see *you* in reality? Never. No, this is a dream."

"You don't have power over dreams," Derek snapped.

Jae shook his head. "No, but I know people who do. Yours are quite something, little Niran."

"Don't call me that."

"I'll call you whatever I please."

Derek took a step back. This was a dream? Jae wasn't really there? But he'd felt Mia and Blair leave. He'd gone outside. He'd....

He couldn't remember leaving the house. He couldn't remember walking down his street. He was in his room, and then he was downtown.

"You definitely aren't as bright as your sister," Jae said with a heavy sigh. "I suppose that's good for me."

184

If this was a dream, Derek decided, ignoring the insult that Jae had thrown at him, then he could wake up. All it would take was for him to....

Derek's eyes snapped open and he gasped.

Blair knew she'd made a mistake the moment they arrived in Australia. The world around them was barren. Sweat beaded on her forehead and she wiped it away, forgetting for a second that they were in summer now. She glanced around her, taking in the Outback. Next to her, Mia whispered something darkly in Chinese.

She knew right away that something was wrong. She'd researched this. She knew where the artifact user lived. She'd seen it in a dream.

But they weren't there.

"Shit," she muttered.

Mia grabbed her arm. "What's wrong?"

Blair shook her head and stepped forward, hoping they weren't going into some trap. A non-seer wouldn't be able to know that she was watching them.

Except for Olivia.

Blair shuddered, recalling the eerie way Olivia had looked at her through her visions. The child had known full well that Blair was having visions about Mia, and Blair was lucky that Olivia had turned out to be on their side. If she'd been on Jae's....

"Let's go," Blair said.

"Go where?" Mia asked.

"This...." She sighed. "This isn't the right place."

Mia pulled away, jaw dropping. "I thought you said that you knew what you were doing this time."

Blair had thought she'd known what she was doing. No, she

still did know what she was doing. All they had to do was find the person with the artifact and convince them to give it up. It wouldn't be difficult.

"I can't predict everything," Blair eventually said. Mia crossed her arms, looking more pissed than Blair felt she had the right to be. "I know that if we get to the person who has the artifact, we'll be able to get it. That's what's important. The fact that we're a little off our destination is—"

"Not a good sign," Mia snapped.

Blair glared at her. She didn't appreciate the attitude. She was doing this for Mia. And it wasn't like Mia was in any great danger here. What was the person going to do? Tell them no if they asked nicely? Blair had no plans to force them to give up the artifact.

"Come on, let's find the artifact," Blair said before stalking off through the night. Mia followed close behind her, glancing over her shoulder at everything.

"Um...."

"What?" Blair asked.

"We're in the middle of the desert. At night."

"So?"

"Animals?"

Blair froze. She hadn't taken the animals into consideration because in her mind, they were supposed to transport right to the artifact. This was another strike against her planning skills, and she wasn't pleased about it. She'd done so much research, put in so much work to make sure that all of this was going to go well.

Already, she was failing. Again.

Blair stopped in her tracks and focused her magic on the ground around them. She'd seen her mom do this with pests in the house. It wouldn't hurt them, but it would discourage them from coming anywhere near the two girls.

When a blue light spread out around their feet, Blair released the magic and the blue light shimmered in the night. Blair stared at it, unable to believe that she had been so off on everything so far.

"There," she said. "That should keep any pests away."

But Mia didn't look convinced. Blair realized that she couldn't see Blair's magic. For all Mia knew, this was some elaborate trick to get Mia to stop complaining. Blair wouldn't do that, but it wasn't like Mia and Blair had been on the same page for anything recently.

"I put up a spell," Blair explained.

Mia looked at the ground, then back at Blair and sighed. "Fine."

Blair stared at her, trying to figure out what to do. How to move this forward so Mia would be more comfortable. "Are you sure you want to do this? We can just go back if you want."

"No." Mia shook her head, and then ran her hands up and down her bare arms. She was wearing a t-shirt and jeans, the same as Blair, but Blair didn't feel the same cold that Mia seemed to.

"Are you sure?"

"I'm sure." Mia answered a little too quickly. She grimaced and stared at the ground. "Let's just get this over with, okay? I have a bad feeling."

So did Blair. But Blair pushed that bad feeling out of her mind so she could focus on the task at hand. There was no bad feeling. Everything was going to go according to plan.

Somewhat.

Blair and Mia trudged on, walking side-by-side toward the place Blair felt an immense power. As they walked, in complete silence, Blair thought about what she was doing and why. Why she was so determined to find these artifacts, because Mia had made it clear that she didn't want this.

But she didn't want to think about that. She didn't want to think about any of this.

Eventually, the girls arrived at a small hut in the middle of nowhere. Blair paused, head tilted as she observed the building. The magic was definitely centered here. The artifact. The person who held the artifact. They were together. She could tell. Maybe it was because she herself was an artifact wielder, or maybe it's because she'd spent so much time with Derek and knew whenever the knife was on him.

Whatever it was, Blair knew that they had made it.

She glanced behind her, wondering why they'd ended up so far away, but pushed it out of her mind and straightened her shoulders.

"Found it," she said, grinning at Mia.

Mia rolled her eyes. "Let's just get this over with."

Blair took a deep breath and entered the hut.

It was small. A single room with a fire blazing in the middle of it. But the hut wasn't warm. At least, not warmer than the outside. Blair's eyes trained to the fire, realizing that it wasn't there for warmth. There was a protection spell in it. She could feel it.

And sitting behind the fire, legs crossed, was a young man with long, thick black hair and dark skin. His eyes were closed, and he breathed in deep when Blair sat cross legged before the fire. She noticed that the artifact was nowhere to be seen, but she had no doubts that it was here.

Mia sat next to Blair and nudged her arm. Blair ignored her, focused instead on the young man. He couldn't have been much older than Blair and Mia. Maybe twenty? Twenty-one? Either way, he was more likely to help them if he was their age. If he understood their plight.

His eyes snapped open.

"You came," he said, though his words did not belong to him. Well, they did, but they came out in a language Blair wasn't used to hearing from anyone outside of Sangota. Her eyes widened, and next to her, Mia tensed.

"You were expecting us?" Blair asked.

He looked between the two girls and cocked his head. "You, yes.

Her, no." He gestured to Mia. "We've heard of her, though. The non-magical girl who keeps showing up in the magical world."

"Great," Mia muttered. Blair nudged her. Mia nudged back.

"How did you know I was coming?" Blair asked.

The young man shook his head. "You haven't heard? The clans are all speaking of you and your connection to the Necklace of Prophecy. The Mauvais Clan has spread rumors that you're not satisfied with your own power, so you're after ours."

"That's not true," Blair snapped.

"So you don't want my stone?" He lifted his hand and unfurled it. The stone was smaller than Blair had expected. Maybe the size of a grape. But the size meant nothing. Its power overwhelmed her and she gasped.

Mia frowned. "That's it?"

The young man snorted. "Of course a non-magical being would see so little in an artifact. Though, there are rumors that you were the original wielder of the Knife of Souls. Is that so?"

"I'm not a wielder of anything," Mia said, though Blair realized she was no longer speaking English. Mia had switched to Mandarin. An instinct. She heard Mandarin, she spoke it. Still, Blair heard the language of Sangota.

The stone was powerful. And useful.

"I can see that." The young man closed his fist around the stone and returned it to his lap. "Now, tell me why you want the artifacts."

"To protect ourselves," Blair said simply. She had to be honest with him. Rumor had it that the stone could detect lies within language. "There are people after us—after Mia in particular—and we know that if the artifacts are all in the same place, they are more powerful than anything else in the world."

"You mean the Gray Spirits?" the young man asked.

Blair and Mia exchanged glances.

"No, not the Iravata," Blair said between gritted teeth. "But their enemies."

"Hm...." The young man stared into the fire. "The stone says that you are telling the truth. But all the clans know that the Gray Spirits are nothing but trouble. Since their queen became free, we've had nothing but bad luck in our clan. Weakening magic. Dying elders. Failing crops. Hostile trade with the invaders."

He looked up at them from underneath long lashes. "Are you here to cause more trouble?"

"No," Blair said simply. "We just want to be safe."

"So, you want my artifact."

"Yes."

"And if I refuse?"

"Then we leave."

Next to Blair, Mia groaned. Blair wished she'd stop reacting, but didn't say anything. She kept eye contact with the young man, hoping, wishing, that he would comply. And for a second, she thought he might. For a second, he looked like he was going to hand over his stone.

Then he laughed. A stark sound. A loud sound.

"I'm not going to hand over the Stone of Language," he said. "It is my right to carry it. You're foolish to think that this plan of yours is going to work."

The fire flickered and grew. Blair stood, backing away. Something was wrong.

And that's when she felt it. The other surges of energy surrounding the hut. Her eyes widened. In the time since she'd been here, the young man must have called for reinforcements.

None of this was going to plan.

"The Cokori Clan was always very full of themselves," the young man said, still sitting, "but to have the granddaughter of the clan leader come and ask for our artifact? Do you really think we don't see what you're doing?"

"I'm trying to protect myself and my friends," Blair snapped. She reached down and grabbed Mia's upper arm, tugging her to her feet. "I have no interest in the Cokori Clan. I just don't want to die."

"Then stop your quest."

"Nope." Blair slipped her hand down into Mia's and pulled her out of the hut, away from the protection spell. She knew they'd be ambushed the moment they stepped outside, but at least there the fire couldn't keep her from going home.

Mia didn't fight her. But she was oddly quiet as Blair burst out into the night, coming face to face with a large group of angry mages.

"Sup?" she said.

Mia gripped her hand tighter and Blair knew that they were done here. Mia was shaking. Looking around at all the mages glaring at them, some with weapons, others with their magic visible on their fingertips.

Shit.

"Return home," she muttered under her breath. The world around them tilted and shifted, then returned to normal. Blair's eyes widened and behind her a voice said:

"Do you really think we hadn't notice your fail safe?"

Blair spun around, letting go of Mia's hand and the young man stood there with a smirk. "You may have been able to run from the Mauvais Clan, but we're not about to let you go. Not when you are responsible for all the pain and suffering of our clan."

Blair couldn't believe her ears. She was responsible for the suffering of the clan? But she hadn't done anything. She hadn't even been the reason for Lady Shion's renewed life. That was all Derek.

"What are you talking about?" Blair asked.

The young man turned and faced his hut, waving a hand over his head. "You'll find out when you stand trial. You may be powerful, but you stand no chance against all of our warriors."

191

Blair glanced over her shoulder at the group of people surrounding them. Men and women of all different shapes and sizes made up the group and Blair tried her best to figure out how to get out of there.

But it wasn't her that came up with the plan.

Mia moved, fast, before Blair could react, and kicked the nearest man in the chest. He flew backwards and Mia bolted. It took a second for Blair to react, but she moved faster than the others. She took off after Mia, letting her magic warm her fingertips. Shouting occurred behind her but she didn't look back. She only imagined a shield around herself, something to protect her from the onslaught of magic she felt coming her way.

Mia was far ahead of her, running like the athlete she was. Then, without warning, she disappeared, leaving Blair alone in the desert. Blair came to a halt, head spinning, trying to figure out where Mia had gone. But there was shouting behind her, and a desert before her, and she was alone.

Breathing heavily, Blair focused all of her energy on home. On her friends. Her family. She called to them, asking for imaginary help, and then she too disappeared.

Chapter Eighteen

Cody had every reason to yell at Lady Shion. She stood in the snow, watching him as he panted and glared at her. Everything he'd just learned about his mother made him want to scream. But he couldn't bring himself to.

She tilted her head, almost as if waiting for him to shout. To throw a fit and blame her for the weirdness in his family.

When he didn't, she spoke, words far more clear and fluent than the last time they'd talked.

"You're angry with us," she said.

Cody scowled. "Why wouldn't I be?"

Lady Shion looked over his shoulder, at his house, and shook her head. "Your mother needed help."

"She doesn't know what you can do!" Cody's voice raised but he lowered it again, not wanting to bring attention to him or the queen. "She doesn't know about magic. She doesn't know about the way things work."

"Are you sure about that?" Lady Shion crossed the field. She reached up and placed a gentle hand on his shoulder. He flinched it away and turned his back to her.

What was she talking about? How could his mother know about magic? If she knew, why had she never told him? Why had she always acted like he was a normal kid? Why had it taken Mrs. Arbour showing him the ropes for him to even understand that he *had* magic?

"She doesn't know," Cody said, maybe more to himself than to Lady Shion. "She can't know. Okay? She can't."

"There are many things about your mother that you do not understand." Lady Shion stepped around to his front, staring him directly in the eye. Her ruby irises sent a chill down his spine. He looked away.

Lady Shion sighed. He'd never heard her sigh before. "I didn't come to speak to you about your mother."

"Great," Cody muttered.

"I came to speak to you about Mia and Blair."

Mia and Blair. Cody's eyes widened. In his rage, he'd forgotten that the two of them had been *stupid* enough to go to Australia. He'd forgotten about his fear for Mia. His anger at Blair. It'd all become about his mother.

"What about them?" Cody asked. Panic rose into his throat.

"They left Willow Creek," Lady Shion said.

"I know that, but are they okay?"

She cocked her head. "You know that they left and yet you have not gone to find them?"

He scowled. "No. I'm not going to try and find them. They want to go off and be stupid…." He couldn't finish his thought. Because as annoyed as he was at both Mia and Blair, for very different reasons, he knew that he couldn't just leave them alone if they were in danger.

Lady Shion held out her hand. "You and Mia are connected. You have formed a bond that no one can break. She needs your help. Bring her home."

Cody had no idea what Lady Shion was talking about. What bond? They were friends. That was all. Mia had made that clear when she'd chosen Chad Rogers. So what if they'd had that moment last spring? So what if Cody had been the one who had always been there for her.

But he couldn't resist. He couldn't stop himself. Because even if she never felt the same way about him, he loved her.

"What do I need to do?" he asked.

"Take my hand and think of Mia," Lady Shion said. "The spell that the others have put on her, that she walked into when she left the safety of her home, will break."

Cody didn't quite understand, but he took Lady Shion's hand and did as she said. He thought of Mia. Of her smile. Her laugh. The brightness in her eyes. He thought of her head resting against his shoulder when they watched a movie and she was tired. And how soft she'd been that night with the wine. He thought of her eagerness to please, the way she worked hard at everything she touched, desperate to gain the approval of a group of people who would never fully understand her.

He would never fully understand her. But he didn't need to, to accept her. He accepted her for who she was and what she did. Even if it meant that he lost her.

Be okay with it, he told himself. *He makes her happy.*

Cody closed his eyes and breathed in, imagining her soft lilac perfume. It tickled his nose, almost like it was really there. And then he heard panting. And then the hand in his changed from soft and lithe to calloused and small.

He opened his eyes. In place of Lady Shion, stood a wide eyed, and panting, Mia. She stared at Cody, and he stared back at her. It took all he had not to pull her against him. Not to wrap her in the tightest hug of her life. It's all he wanted to do. Weeks of not speaking was getting to him.

He'd missed her.

Her. Not the thought of them dating. But her.

"What?" she asked between shivers.

Cody let go of her hand, reluctantly, and pulled off his jacket, wrapping it around her to keep her warm.

"I heard you were in danger," he said. "So I brought you home."

He didn't understand how he'd done it, but he decided not to question it. It wasn't just his magic that had pulled her back, but Lady Shion's. All of his anger at her, at the Iravata for what they'd pulled with his mother, disappeared.

He was just glad to see Mia safe.

Mia's head jerked around. "Where's Blair?"

"Don't know," Cody said, running a hand through his hair. The chilled afternoon nipped at his skin and he shivered. "But we should—"

There was a flash of light and out of nowhere, Blair tumbled into the snow. Mia yelped, then knelt by her friend, fussing over her, asking if she was all right.

"Where the hell did you go?" Blair asked, looking between Mia and Cody. "I thought for a second that they'd gotten you."

Mia shrugged. "I don't know. One second I was running and the next I was here." She glanced at Cody. "You'll have to ask him what happened."

"Oh, you pulled her out of there?" Blair asked, rising to her feet.

Cody took a step back. It'd been a while since he'd heard that tone out of Blair's mouth. Not since they'd decided to stop fighting.

"I…." Cody glanced behind him, desperate for Lady Shion to come back, but she was long gone. Her mist, her body, and her magic. "I just did what Lady Shion told me to do. I don't—"

"You couldn't have gotten me out of there too?" Blair asked, rounding on Cody.

Mia stood between them, holding out her hands with wide eyes and a half open mouth.

"You seem to have gotten yourself out of *your* mess just fine," Cody snapped back at her. "What were you even thinking, taking Mia? When we went to France it was one thing. There were two of us and a surefire way to get out of there. But this time? What even happened?"

"None of your business!" Blair threw her hands up. "You stopped talking to everyone and I needed to make sure that I got the artifacts. Okay, it didn't go as planned, but at least I'm *trying* something unlike you, who just sits at home and mopes all the time."

Cody scoffed. Blair didn't know about his mom, but she had to know something was up. "I am not sitting at home moping."

"Oh yeah, you aren't upset that Mia is dating Chad?"

"I don't care about that!"

"Sure you don't."

"Stop it!"

Mia's voice rang out across the clearing where they stood, high pitched and shrill. Both Blair and Cody fell silent, and Cody took a step back. He hadn't meant to scream at Blair. He hadn't meant to get into a fight with her. Especially not in front of Mia.

"Mia…," he said, but Mia shook her head and backed away.

"No, you two need to stop. I thought you were better, I thought you'd figured out your problems, but you're both still so angry at each other and I'm tired of it!"

"Mia." It was Blair who spoke this time, stepping toward Mia.

But Mia backed away more. She took off Cody's coat and threw it at him. "Just…leave me alone, okay? I want to go home." There were tears in her eyes, but she wiped them away. "I want to go home and I want things to be normal. But you all are making that impossible so just leave me alone!"

She took off before anyone could say anything else.

Cody thought about following her, but he had no idea what she'd been through in Australia. She'd been running....

Cody faced Blair. "What exactly happened?"

Eventually Mia slowed to a walk, when she was sure that the others weren't following her. She wiped away tears, trying to get herself under control. From the moment she'd entered that tent, she'd had a feeling that something would go terribly wrong. The guy with the stone had been a jerk, even if he was right to tell them no. But he'd had no right to try and keep her there.

She shuddered, probably from the cold, but maybe from the idea of being kidnapped again. She ran her hands up and down her bare arms and glanced around at the snowy terrain. It was better than a desert, that was for sure.

I never should have gone with.

She'd known it was a stupid decision. She was reliving it. Over and over. The moment in the airport. Being dragged off against her will. The bedroom that looked like hers.

It didn't look like hers anymore. But the memories were like needles stuck in her mind, just out of reach of a pair of tweezers.

More tears streamed down her face, chilling in the winter air. She picked up the pace, knowing that she needed to get inside before she caught something. A cold. More memories. She needed to get into her room. Her real room. The one that her mom had helped her paint. The one with the new furniture and clothes.

That would ground her.

After a few minutes, she turned down her street, eager to get home, when she spotted someone out of the corner of her eye. Fear tickled her stomach and she spun around, wondering if Jae had decided to come reprimand her for going to Australia. But it wasn't Jae. It wasn't Lior or Adelia.

It was Lady Shion.

Mia froze. She wasn't used to Lady Shion appearing before her. The last time she'd seen the queen, it'd been back at Shubishi's house. Even then, Lady Shion hadn't looked Mia in the eye. She hadn't acknowledged Mia's existence. The others had. They asked her how she was doing, offering to help her heal in whatever way they could.

Not Lady Shion. Not the queen of the Iravata, who had all the power in the world. Who took an interest in Cody.

"What do you want?" Mia asked, wiping away more tears. She needed to stop crying. She needed to stop shivering. She needed to stop blaming the Iravata for what had happened to her.

Lady Shion dipped her head, but said nothing before disappearing into the shadows of the house she stood beside. Mia watched the shadows, and then the frustration overtook her.

She stormed to her house before realizing that she didn't have her keys. She hadn't expected to appear in the woods with Cody. She'd thought they would be back in the living room, no problem. Luckily for her, at least, her parents weren't home, so it was safe to ring the doorbell.

Derek answered it at once, panting. She didn't wait for him to say anything. To scold her for leaving. To lecture her about leaving Willow Creek again. She didn't want that.

She pushed past him, desperate for warmth, and went immediately to the kitchen to make herself some tea. Derek followed her, but she ignored him. Even as he watched her. Even as she desperately wanted to tell him that she was sorry for bringing Blair here. That Blair's recklessness was ruining everything.

"Are you okay?" Derek asked.

Mia ignored him and he sighed.

"I know you're not okay."

"I don't want to talk about it."

"Is Blair coming back over? She left her jacket and her stone."

"No." As far as Mia was concerned, she needed a break from Blair. A real one. One where Blair didn't try and do anything for her. She wanted to be free of this magical world as much as possible. She couldn't divorce herself from Derek, but she could from Blair. She could from Cody.

She wiped away more tears and before she knew it, Derek was by her side, gripping her iced hand. This time, she didn't push him away. She didn't try to fight him or explain that she wasn't in the mood for his comfort. She wanted it. She wanted him to take away these bad feelings and put her to sleep. Just like in the hospital.

"Mom and Dad will be back soon," Derek said. "Do you want me to tell them you aren't feeling well?"

Mia nodded.

"Do you want help?"

She nodded again, and the warmth of his gentle emotions flooded her body. The tea kettle clicked, boiling water the only sound in the kitchen, but Mia ignored it and let Derek lead her to her room.

Derek closed the door to Mia's room and leaned against it, staring at the ceiling. He'd had almost no time to process his dream before he'd felt Mia's distraught emotions overtake the entire house.

He didn't know what had happened, and he wasn't about to ask Mia. Whatever it was had rattled her to the point where she'd looked like she had when he first saw her at Shubishi's house. How scared she'd been in the hospital. He wanted nothing more than to comfort her. To make her understand that she was safe here.

But was she safe here?

His dream pricked at his mind. He hadn't realized it was a dream until Jae had said something. It'd felt so real, just like his other dreams, but those were of Niran. Not of Derek's normal life. He'd never been in Willow Creek before.

He breathed out. It was okay. He was safe. Jae couldn't get to him here. Maybe he could access Derek's dreams, but Derek had power in those. He had enough power to wake up if he needed to. Even if he couldn't even remember falling asleep.

The front door opened and low voices echoed in the entry way. Behind him, Mia's emotions were calm and warm. She was asleep, and he didn't want to disturb her. Her headed back toward the front door, putting on a smile.

"Hey," he said to his parents. They looked up at him and smiled as well.

"How were things?" Intira asked. "Did you and Mia have a good time?"

No. "It was okay. Mia didn't feel well so she went to bed early."

Her mother's smile vanished in seconds. "Not feeling well? What do you mean? Is she all right? Does she need to see a doctor?"

Yes. "No, I think she just needs sleep."

His mother clearly didn't believe him. She looked at Liang, who nodded and passed Derek, heading up the stairs to his room and office.

Derek grimaced. "Mā, I'm serious. Everything is fine."

"I've never been good at knowing when you're lying to me," Intira said. She gestured for him to follow her and the two headed to his room. She closed the door and sat on his desk chair. He settled on the bed and looked anywhere but her. "Ever since you were a child, you've been amazing at lying. But I know enough to know that Mia is not okay, and neither are you."

Derek didn't know what to say. Honestly. He'd tried. He had.

But he hated lying to his mother.

"Mia went off somewhere with Blair and it shook her up," Derek said. "And I had a dream. Mia's kidnapper visited me."

Intira looked like she'd been hit by a train. She blinked, looking around Derek's room, and then finally back at him. "Mia went somewhere with Blair?"

"I don't know where," Derek defended. "She didn't tell me before she left. But she came back rattled. I helped her sleep."

"I see." Intira glanced at the wall, toward Mia's room. "She's asleep now?"

"Yeah."

"You can tell?"

Derek nodded. "Emotions are different when someone is asleep. They're there. They exist. But they're quieter."

"I see."

Derek didn't like how quiet his mother was being. She usually had a million things to say on all topics, but today.... "I know we're supposed to be good, but please don't tell Mia I told you. I think she regrets going enough as it is."

Intira sighed. "I won't say anything. And this dream of yours... you've mentioned before that you have odd dreams. Do they always involve the man that stole away your sister?"

"Never have before."

"Do you think it was just a dream, or did he really visit you?" She breathed in at the last words, then shook her head. "This is so strange. Someone visiting you in a dream...that shouldn't...none of this should be possible."

Derek could only laugh. A stark, short laugh, but laughter nonetheless. He may have lived with his magic all of his life, but that didn't mean he was immune to the idea that all of this was batshit insane.

"He visited me," Derek said. "He said he knows someone with

the power of dreams. Probably one of the Natara he took care of. I guess he wanted to see who I was?"

Though, if he'd been watching Mia all of her life, then why couldn't he also have been watching Derek? Why didn't he know about Derek from his stalking of Mia?

He shook his head. Intira remained quiet, so Derek continued. "These dreams worry me, you know? They feel so real. It's like I was actually downtown. It's like Jae was actually there and talking to me. I was so scared that he'd found a way around the barriers that Mrs. Arbour and the Iravata put up, and now I'm scared that he can visit Mia in *her* dreams. She doesn't need that. She doesn't need to feel unsafe again."

But she already did feel unsafe again.

"Shit," Derek muttered.

Intira moved until she was sitting on the bed next to Derek. She wrapped an arm around his shoulder and pulled him against her. He didn't fight it. It was warm. And safe. His mother's arms had always been warm and safe.

"You know, when you were a little boy, you used to have dreams," she said. "You were very small. You could barely speak, but you always mentioned being in Thailand, I think. It sounded like the area my family came from. We never thought much of it. We'd visited the place when you and Mia were very small. But you always cried when you had those dreams."

Derek pulled away from his mom. "I dreamed of the Mekong River?"

"Yes."

He shook his head. "Why can't I remember that?"

"Oh, you were so young. You stopped talking about it eventually and moved on to other things. I think it was around the time you started school."

He'd been having these dreams all of his life. They hadn't started when the queen was unsealed.

"Oh." He didn't know what else to say. There was nothing else *to* say. He was certain that whatever was going on with him and Niran, it had started when he was very little. Possible from the moment of his birth. And that made him uncomfortable.

Intira stood. "I'm going to check on your sister. Just to make sure she's still asleep."

She was, but Derek didn't want to take this moment away from his mother.

"I'll talk to Mrs. Arbour in the morning about protecting your dreams," Intira said. "Hopefully she has something that can help keep you both safe."

Derek hoped so. Intira left the room and he sat quietly by himself, staring out the window across from his bed. It was getting dark. Flakes of snow drifted from the sky, and he closed his eyes, feeling out for Blair and Cody. For their emotions and their magic. He didn't normally check on them, since they'd asked him not to, but if Mia had been freaked, then there was a good chance the two of them were not okay either.

He searched. And searched. The entirety of Willow Creek, and found neither of them.

His eyes snapped open. Had Blair not come back with Mia? Had Cody gone to find her? Should Derek be worried?

WORRY NOT. THEY'RE FINE.

Get out of my head.

STOP WORRYING SO LOUD.

Derek rolled his eyes and turned on the small TV in his room so he could play some video games and maybe quiet his consistently worried thoughts.

Chapter Nineteen

"I knew you were going to go."

It was a familiar voice. Blair blinked and turned away from Cody, fists clenching. She shivered, trying to keep her body from freezing too much, but it was difficult to do with snow sprinkling from the sky. Behind her stood a familiar face. One that Blair had hoped they would never see again.

She had changed. Older. A little taller, face with a little less baby fat. Her hair was longer, curly and dark, but she was paler.

"Olivia?" Blair asked.

Olivia stepped forward, out of the shadows, and smiled. "It's good to see you two are as lively as ever."

She'd never really spoken like someone her age, but today she was particularly formal.

"What are you doing here?" Cody asked. Blair wanted to round on him again. To yell at him for rescuing Mia but not her. For making her worry about Mia. For getting involved at all when he'd been moping around for the past few weeks.

Instead she focused on Olivia. She tried her best to quell her anger. It had scared off Mia. She didn't want to scare off Mia anymore.

"I came looking for you two," Olivia said.

"And you'd knew we'd be here," Blair said.

"Of course."

"But why?" Cody stepped forward, holding out an arm to block Blair. She glared at him, but said nothing. Cody continued, "Why are you looking for us? We want nothing to do with you or Jae."

"Cody," Blair chastised. "Come on, she helped save Mia."

Cody snorted. "Only because she knew we were going to win. She knows everything, remember?"

How could Blair forget. Olivia was the only person who had known that Blair was spying on her. The omniscient Olivia.

"No, it's fine." Olivia slipped her hands behind her back and smiled wider. "I know that you two have every reason to be suspicious of me. But I promise, I'm not working with Jae. I came here to warn you."

"Warn us? Of what?" Blair asked.

"Enya," Olivia said, brow furrowing.

The name sent a shiver up Blair's spine. She hated the name. Enya.

"She's...."

Olivia gasped, eyes going wide. At first, Blair thought that she was injured, and immediately ran to her side. But Olivia didn't faint or collapse. She merely stared over Cody's shoulder, and Blair followed her gaze.

In the snow, far away, stood Shubishi, wearing a heavy winter coat. He stared at Olivia, eyes wide. Olivia stared back at him.

Blair backed away from Olivia, joining Cody between them and her head swung back and forth as she tried to take in what was going on.

"Shubishi," Olivia said, voice lower, taking on a more mature quality.

"Nadine?" Shubishi whispered.

Nadine? Who the hell was Nadine? Why was that name so familiar to Blair? Why did she feel like she'd seen something like this before? In a distant dream? In a far off memory?

A shot of pain spiked in her mind and she doubled over, grabbing her head as images flashed across her eyes. Images of Shubishi. A younger Shubishi with a girl who must have been a few years older than him. Playing together. Laughing.

Shubishi and Nadine.

"Blair!" Cody's voice broke through the images, shattering them into dust.

Blair opened her eyes, panting, and found Olivia collapsed in the snow. Behind them, Shubishi was gone, and in his place stood Lior and Adelia. They ran toward the kids, both with frantic looks behind their eyes.

"What happened?" Blair asked.

"I don't know," Cody said.

Lior crouched next to Olivia and turned her over, lifting her from the ground. "Something is wrong here," he said. "We need to get her help."

Help? How could they help her when they didn't even know what was going on?

She'd come here to warn them about Enya, and now she was asleep? Collapsed? Why had Shubishi said the name "Nadine"? Where had he gone?

There were so many questions and Blair didn't have the energy to ask any of them. Cody hefted her to her feet, but she wobbled. She hadn't been like this in months. Even her visions, which had been small, but frequent, revealing almost nothing about the future or the past, hadn't taken her out like this.

So why...?

"The hospital in Denver," Cody said. "Can't they help with things like this?"

"That's for mages only," Blair managed to say.

"Yeah, but they won't know that Olivia isn't a mage."

"Yes they will." It was Adelia who spoke, coming forward. She faced the teens and shook her head. "But it's our only choice if we want her safe. We can make it work."

Cody tensed, gripping Blair's arm tighter. She flinched and looked up at him, confused.

"You mean like you did with my mother?" he asked.

Adelia observed him for a moment, and then sighed. "Yes, like with your mother."

Cody snorted. "We don't need your help. We can get Olivia into the hospital without you."

"No you can't." Adelia's voice was firm. "But we won't stay long. That place gives me the creeps."

Blair didn't want to go to the hospital. She didn't want to be in the same place as Leo. But what else could she do?

"All right," she said.

"Blair…." Cody's voice warned her. She didn't know what he was talking about, with his Mom, but she had no interest in finding out.

"We should get going." She pulled away from Cody, stumbling, and caught herself on a nearby tree.

Lior and Adelia nodded, and then without warning the woods around them morphed and changed into the familiar green grass of the hospital where Blair's brother waited for the day when his magic would return to him. A day that would never come.

Cody sat in the waiting room, ignoring all the people staring and whispering. He didn't want to think about them. He didn't want to be here at all. All the sick people. All the broken and shattered mists.

One broken and shattered mist in particular.

Leo's mist had never been the same since that day. While the other mists still retained their color, his was completely devoid of any part of the rainbow. It wasn't even white. More clear. Not invisible, but clear. Cody could still see it every time he looked at the room where he knew Leo waited to talk to him.

He couldn't explain how he knew. It was a calling. A use of the mist to attract Cody's attention. He kept looking at the room. Even when he didn't want to, he found his gaze trailing to the door. Leo may not have magic, but he certainly knew how to manipulate things to get his way.

A different door opened. Cody stood, tearing his gaze away from Leo's room again. He wished that Olivia had been put on a different floor, but what could they do?

Blair walked out of the room, closing the door behind her. She and Cody made eye contact, but neither spoke. All of this was madness.

Shubishi knew something. Something he wasn't telling anyone, and there was nothing they could do about it. The Iravata had told them their story, but there were things they'd left out. Things they'd admitted to leaving out, and things they hadn't.

Finally, Blair sighed and pushed away from the door. "They said they'll take care of her, even if she isn't a mage. She's in a coma and they can't figure out why, but they'll make sure she's all right. She's just a kid, after all."

Cody thought to his conversation with Heba and Parker. The two of them had spoken before about how the rest of the world, especially the mage world, hated them, so he had trouble believing that the mage hospital cared whether or not Olivia was a child, but he wasn't going to argue with Blair. Not when she looked so distressed.

"That's good." He glanced over his shoulder again. At Leo's room. Before catching himself and forcing his head back in Blair's direction.

She raised a brow. "Leo?"

"Yeah." There was no point in lying to her. "I think he wants to see me."

Blair gestured toward his room. "Then go. It's not like he can hurt you anymore."

Oh, but Leo had never been one to be physically harmful. It was all about his words. The way he talked to Cody had shaped so much of Cody's anxiety. Every time he thought he was over it, Leo's voice entered his mind and reminded him that he wasn't safe. People weren't safe.

He shuddered, but nodded. Her mist shifted, but she said nothing about Leo wanting to see him and not her.

He glanced over his shoulder at Blair, waiting to see if she would glare at him, but she'd turned her attention away, focusing on Olivia's door. With a deep breath, Cody entered the room, but stayed close to the door, hand on the handle.

Leo sat in his wheelchair, staring out the window. At first, Cody thought he might be sleeping, but his mist, clear as air, danced around him. Cody watched it, unable to tear his eyes away from it. It used to be the prettiest shade of blue. Prettier and stronger than Blair's. And now it was like it had never existed.

Another shudder.

"I'm surprised you're here," Leo said in a gravelly voice. His chair turned so he was facing Cody.

Cody gasped. He hadn't seen Leo since the accident and the boy had changed so much. Hollow eyes. Sallow skin. Cheekbones prominent. He looked emaciated. Cody took a step back, wanting to run. Run from the look Leo was giving him. Run from the memory of that night.

Run from the fact that he did this to someone, and he didn't even know how.

"Afraid of me?" Leo asked.

Cody said nothing.

Leo chuckled. "I guess I deserve that. I was pretty awful to you. I regret it."

Still, Cody said nothing.

Leo moved closer to him, but Cody stepped back, prepared to slam the door shut.

"I didn't think you'd be so tall." When Cody still said nothing, words lost in the back of his throat, Leo sighed but continued. "I was going to ask you if you could give me back my magic, but it would seem you're too afraid of me to even speak. Guess I'll let you leave."

Cody blinked and finally the words came out. "Give you your magic back?"

Leo glanced up at him. "Of course. You took it. You can give it back."

Cody's eyes trailed to his hands. "I…."

"You can't."

"I don't even know how I took your magic."

Leo scoffed. "Of course. You haven't learned anything since we were kids. Why am I not surprised?"

He'd learned so much, though. He'd learned how to control so much of his magic that he was an entirely different person now. Even though they were in Denver, the mists didn't bother him as much. Even though he was surrounded by crying mists, he wasn't about to have a panic attack.

He was nothing like he'd been as a child.

"That's not fair," Cody said, voice quiet. "It's not like I go around taking people's magic from them. I don't train that part."

"Why not? Wouldn't it be useful?"

It would be very useful, but Cody could still remember how it felt. Like ripping apart steel with his bare hands. Painful. Difficult. Terrifying.

"I should go," Cody muttered. "Sorry I can't help you."

Leo waved him off. "Go ahead. Keep running. It's what you do best."

Cody wasn't sure if Leo had meant for the words to hit as harshly as they did, but it was true. All he did was run.

He'd run from Leo.

He'd run from his mother.

He ran from Mia.

He didn't like confrontation. He didn't like having to deal with the problems at hand. He just wanted to pretend that none of it existed so he could go on with his life with his fingers in his ears.

But there were also times when he didn't run. He'd faced Jae. He'd faced Kathleen. He'd confronted Blair about the way she'd talked to him.

He didn't always run.

This time, he did run. He closed the door and stared at it, hand still on the doorknob. He couldn't fix Leo. He wasn't sure what happened to Leo's magic when he took it. If it was still in him or if it had returned to the cosmos. Regardless of the answer, he couldn't do anything about it.

So, he might as well run.

"How is he?" Blair asked.

Cody shrugged. "The same."

"Really?"

No, not really. There was a softness to him that hadn't existed when they were children. Cody didn't tell her this. Instead he turned. "Let's go home."

Home. Home where everything was a mess. Home where he

had no more friends. Where Derek and Mia wouldn't talk to him. Where Blair would still, and forever, blame him for the wrongs in her life.

Home.

He didn't want to go home.

Part Four

Chapter Twenty

Derek watched from the living room as Mia and Liang busied themselves in the kitchen, preparing for the Lunar New Year feast. Really, he didn't care about his father. Liang had adjusted to the idea that his children were involved in the magical world and everything he thought he knew about his connections and his job were not exactly the truth. Not a lie, per se, but a little bit of a lie.

Really, Derek was concerned with his sister. The one who, only a few weeks before, he'd had to help fall asleep. Mia still hadn't talked about her trip with Blair. She hadn't told him where she'd gone, and he didn't press, fearing that it would awaken more terrible memories for her.

She laughed loudly, rambling something to Liang as he held up a pair of chopsticks with a sticky rice ball between them. Mia pushed it away.

"If I eat any more of them I'll be too full for dinner!"

"But I need to make sure that this batch is as delicious. It's not every year we have someone new at our table," Liang said.

"Ask Māmi or Derek." Mia laughed again and turned her back

on their father.

Derek couldn't stop watching her. She moved differently. It was like two years ago. Mia and Liang always took over the kitchen for the big feast, often with Blair or Cody asking questions.

This year, there was no Cody. There was no Blair.

There would only be Chad.

Derek's brow furrowed. He didn't want to admit to Mia that he didn't like her boyfriend—though she insisted Derek not call him that. For some reason, he made her happy. He made her feel stable. When Mia was with Chad, with his friends, her emotions evened out and she came home happy and able to sleep on her own.

She spent a lot of time with him.

She did not, however, spend a lot of time with Cody or Blair. Derek let it be. This was her battle to fight, and he had no interest in trying to make things better between the her and the two people causing her stress.

"Derek!" Mia hopped into the living room and grabbed his hands, pulling him away from the back of the couch. "Come on, Bà wants you to try something."

"I said I needed *you* to try it," Liang called with laughter.

Derek smiled. "It's all right, I can try it."

He followed Mia into the kitchen. Her emotions were a mix of nerves and excitement. Not a hint of fear. Not a hint of negative anxiety. Just happiness as she prepared to welcome Chad into their home.

He honestly never thought she'd date in high school. Boys had shown interest in her before, but she'd been so oblivious to it. He figured she'd end up finding someone in college who was a lot better at expressing their emotions than anyone at Willow Creek High. Last year, when she'd gotten involved with Steven, he'd been too focused on himself to really notice it, but he noticed the difference with Mia when she was with Chad.

Derek grabbed a pair of chopsticks and plucked one of the sticky rice balls out of the water they were boiling in. He blew on it, then popped it in his mouth, flinching at the heat. The gooiness of it stuck to his teeth, but it was delicious. Just sweet enough to be noticed, but not enough to make him want to drink a gallon of tea to balance it.

"Tastes good to me," Derek said.

"Good." Liang returned to the stove, Mia hovering next to him, and Derek retreated back to the living room, still watching his sister. Her movements were so much lighter. She laughed again.

She was returning to normal.

And it wasn't because of him. It wasn't because of Blair or Cody. It was in spite of all of them. In spite of the magic that still ruled her life. Their lives. She was rejecting it, and was so much happier for it.

This was why he'd never wanted to tell her. She'd gotten angry at him for keeping her in the dark, and he'd blamed himself for it for years. But this was why. He knew that she couldn't handle it. Not because she was weak, but because she wasn't. Because she couldn't balance the two worlds. And she didn't have to, because she wasn't part of it.

"She looks happy." It was his mother speaking.

He tilted his head to look at her. "Yeah."

"I honestly never thought I'd see her happy again." Intira joined him leaning against the couch, the English sounding foreign on her tongue. "She's always been strong, but this summer broke her in a way I'd never seen."

Derek knew she would recover. He just hadn't known when. Or how.

"It's a shame that Cody and Blair aren't coming this year," Intira continued. "I know that things are rough between the four of you, but I was hoping that you would make up before the holiday. It's such an important time of year for all of us."

"They're a reminder," Derek said without thinking.

"Of what?"

"Of when she was kidnapped." He'd done a lot of thinking. Observing his sister's emotions. Keeping track of them throughout the day, even if it meant not paying attention in class. "They keep dragging her back into that world when all she wants to do is move on. They're obsessed with finding these artifacts to protect her without realizing that she doesn't need protection. She just needs time."

Intira hummed, nodding. "I suppose that's true. But what about you?"

"Me?"

"You've gone through a lot over the past two years. Do you need time too?"

Derek hadn't realized that his mother was worried about him. He looked at the ground, shuffling his feet. "I'm fine."

"Are you?"

"Yes." He hated lying to his mother, but he didn't want her to worry about him. It was Mia who needed the help. She was the one who could escape from the trauma that was magic. Derek couldn't. No matter what he did, he was stuck on a path he didn't want. Having dreams he didn't want. Keeping secrets he didn't want to keep.

He looked up, straight into the green eyes of Niran. Niran grinned before vanishing and Derek shook his head.

"Chad's probably going to be here soon," Derek said.

"Yes. He's a very sweet boy."

"Yeah. Sure."

"Something you know that I don't?"

Derek shrugged. "Just that he wasn't always so sweet. To Mia or to anyone else."

"Well," Intira said, placing her hands on Derek's shoulders, "it's a good thing people can change."

Derek smiled as his mom headed into the kitchen to join her husband and daughter. He, meanwhile, stayed behind, staring at the happy family. He thought back to that dream. The one with Niran telling him that he didn't have much time left. That he was either going to die or become Niran, just like the choice that Niran had made thousands of years before.

And he decided to pretend like it had never happened. He didn't want to disappear or die. He wanted to continue living his life with his parents and his sister. They were what mattered here.

Niran smirked at him again, appearing like a ghost. Derek raised his head high and walked straight through the ghost to join his family in the kitchen.

Blair sat on the swings at the park, kicking at the ground. She refused to look at her phone, to see the time, because she didn't want to think about what she was missing.

It wasn't until another person joined her that she looked up from the sand, wet from months of unrelenting snow.

"You weren't invited either?" Cody asked, hands in his pockets.

Blair eyed him. They hadn't spoken much since the trip to Denver, and she couldn't tell if it was because he was rattled or angry at her for snapping at him. She hadn't meant to. But the stress of everything had settled on her shoulders and, well, old habits die hard.

"No," she finally said. "Wasn't invited. Didn't think I was going to be."

"Me neither." He joined her and swayed in the opposite direction of her swing. "But I kinda hoped things would be normal now. That things would be back to the way they were."

Blair knew what he meant, and she had to resist from telling him that nothing was ever going to go back to the way they had been. She didn't want to admit that things were messed up beyond fixing. She could feel her safe, stable life slipping away from her.

She needed it back.

"I have one more artifact to try and get," Blair said.

Cody stopped his swing and stared at her. "Are you serious? You're still on that? It hasn't gone well *any* of the times. Including getting the necklace."

"Yeah, well, I have a good feeling about South Africa." She did not, in fact, have a good feeling about South Africa. She'd been having minor visions recently, but nothing about the artifact. It didn't matter how much she focused on it, all of her visions were about something ominous. Fire. Screaming.

She didn't like them. Not that she'd ever liked her visions, but at least they used to be helpful sometimes. These just made her want to tear her hair out. To do *something* to stop whoever was screaming.

Cody sighed. "Blair, maybe we should stop this. I don't think Mia cares. She's been happy recently. Her mist has never been brighter. She's safe. We don't need to risk our lives for her anymore."

But it wasn't about Mia anymore. It was, on the surface, about protecting her best friend, but Blair knew there was something deeper to it. She needed to find the artifact so she could prove that she was good enough to do something. Cody had saved Mia. Derek could protect her emotions. The Iravata and her mom could keep her physically safe.

All Blair did was get her in trouble.

All Blair did was make things worse.

All Blair did was mess up.

And she didn't want to be that person anymore. She wanted to prove that she could do this. To herself. To the world. To her best friend who wouldn't speak to her anymore.

It was all she had.

"I'm going whether you come or not," Blair said. She jumped off the swing. Tonight was a perfect time to go. It wasn't like she had a Lunar New Year dinner to attend.

Cody sighed. "Fine. I'll go with. But after this, you need to drop it. Once the wielder says no, we leave. We don't stick around to argue or make our case. We just leave. Got it?"

Blair did not want to agree, but she knew Cody wouldn't come with her if she didn't, and she didn't want to go alone. "Fine."

"Good."

Cody slipped off his swing and faced her, arms crossed. "So, what are we going to do? You don't have that stone with our names on it."

"Don't need it." Blair held out her hand. Cody eyed it before placing his hand in hers. "I've been growing stronger. Coming back from Australia without anyone's help made me realize I don't need a magical stone to help. I can get us there and back no problem."

Cody frowned. "Why don't I believe you?"

"Because you've never trusted me." She gripped his hand tighter. "But I know what I'm doing."

She certainly hoped she knew what she was doing.

Maybe it was because he didn't have anything to lose either, but Cody gripped her hand and nodded. "All right. Take us to South Africa."

Blair grinned and closed her eyes, imagining the artifact. Not the person who wielded it, but the actual artifact this time. She wasn't going there to argue. She wasn't going there to bargain. She was going there to make sure that she came back with an artifact, even if it got them into massive trouble.

She breathed in, focusing, and let the warmth of her magic spread through her body. Into Cody's body, calling on his magic too.

It responded and sprang to life, spreading white hot magic through her body. She gasped. She'd always known that Cody was powerful, but she'd never imagined how much power he really had.

This was a lot.

"Ready?" she asked, opening her eyes.

Cody nodded, and then the world around them shifted. Changing from forests and snow to a village deserted because of the night.

Derek continued to watch his sister throughout the night. She couldn't stop smiling. Trying to get him to engage in conversation, but he wasn't feeling particularly chatty. He was more in an observational mode. Waiting for the moment when his sister would break down.

He didn't want to think of her as fragile, but he knew how she worked. She would have great moments. Moments where everything was fine, but then something would change and she would slip back into the depression.

But all through dinner she seemed ecstatic. Chad, too, appeared happy, constantly staring at Mia with gentle eyes. His emotions whenever she focused on him went haywire. A mix of happiness and desire. Derek tilted his head, wondering if there was love in the mix. He didn't feel any of the slippery lust against his skin. And he was glad. Happiness and desire were good enough, especially since the desire didn't seem to be about touching Mia. He wanted to be around her.

"Derek, stop spacing out," Mia said with a laugh. "We're trying to talk to you."

"Hm?" Derek glanced between all the members at the table, and then at his food, which he'd hardly touched.

"I was talking about plans for college," Chad said. "I got scouted so I'm planning to go to Harvard and get a comp-sci degree."

Derek had to resist sighing. There was absolutely nothing wrong with Chad's plan, but it wasn't what he'd pictured for Mia. Not that he had any say in what her picture was going to look like, other than he was in it. It was just…a computer science guy? Mia had so much ambition.

"Have you finished applying to schools?" Chad asked. A hint of worry licked at Derek's skin. Chad wanted to get on his good side.

"Yeah," Derek said, thinking back to the applications he'd half-assedly filled out. His essays were stellar, thanks to his mom's insistence on editing them, but the rest…he didn't care about college. He'd used to, but that was before….

"That's cool. Any top choices?"

"Derek's always wanted to go to New York," Mia explained for him when he hesitated. "NYU. Maybe Columbia, but who knows. It's hard to get into both those schools and Derek doesn't take school seriously."

"Hey, I do too," Derek protested.

Mia stuck out her tongue at him and he smiled.

He hoped that this mood of hers lasted forever. He wanted her to be happy. To know what safety felt like again.

"I can't believe you're all going to university next year," Intira said with a sigh. "You've all grown up so quickly."

Derek couldn't help but roll his eyes. Intira always got nostalgic around this time of year. Something about Derek and Mia's birthday being in a few months. They were going to be nineteen. A year older than all of their friends, but that was the consequence of moving to another country when they were kids.

Dinner continued on and Derek fell back into his silent observations. But as he watched Mia and Chad together, him flirting with her, her turning red because of it, he realized that he didn't want to be there. At least, not without Blair. Last year it'd been him and Blair who had been nauseating. Last year she'd been at the table with them, eating food and having a fun time.

He missed her.

He really missed her.

Closing his eyes, he reached out for her emotions, wondering where she might be, but found she was missing from Willow Creek. Again. He opened his eyes, considering excusing himself to go find her. To bring her back and tell her to stop being ridiculous. To stop leaving the safety of their home.

But he didn't. Because deep down he was still angry with her, and he didn't want to interrupt his family time to go find someone who had betrayed him.

Even if he also really did.

Instead he returned his focus on the table, trying his best not to wonder where Blair had gone this time, and if she was having any better luck this time around.

Chapter Twenty-One

B lair wasn't sure how to react to the bowl sitting on a table in front of them. She knew it was the artifact. As plain and simple as it appeared, it blasted her with magical energy, more than any of the other artifacts. She tried to imagine why that could be. The Knife of Souls barely registered on her radar.

Then there was the Staff of Storms, which had always been a heavy presence upon the school. But still, it didn't compare to the bowl sitting in front of her.

The necklace too couldn't compare, but Blair had a feeling that had more to do with the fact that she was the wielder.

And the Stone of Language...she hadn't been able to tell if it was the magic of the stone or the magic of the wielder that she'd felt.

The Bowl of Transportation was another story altogether. She knew that the power emanating from it wasn't part of another person's magic. It was powerful. It was *loud*. She was afraid to go near it.

"Is that it?" Cody asked, voice a little hoarse. Blair glanced at him, noticing that he rubbed his hand up and down his throat. It must have been a side effect of her transporting them.

"I think so." Her own throat burned when she spoke and her hand flew to it.

"You probably should have used something to help us get here," Cody whispered. "That was not fun."

"Sorry." She took a step toward the bowl and tried her best to keep calm and focused. She wasn't actually sorry. She just didn't want Cody to chastise her.

"Think it's a trap?" Cody asked.

"No idea." She took another step forward and then closed her eyes, feeling for the magic of anyone else. But the Bowl of Transportation drowned out all possibilities of magic. Even Cody's magic was nothing more than a whisper compared to the artifact.

It wasn't until a figure emerged from the night that she tensed, ready for a battle. Because dammit, she was going to get this artifact, even if it almost killed her.

"Who are you?" Blair asked the woman emerging from the shadows. She looked different than the young man in Australia. He'd had life to him. Excitement behind his eyes. But she glanced around her, nervous. Her hands wrung together, nervous. Her shoulders were tense. Nervous.

"My name is not important," the young woman said. Her eyes trained to the bowl in front of her. "You two...you're trying to collect artifacts, correct?"

Was this a trap?

"Yes," Blair said.

The woman looked up from the bowl and directly into Blair's eyes. When she spoke again, her thick accent made it difficult to understand her, but the intent behind her tone was crystal clear.

"Take it. I don't want it."

Blair blinked. This was a trap. They were waiting for Blair to take it so they could jump her. She wouldn't be able to use its power because she didn't know how. There was no way in the world that a wielder would give up their artifact. Especially not to a stranger from another clan and a stranger who wasn't even a mage.

"What?" Cody asked. "Why don't you want it?"

The woman reached forward and grabbed the bowl before storming toward Blair. Blair stumbled away, only to bump into Cody and the woman caught up to her. She grabbed Blair's hands and shoved the artifact into them.

Immediately, the magic from the artifact clung to Blair's own, and she gasped, nearly dropping the artifact in the process. She managed to keep a hold of it, but the electricity in her skin made her shudder.

"I give you, Blair Arbour, the Bowl of Transportation. Use it to protect yourself and your friends. Use it to defeat the woman with red hair. Use it to restore balance to the clans. Use it however you please, just get it away from me!"

The woman backed away, hands wringing together.

"Wait!" Blair called out, but before she could say anything else, the woman was gone. She wasn't gone in the way that Blair had transported her and Cody. There was no hint of magic. She was just…gone. Transported away with a gift that Blair hadn't realized existed. Blair turned to face Cody, whose eyes were wide.

"She just…." Cody tensed before he could finish his sentence. "People are coming. We have to go."

Blair looked down at the bowl. With it, there would be no trouble getting to where she needed to go. She'd actually gotten an artifact. But something about all of this felt wrong.

That's when it hit her.

A vision.

Not one of fire and screams, but one of anger and malice. She collapsed to the ground, dropping the artifact. It clattered against the paved road as her mind went wild with the anger of the clans.

But was it old anger?

Was it new anger?

Was it already happening anger?

Blair couldn't tell, and before she could look deeper into the rising voices, they vanished and the world returned. She stared down at the bowl. Cody shouted something at her, but she barely heard him. All she cared about now was getting home. Getting to Mia to show her that Blair wasn't crazy. That this was going to work.

She snatched the bowl from the ground and stood before grabbing Cody's hand. She had no idea how to use the bowl, but she pictured the playground. The swings. She imagined the world as it should be, not the world as it was.

There were more voices. Shouts. Real shouts.

And then there was silence.

Cody wasn't sure what happened. One second Blair was on the ground, and the next they were back in Willow Creek, standing together in the park with the Bowl of Transportation in Blair's hands. It'd all happened so quickly that Cody barely had time to process what had happened.

Snow fell from the sky. Drifting down like white ash, slow and menacing. He shuddered.

"Blair," he said. "What?"

She looked at him, brown eyes wide and confused before she said, "I have no idea."

Great. Clearly things hadn't gone according to plan, but that's how everything else had gone, so what had Cody really expected? Nothing much, if he was being honest. He'd gone into this thinking it would be the last ditch attempt to get an artifact and then they could all go back to normal. Blair could stop this tirade, and maybe Mia would start speaking to the two of them again.

He just wanted things to go back to normal. Back before anyone but Blair knew about his magic. Hell, he'd trade Blair's friendliness for Mia's. He knew how to handle Blair's hostility. He didn't know how to handle it from either of the twins.

"Are they going to follow us?" Cody asked in a low voice.

Blair shook her head. "They can't. Mom has too many barriers up and they can't track us if we travel with the bowl."

That was convenient. Cody breathed out and stared at the bowl. He could feel the magic bleeding off of it. It called out to him, begging him to take it. To travel. To leave this place where everything felt wrong.

But he also knew he wouldn't be able to take it. The wielder had given it to Blair. Not him. She was the new wielder and that scared him. He didn't know much about the artifacts, but one thing he did know is that one person was not supposed to hold onto more than one at a time. Blair had two.

Well, one. But two.

"We should tell Mia," Blair said, grinning at the bowl. "Hopefully she'll be happy. Finally."

But she was happy. Happy without them.

He didn't have time to tell Blair this. Blair took off away from the park. Toward Mia and Derek's house.

Cody jogged after her, struggling to keep up as she rushed to tell Mia the good news.

"Blair, maybe we shouldn't," Cody said, out of breath. Blair waved him off and he groaned. "I'm serious. She's not going to appreciate seeing either of us, and you're going to have to interrupt her dinner and–"

He fell silent in part because Blair stopped, and in part because he could feel two mists down the street. Near Mia's house. He looked up and the first thing he noticed was Mia.

She was staring at the sky, mist white and bright. It was too far away for him to see her expression, but he didn't need to, to know that she was smiling. He always knew when she was smiling.

The second thing he noticed was Chad Rogers.

He stood in front of Mia, also looking at the sky. His mist shifted as if he were nervous. As if he were going to do something unexpected and brave. Cody watched. He watched as Chad tilted his head down to look at Mia. He watched as Chad said something. As Mia looked into his eyes. As he cupped her cheeks and leaned in.

He didn't watch the kiss. He spun around and stormed off, ignoring Blair shouting his name. Ignoring her footsteps following him through the snowy evening. Going to Mia's house had been a bad idea. He'd had no idea that she'd invited Chad to dinner. She hadn't told Cody.

He hated it. He hated it so much that it made him want to scream.

"Cody!" Blair caught his arm and he came to a stop.

He didn't look at her, but he felt out for her mist. Dark and blue. She hadn't liked what she'd seen either.

"Cody, are you okay?"

He was not okay. Seeing Mia with Chad had hurt. It tore at his heart and sent him into a panic. Because he didn't know if he could ever love someone else. He didn't know if anyone could love him. Mia was rejecting him. She had to know how he felt. She had to know that not being in her life was painful. But she kept doing it. She kept choosing Chad.

"I want to go home," he said, pulling his arm out of her grasp. "I don't want to talk about it. Show Mia the bowl later. She's clearly busy."

"You cannot be angry at her for wanting to be with someone

without magic," Blair said.

"I'm not angry at her."

"You are."

"I'm not!" He spun around. She didn't flinch. She didn't back away. She stared him straight in the eye, holding the bowl under her arm. He stepped back. "I said I don't want to talk about it."

"Okay, fine. Don't talk to me about it. Talk to Mia."

"Mia doesn't want to talk to me."

"She doesn't want to be reminded of magic," Blair snapped. "But she cannot escape from this world now that she's in it. That's why I never wanted her to know."

Him either, but she did know now. "We can't protect her."

"We can try."

"She doesn't want us to."

"Well that sucks for her."

Cody rolled his eyes and backed away from Blair. He just wanted to go home and forget everything.

"Goodnight, Blair. I'm glad you won this one."

He didn't wait for her to respond before he took off, heading into the night as the snow grew heavier and the temperature dropped all around him.

Chapter Twenty-Two

Mia couldn't stop smiling. All night. The house was warm, the food was delicious, and the company was excellent. Derek was a little quiet, and she noticed him watching her all night, but she figured it was because her change of mood shocked him. And she was okay with him worrying about her, because there was nothing to worry about.

For the first time in a while, Mia didn't feel a weight on her chest. She didn't look over her shoulder at every turn. She didn't have nightmares. She didn't need Derek to help her sleep at night.

Things were good.

When dinner came to an end, her mom pulled her aside and told her to walk Chad out. They would take care of the dishes. Mia didn't argue. She wanted to spend some alone time with Chad. He'd been so wonderful, making conversation, asking questions about their customs and culture, and getting to know her family. He didn't feel like an outsider. He didn't act like an outsider. It was warm.

So warm that she barely noticed the cold when they went outside. She stared up at the night sky, holding Chad's hand with a tight grip.

"That was a lot of fun," Chad said. The two of them came to a stop, Mia still staring at the sky. "Thank you for inviting me."

Mia looked down and grinned. "Thanks for coming. I hope the food was good."

"The best."

"And sorry my dad and Derek were so quiet. My dad gets embarrassed about his English sometimes, and who knows with Derek."

"No need to apologize! They spoke the perfect amount."

Mia giggled. "You know all the right things to say."

"It's easy when I'm with you."

Her cheeks burned and she stared up at the sky again. The snow was beautiful. She hadn't seen the beauty in snow in a long time. Last year, it had been a reminder of the forest, and this year it was a reminder of being locked away. Of the cold room and the cold way that Jae treated her when he was angry.

Tonight it was beautiful, and she wanted to keep staring at it.

"Hey, Mia?"

Mia looked down, into Chad's eyes and smiled.

"Yeah?"

"I…." He took a deep breath. "Can I kiss you?"

Her eyes widened. He hadn't tried to make a move or pressure her into anything. He'd been so patient with her.

She smiled. "Yeah."

His hands came up to her cheeks, chilled against her pinking skin. He tilted her head up and leaned in slowly, almost as if waiting for her to push him away. But she didn't want to push him away. He was so gentle with her. So kind. So amazing.

But then he kissed her, lightly, and she was back with Steven, sitting in his room as she kissed him for the first time. Then that night…the night she'd spent alone with him. It all came back to her and she didn't kiss Chad back. She pulled away, tears spilling down her cheeks, eyes wide.

"Mia?" Chad asked.

She realized how it must look and she shook her head, wiping away the tears. "I'm so sorry. I...I just...I remembered...."

She stopped, realizing that Chad didn't know who Steven was.

More tears spilled out of her eyes, coming against her will and she turned away from Chad, trying to get control of herself. This wasn't the time to cry. This wasn't the time to think about Steven. She was supposed to think about Chad. About kissing him.

Warm arms wrapped around her, blocking out the chill of the night. He pressed his nose to her hair.

"No, I'm sorry," he said. "I shouldn't have asked."

Mia placed her face in her hands and pressed against his body, seeking out the warmth that was once there. She wasn't sure how long they stood there like that, but it was long enough for the tears to finally stop and for the cold to take over both of them. She pulled away and faced him again, wiping away the remaining tears.

"Thank you," she said. Then she leaned up and pressed a kiss to his lips. Sweet and gentle.

"I should get inside." She backed away, and he stared at her with a dazed expression. She waved goodbye before heading into the house where she closed the door and stared at the ceiling for a moment, trying to collect herself.

Steven was gone. He would be gone forever. Derek had killed him. There was no undoing that, no matter what anyone said. Even if Mrs. Arbour said anything was possible with magic, the dead couldn't come back to life. Even Death himself couldn't reverse someone's life ending.

"Mia."

Derek stood in the doorway to his room. From the kitchen, Mia heard her parents clanking about, cleaning up after the wonderful dinner where everything had been warm. She could go back there.

Pretend like nothing had happened. Like she hadn't cried when Chad kissed her.

But she couldn't do that anymore. Hiding from her emotions only made things worse. So she turned and followed Derek into his room.

Derek hadn't meant to spy on Mia, but the change of emotions had caught him off guard. She'd gone from happy to distraught in a matter of seconds. He hadn't heard the conversation, but he'd seen Chad hug her. He'd seen her kiss him, but there was no love there.

Mia didn't love Chad.

"What happened?" Derek asked once they were in his closed room.

"Nothing," Mia said. She settled on his bed and stared out the window. Derek didn't believe her for one second, so he joined her on the bed with a heavy sigh.

"Okay, if you don't want to talk about it, we don't have to. But I'm here for you if you need to talk. Okay?"

Mia wrung her hands together, emotions a tangled mess. She wanted to tell him. He could tell. But the question was: would she? Would she keep what was going on inside her mind a secret, or would she finally open up about why she had let Chad kiss her? Why, when he did, had she cried?

What was going on with her?

"Derek," Mia whispered, "I don't know what to do."

"About what?" Derek asked.

She bit her lip. "About Chad. And…Steven."

Derek flinched. He didn't like hearing that name. He didn't like thinking about Steven. He didn't like remembering the moment when Steven's emotions had disappeared forever. It'd taken him a long time to be able to go back in the woods after. Months of avoiding it. Months of staring at the knife in his drawer, unable to touch it without memories of it going into Steven's body.

He swallowed. "What about Steven?"

She curled up in a ball, placing her forehead on her knees. "You don't want to hear this."

"I do." He took a deep breath. "Look, we've never talked about what happened with Steven. I know that I…I know that it didn't end well. At all. But that doesn't mean we can't talk about it. You never mention his name around me. You don't bring him up and, well, I guess that leads to you crying because a boy shows interest in you."

Mia tensed. Her emotions assaulted Derek's skin, but he ignored them, as well as the urge to calm her down. She needed this.

Finally, she looked at him, eyes red. "You know that night when I didn't come home?"

Derek remembered that night not so fondly. It was when everything was getting worse with the dreams. Before Niran started showing up in real life, but right at the start of his exhaustion. He'd made so many mistakes in that moment. That entire night.

He nodded.

"I…." Mia sucked in a breath and looked at the ceiling, blinking rapidly. "Steven and I…."

She didn't need to say more. Derek knew what she was going to say, and he couldn't stop the tangle of emotions building in his gut.

"Oh." He said, trying to control his own emotions. They stabbed at his stomach. Tore at his heart. He'd known that Mia and Steven were close. Dating, maybe. He'd known that Steven had actually felt something for her. But he hadn't known that Mia had actually *slept* with him.

He hadn't noticed. No wonder Mia had been so distraught about his death. He'd meant more to her than any other person ever had.

More than Cody. More than Blair. More than Derek himself. Steven had been her first. Her first kiss, her first love, her first....

"And now Chad...." She closed her eyes as a tear fell from them. "He's so kind and understanding. He never pressures me into anything, and I want to be happy with him. I want to live the life that he can give me right now. But every time something happens, every time we get closer, I think of Steven. I know he manipulated me. I know he betrayed me. I know he's dead. But he was my first love and I don't know if I'll ever get over what happened."

Derek wrapped an arm around her shoulders, closing his eyes as well. "You will. You'll move on eventually. You just need to find the right person. Steven isn't the only person you'll ever love."

"What about you and Blair?" Mia asked. "Will she be the only girl that you'll ever love?"

Another name Derek didn't want to hear. He pulled away from his sister and stood, going to the window. He'd felt her emotions earlier. Returning to Willow Creek. He knew that she'd succeeded this time, and part of him wanted to go out and ask her what she'd gotten. But he knew better. Any open door and he might forget everything she'd done to him.

He might forgive her.

But he wasn't ready.

"Blair is not the only girl I'll ever love," Derek said in a low voice. "And even if she was, it'd be different because–"

"She's alive?" Mia asked.

Derek bowed his head. "Yeah."

"Right." Mia rested her head on Derek's shoulder. "I don't think I love Chad. I think I like the normality of him."

"I think that's fair."

"It's not fair to him."

"Maybe let him decide that."

Mia nodded and then pulled away. Derek watched her walk to

the door, stunned by the contrast of her emotions. Earlier today she'd been so happy and now it was like all of that work was out the window. All because of one kiss. One stupid freaking kiss.

"Thanks for letting me talk," Mia said. "I'm going to go to bed now."

Derek nodded and Mia left the room.

This time, it was obvious it was a dream. Derek sat by the edge of the Mekong River, staring out at the beauty of the water, when Niran sat beside him.

"Come to mock me some more?" Derek asked.

"No." Niran shook his head. "I'm here to talk to you about the knife."

Derek didn't look at him. He didn't want to look into his own eyes. At his own face. Into his reflection. "I don't need you to talk to me about the knife. I used it to kill Steven. That's all there is to it."

"Yet, you carry it around with you at all times."

Derek scowled. He willed himself to wake up, to escape from this madness, but it didn't work. If anything, the world became more real. It felt more like Derek was awake and talking to his twin brother. Except he didn't have a twin *brother*.

"The knife is dangerous," Niran said. "It takes away people's souls."

Derek glanced at him. "So that's why Steven...."

"Yes." Niran nodded. "I wanted to warn you earlier, but I was too weak and then Shubishi...."

Derek didn't want to hear about Shubishi. He pushed himself off the grass and turned away from Niran. Maybe if he walked, he could find his way to the waking world. Or, at least to another dream. A better dream.

Niran appeared beside him. "You can't run away from this, Derek. As long as you are the wielder of the knife—"

"What if I don't want to be the wielder anymore?" Derek asked. All the knife had done was bring him pain. Brought his sister pain. "It didn't even choose me anyway. It chose Mia."

"And Mia chose you to take it," Niran countered. "She couldn't wield it anyway. She has no magic. The knife attaches to magic and helps the wielder steal souls. The more souls it takes, the more powerful it gets until finally it can take away the soul of someone immortal."

Derek halted. Enya had given Niran the knife to kill Lady Shion. She must have known that tidbit. But…Derek stared at his hands. How many people had the knife killed? Why did it have that power? Where did the artifacts get their power from anyway? Why was it if they were all together that they would be able to protect Mia? There were so many questions.

Niran stepped in front of Derek and grabbed his chin, forcing him to look into Niran's eyes.

"You need to be careful with the knife," he said. "I made the mistake of not taking the power seriously and it ended up in disaster. You cannot, and I repeat, cannot, let it get into the wrong hands."

Derek jerked away. He stared at Niran, who stared back, and then Derek smirked. "Don't worry. I won't. After all, I'm not you."

Part Five

Chapter Twenty-Three

Cody didn't know what to do.

He sat in the kitchen, staring through the window at the front porch. In one hand, he held a pencil. In another, his history textbook. But he wasn't paying attention to the essay he was supposed to be writing. Instead, he focused on his mother who sat on the creaky porch swing and stared out at the coming spring.

He didn't want to admit that his mom was starting to fall again. He didn't want to talk to his dad about how she cried sometimes when she thought no one was listening. He didn't want to do anything, really, but obsess over her mental state.

Even though he'd spoken to Lady Shion, he still wasn't one hundred percent sure what Eran had done to her, or why. The why was what killed him. Why did the Iravata care about her? Why were they messing with her mind? Why? Why? *Why?*

He wanted to talk to Mia about it, but she stuck to Chad like glue since they were "officially" dating now. Cody couldn't speak to her like that. He couldn't divulge one of his greatest secrets to Chad, or even let Chad know that there was something going on.

Instead, he watched over his mom in silence. He went to school but often ditched the classes he knew he was going to get an A in regardless of attendance. When he was home alone with her, he didn't do his homework, instead watching her sit out on the front porch until Dylan got home.

It was exhausting, but he didn't know who to talk to about it.

He'd tried with Blair. He had. He really had. But she'd been so obsessed with the artifacts that any irrelevant information…well, she didn't give a shit about it. Her words, not his. She was planning something new, now that she had the Bowl of Transportation, but he was trying his best not to get involved.

He had too much on his mind to get involved.

The sound of a car door slamming startled Cody out of his thoughts. He looked down at his textbook, which had highlights from previous students, as well as notes written in the margins. His eyes glanced over them, trying to take in the information, but none of it wanted to stick.

He'd always been good at getting information to stick. But it was almost like learning about a false history wasn't that important. Not when he knew there was more out there, with the mage clans having their own records and the Iravata having actually lived through it.

He wanted to ask them more questions, the Iravata. Not just about his mother, but about himself too. The longer he thought about it, the more certain he was that he knew who his father was. Who Jae's father was. But he didn't want to admit it to himself. Admitting that he wasn't Dylan's son was difficult.

So, he didn't ask them questions. He didn't dig deeper into his own history, much less his mother's. Because he was afraid if he did, she would break and he would be left without his mother again.

Sighing, he closed his textbook and put down his pencil, giving up on doing any work today. He got up and headed outside to see if his mom was okay. If she needed anything. It was mid-March and as the rest of the world flourished anew with greens and flowers, he watched his world fall apart.

"Mom," Cody called out once he was out on the porch. She glanced at him, eyes dead, and said nothing. "Are...do you need anything?"

"I'm fine," she said. "Just looking out at spring. Isn't it beautiful?"

Cody settled on the swing next to her. "Yeah. It's beautiful."

"Are you okay?" She smiled at him, but there was something off about it. Almost like she was reading from a script.

"Yeah. I'm okay." He didn't know what else to say. He wasn't okay, but he didn't want to worry her.

"You know," she continued as if he hadn't spoken, "I remember springs from when I was young."

Cody blinked. She'd never spoken about her life before. When she was young.

"You do?" he asked.

"They were so different back then," she said with soft eyes. "It was planting time. Everything was growing. But there was no snow. We didn't have to worry about a spring snow fall. Not like here. Daddy used to tell me that I was meant for something greater. Every spring. You know, my birthday is in the spring."

Was it happening again? The memories of somewhere else? Something else? She'd said that's what got her in the hospital in the first place. Did she need to go back? Was what Eran did not sticking?

"Mom," Cody said, touching her arm, "your birthday is in the fall."

She let out a laugh. Boisterous. Fake. "No, sweetie, that's the birthday they gave me, since they found me in the fall. But I was born in the spring. Across the sea. In a place where it never snowed."

"Where?" Cody asked, voice low.

But then she fell silent. Any joy in her expression vanished and she went back to staring out at the street.

"Mom?"

She blinked and stared at him. "Hm?"

"You were...." He halted. It was obvious there was something wrong. Anyone could see that, if they bothered to pay attention. The problem was, very few people paid attention when it didn't concern them. Cody's dad wasn't paying attention. As far as he was concerned, he'd gotten his wife back and everything was good.

But things weren't good.

"I was what?" she asked with that fake smile.

"Never mind," Cody muttered. He stood. "I'm going to go on a walk. Clear my head."

"Okay, dear. Take care."

He nodded before heading off down the porch steps, down the street, away from his almost catatonic mother with her fake smile and her blank eyes.

Blair sat on her front porch, books scattered about her. She jumped from one to the next, trying to figure out what to do about the artifacts. So far, there hadn't been any noise from the clans. She knew it was coming. It had to be coming, and she had to be ready for it.

She'd tried to tell Mia about the good news, but Mia was always with Chad. They were dating, apparently. Not just going on dates, but called each other girlfriend and boyfriend.

The idea sickened Blair, but it made Mia happy, so Blair ignored it. They spoke sometimes. Randomly. Usually about school, since Chad was always there. He was Mia's freaking security blanket.

Blair pored over her books. Esther tried to get her to stop. She'd said that it was dangerous to seek out the rest of the artifacts, even with one already in her possession. Blair had gotten a massive lecture when she'd brought the bowl into the house, and Esther had taken it and hidden it, saying what was done, was done, but Blair had to stop.

Blair didn't want to stop.

At this point, it had nothing to do with Mia. Mia was fine. Mia was safe. Mia was happy. No. This was about Blair. About the fact that everything in her life was falling apart.

A couple kids screamed down the street, and Blair looked up from her books, tensing in case they were screaming for a real reason. But when the screams dissolved into laughter, she scowled and returned to her studying. She wasn't getting anywhere. They all said the same information:

The artifacts were powerful. The artifacts were as old as time itself. The artifacts could bring the wielder unbelievable power.

Blair knew that she had to get the others. It was the only way to make things go back to normal. Maybe then she could trust her grandmother. Or maybe, if things went really well, she could have her best friend back. But there was nothing to indicate that would ever happen again.

Eventually, she would give up. She knew that. Eventually she'd run into something that made her stop in her tracks. But she hadn't run into that yet, and she was going to keep going until a roadblock made her halt.

Blair considered going back inside. No one was home. Since it was Saturday, Esther had decided to take James to the park to get out some of his energy, while her father was at work doing parent-teacher conferences. They wouldn't be home for hours. She could go inside. Take a nap. Relax for a moment.

Just as she was collecting all of her books, the wind shifted, bringing with it a soft but powerful magic. Magic that Blair recognized.

She looked up from her books to find Enola Demini standing at the edge of the driveway.

Blair put her books down and headed down the porch steps. The children screamed again, but it was more distant. Like a bubble had surrounded Blair and her grandmother, keeping the rest of the world ignorant to their conversation.

"Grandmother," Blair said, voice cold.

"I've heard through the grapevine that you've been causing trouble with the other clans," Enola said.

Blair shrugged. "Not much."

"You stole one of their artifacts."

"It was given to me." Blair crossed her arms. "I went to talk to the person and she just…gave it away. Made me the wielder. You know as well as I do that you can't just *steal* an artifact."

Enola sighed, but didn't move from her spot. "Blair, I'm begging you to stop this nonsense. Come back to the clan. Take your place as leader. Forget about Mia and Derek and…Cody. You belong with your family."

"My family is right here," Blair snapped.

"Really?" Enola laughed. "I don't see them."

"Of course not. You came when they're all out. But I'm not leaving Willow Creek. This is my home."

"So, what do you plan to do when you graduate from high school?" Enola asked.

Blair hesitated. She hadn't applied to any colleges. She figured she'd go traveling. Maybe get a job. Anything to stay out of school. But all of that was a while away. She had months to figure out what she wanted to do. Sure, her parents were upset that she'd thrown out all her college applications, and Esther had made it clear that Blair wasn't allowed to stay with them if she didn't go to school, but Blair knew that wasn't the right path for her. Whenever she thought about after high school, whenever she had dreams about after high school, she came up with nothing.

Nothing but fire.

"You cannot stay here forever," Enola continued. "You cannot run from your destiny. I've seen it. I've seen you take the mantle at the head of our clan. I've seen you accept what has been yours from the moment of your birth. You are destined for great things, Blair. If only you weren't so stubborn."

Blair's eyes trained to the ground, and she said nothing. If her grandmother had seen it, then it must be true, but she also knew that visions weren't set in stone. Sometimes they changed. Sometimes they were warnings, rather than a future reality.

Enola sighed. "I love you, Blair. You are my granddaughter. My *only* granddaughter. I don't want to live out my final days without you. You don't have to come back now, but I want you to think about what I've said."

Her final days? Blair didn't appreciate the guilt trip, and she held her head high. "I'm firm in my decision. I won't be coming back. I won't be taking the mantle over. I'm done being lied to and manipulated."

Enola sighed, but bowed her head. "I understand you're angry. Hopefully soon you'll see why I kept it a secret. Why I never told anyone why I was a seer. I never meant to manipulate you, Blair. I just wanted—"

She didn't finish her sentence. Instead she turned, drawing Blair's attention away from her grandmother and to the boy she so desperately loved.

She didn't know why Derek stood there, watching Enola and Blair with cautious eyes, but she was certain that she hadn't wanted him to know that she'd spoken to her grandmother. More than once.

Enola vanished.

Chapter Twenty-Four

Derek watched Enola Demini disappear and the world return to normal. His eyes then flickered to Blair. He wasn't sure why he was there. He'd woken up and decided to try and make things right with her. But he hadn't expected her to have company.

Especially not *her.*

"Derek," Blair said.

Derek considered turning around and going home. He thought about leaving Blair to wonder. After all, Enola had tried to stop Blair from saving Mia. Enola had refused to help save Mia. Why the hell would Blair want anything to do with her grandmother?

His feet didn't take him away, though. They took him toward her, anger flaring in his stomach. Why the hell was she talking to Enola? After everything the woman had done? Derek may have been angry at Blair for what she'd done to him, but he was still empathetic to the fact that Enola had tried to screw Blair over. He'd thought that Blair had given up her position in the clan. That she was done with a group of people who treated her like shit, who she couldn't even be honest with because she was so afraid of what they might do to her.

"Okay, so you're angry," Blair said, stepping back. "Look, I didn't invite her. She came of her own free will. Every time she's come I–"

Derek stopped in his tracks, maybe halfway up the driveway. Blair had backed onto the porch, but stopped when he did.

"Every time?" Derek asked, voice low and dark. "What do you mean, every time?"

Blair grimaced, her emotions a range of textures. "I just…I mean that…she's come a few times, okay? What do you want me to do? She's my grandmother."

Derek knew he shouldn't be as angry as he was. Blair was right. Enola *was* her grandmother, and family was always complicated. But Enola had messed with Derek's family.

"So you're just okay with the fact that she wouldn't help Mia?" Derek snapped.

Blair's worry and concern disappeared, replaced instead with anger.

"Of course not!" Blair exclaimed. She groaned. "I'm not going to fight with you. You don't care about me or what's going on in my life, so you don't get a say about it."

She turned, collected the books that were scattered about the porch before storming inside.

Derek followed.

"I never said I didn't care about you," Derek said. He followed Blair into the living room where she shoved the books on a bookshelf. "But this has to do with my sister. You know, the one who is traumatized because of us?"

"Don't you dare put that on me!" Blair spun around, hair flying into her face. Derek had gotten used to seeing it down, but it didn't change the fact that she looked so different without her braids. With her hair getting longer, way past her shoulders.

"You're the one that Jae wanted to kill," Blair continued. "You're the one who kept Mia in the dark your entire lives. You're the one with the priest's soul. None of this is my fault. None of this is because of anything I did."

"So why do you feel so guilty?" Derek asked.

Blair's eyes widened. "Stop feeling my emotions."

"Stop emoting so much."

She scowled. "I don't feel guilty."

"Your mouth lies, but the emotions always tell the truth," Derek said, crossing his arms. "You want to pretend like all of this is my fault? What exactly did I do to deserve any of this? I didn't ask to be a reincarnation. I didn't ask to have magic in a family who didn't know magic existed until recently. If it's my fault Mia is traumatized, then it's your fault too. It's all of our faults."

"Oh, screw you," Blair said with venom in every word. "You don't get to lecture me about anything. Got it?"

Derek's eyes narrowed. He wasn't sure what to do now. How to proceed. All he could think about was Blair with her hair down. Blair glaring at him like she used to. All he could think about was her.

"You should go," Blair said, pushing past him. "You don't want anything to do with me. I get it. You're mad because Mia is hurt. Well, news flash, buddy, your sister is doing *just fine* without me or Cody in her life. Maybe you should leave it too so she can finally be at peace. She's moving on, and so am I."

Derek wasn't sure what he was doing. The idea of Blair moving on stabbed him in the gut. The idea of her forgetting about him. Leaving him. Vanishing from his life.

He grabbed Blair's arm, spinning her around. She gasped, magic welling up as if she were ready for an attack, but he didn't want to fight her. Even if her words stung, he knew they were because she was hurt, not because she meant them. He knew that she was in pain. That he was the cause of that pain. No, he didn't want to fight her.

He placed a hand on either side of her face and pulled her in, kissing her so intensely that her gasp was caught in her throat.

Her shock overcame him. Needles on his skin. So sharp that he didn't fight when she pulled away, eyes wide.

"What are you doing?" Blair asked in a shaky voice.

Derek moved in closer. He could barely think. His mind was a battlefield. One side wanted him to run. The other wanted to kiss her again. "I don't know."

There was a moment. A stalemate. Her body was pressed against his. His hands were still on her cheeks. She stared up at him, the silk of lust consuming all of her emotions. He could only think about her. Only about the way her hair felt tickling his fingers. How her skin felt beneath his palms. How she smelled of roses. Her shampoo. After a moment, she breathed out.

"Okay," she said before wrapping her arms around his neck and kissing him back.

Cody walked. And walked. And walked. He walked so far that he wasn't sure where he was. Somewhere in the woods, that was for sure. He'd be able to find his way back, but for now, he was content on being as lost as he felt.

His legs grew sore. His lungs ached from the increase in altitude. He panted, leaning against a nearby tree, before he sunk to the ground. He wished he had someone to talk to. Someone who could understand what was going on in his life.

Mia and Derek. Blair. None of them would ever understand. They had their mothers. They had stability in every aspect of their life. He didn't.

He realized, though, that he did know someone who understood. Two people. People who he'd only spoken to a few times, but would get it.

He pulled out his phone. It was almost dying, but he sought out Parker's number anyway and sent him a quick text.

It took only a few seconds before Heba and Parker appeared. Cody stared at them. They stared at Cody. And for a moment, he thought they were going to get angry at him for calling them out here, especially with no real reason.

But they didn't yell. They didn't lecture. They merely sat on either side of him.

"What's going on?" Heba asked. She twisted her hands together, creating sparks of fire. Cody watched it, wondering if it was safe for her to create fire, especially with the drought going on.

Without more pressing, Cody explained everything. He spilled his guts about what was going on with his mom, what was going on with Mia, with Blair, with Derek. He talked about school and his fears and how much he hated going home. How he wasn't focusing. How everything was a mess.

And the two of them listened. They listened and didn't judge. Their mists didn't twist and turn into something dangerous. They stayed calm, listening to Cody explain exactly why his world was falling apart.

When he was done, silence fell over the three of them. Cody breathed out, closing his eyes and wondered if he'd gone too far. If he had any right to complain to the two of them, when they were currently homeless.

"That's…a lot," Heba said. "I'm sorry you're dealing with all that."

"Seriously." Parker placed a hand on his shoulder. "But why call us? Why not try and talk to any of your friends?"

There was a reason Cody called them there. Because all three of them were Natara. And maybe they would understand what was going on with his mother.

"I think something happened to my mom," Cody said. "I think that she's been messed with, and I was wondering if the two of you knew anything more about what happened to moms who have Natara children. Since…well, you're also Natara and you lived with a bunch of kids who I'm guessing didn't have great relationships with their mothers."

Heba fell quiet, looking out at the woods, but Parker spoke with a sense of authority.

"Yeah. It's complicated. Women who have Natara children often lose it. They start imagining things, or hallucinating. You know that what you are, half mage, makes it even more complicated, right?"

But was he half mage? He stared at his hands. Was he half mage, or was that the magic of Leo that he'd stolen when they were kids?

He closed his hands into fists. "So, what's going on with my mom is pretty normal?"

"Nothing about us is normal," Parker said with sad eyes. "We aren't supposed to exist. Most Natara children don't live as long as we do, for whatever reason. Miscarriage, SIDS, murder…. The world doesn't want us. You're one of the lucky ones, having a mom and a dad who are around."

"Yeah, I know." Cody sighed. "I know that I'm lucky but I feel like it's only made things worse. Now I gotta worry about my mom. Now I have to worry about my dad finding out he's not my father. And it's so much pressure."

This time, Heba piped up. "I know that you're under a lot of stress, but just remember that you have a home to live in. Maybe the Iravata can help your mom. They probably know more about all of this than we do."

Except Cody didn't trust the Iravata anymore. Not after messing with his mom's head like they had. Not after making her seem so fake, and even that hadn't stuck.

"I can't ask the Iravata," he said. "I don't know what to do."

Heba wrapped an arm around his shoulders. "Trust me when I say we get it. My mom lost it when I was about six. Parker's when he was eight. We found each other and have stuck by each other's side ever since. You haven't had anyone who understands. But I guess that's what we're here for."

Cody nodded and closed his eyes. It was like his heart was healing just a little bit. He didn't have Mia to talk to anymore. Or Derek. And Blair was, well, Blair.

But he had Parker and Heba.

That may not have been enough, but for now it would do. And for now, he would have to pay more attention to his mom and maybe stop caring for a moment what happened to Mia. He was stretched too thin, worrying about her and his mom. She was doing okay. She was happy with Chad.

That's all that mattered.

Mia remembered when they were kids, they used to come to this park. She hadn't been back since the trip to Australia, and she wasn't sure why Chad had asked her here. All she did know is that she was getting antsy, sitting there on the swing.

"Mia!" Chad called out to her the moment he saw her, and she smiled at him. Being his girlfriend had been interesting. She'd branched out and hung out with his group of friends a lot more. They made her uncomfortable, especially the girls who used to bully her, but she was used to being in uncomfortable situations.

So, instead of focusing on them, she'd focused on Chad. On the happiness his normality brought her.

After her talk with Derek during the new year, Mia had decided she was going to forget about Steven. She was going to move on with her life. After all, he was dead and she was not. There was no use in obsessing over a boy who had manipulated her. Who had lied to her. Who had almost gotten her brother and friends killed.

She would focus on Chad. On how he was so respectful of her. How he didn't pressure her into anything. He was okay with just cuddling. He was okay with just an occasional kiss. His buddies made fun of him for it, and he chastised them for making fun of him. He was gentle and kind and perfect for what she needed.

But she didn't love him.

She knew she didn't love him.

And that didn't matter to her. Because both of them were happy.

"Hey," Mia said. "What did you ask me out here for?"

Chad came to a stop, breathing heavily from having jogged all the way here. "Okay, so, I was going to do something big, but then I figured you wouldn't want all that attention on you, so I figured I'd ask you in private."

Mia tensed. "Ask me what?"

He blinked. "Oh, it's nothing bad."

Still, Mia kept her hands clenched around the chains of the swing. Just in case. He wanted to ask her something? She couldn't figure out what it could be. At least, not until he pulled a piece of paper out of his pocket and unfolded it.

Written in his messy sprawl was the word, "Prom?"

Prom. Mia had completely forgotten about prom. With things rocky with her, Cody, and Blair, she'd put it out of her mind. The four of them were supposed to go together. They were supposed to have a good time, sneak in some alcohol, and then go hang out at Mia and Derek's house while they sobered up.

They'd been planning this since freshman year.

"Mia?" Chad asked. His eyes were so hopeful. She could tell him no. She could explain that she didn't want to betray that moment with her friends. Her old friends? No, they would be friends again.

259

She just needed time. They all needed time.

And she couldn't tell him no.

"Of course I'll go with you," Mia said. "I can't wait."

But she could wait. Prom was in a few weeks. She'd have to go to Denver to find a dress. He was asking her kind of late, but that was okay. Because he made her happy, and going to prom with someone who made you happy was the point.

Wasn't it?

"Great!" Chad grabbed her wrist, pulling her off the swing, and embraced her with such gentle warmness that Mia couldn't help but smile. She hugged him back, disappearing into his massive chest.

When he let go, she couldn't stop smiling. That is, until she looked over his shoulder and saw the last person she wanted to see.

"Um...I gotta head home," Mia said. "Homework."

"Right." Chad laughed. "Well, I'll see you tomorrow, yeah?"

"Of course." She leaned up and pressed a chaste kiss to his lips. "I'll see you tomorrow." For their date. Which she hadn't forgotten about, she'd just put it out of her mind. Chad waved goodbye and jogged off toward his house, leaving Mia seemingly alone at the park.

But she had no intention of going home. Instead she stared at the man standing at the edge of the park. The one who wasn't really there, but who haunted her anyway.

"Go away," Mia said, stepping back. "You know I don't want to see you. Why do you keep harassing me?"

Jae didn't move. He reached up and brushed some of his hair out of his face, and then sighed.

"He makes you happy," Jae said. "He's not part of the magical world."

"No, he's not, and don't you *dare* do anything to him!" Mia knew better than to trust Jae in this kind of situation. She knew better than to trust him at all, but anytime anyone got close to her...well,

Jae didn't like that.

Jae stepped forward. "I'm not going to do anything to Chad Rogers. He's a nice boy who only wants to make you smile. I'm okay with that."

Mia said nothing.

Jae continued. "All I want is for you to be happy, Mia. That's all I've ever wanted for you. And if this makes you happy, then that's good. But the others…they don't want you to be happy. They want themselves to be happy, regardless of what it costs you and I won't stand for that. I suggest you stay home this week. Don't get involved in the fight that's about to happen."

Mia blinked. "Fight? What fight?"

"I see you haven't been speaking to Blair."

"I–" She hesitated.

"That's good," Jae said. "She can't hurt you if you aren't involved. Just remember, Mia, that I will do anything to protect you. Even if it means hurting myself, I will protect you from all those who want to cause you pain. Even if you don't agree with me. Even if it takes time for you to understand why."

Mia opened her mouth to say something, but Jae was gone before she could.

Blair wasn't quite sure what had happened. One second she was screaming at Derek and the next he was kissing her. The next he was taking off her shirt. The next she was leading him up to her room, undoing his pants.

The next they were lying in bed together, naked, with his arms around her.

She looked up at him. His eyes were closed, breath even, but he wasn't asleep. She knew that he was still angry with her, and maybe that's all it was. Just a burst of hateful emotions. Hate sex, she believed they called it. But she didn't care, because this was the closest the two of them had been since Denver.

"Derek?" she asked in a low voice.

"Hm?"

"What just happened?"

Derek pulled away from her, leaving her cold, and sat up. "I'm not really sure. I…I was just…I just…I missed you."

Blair sat up as well, grabbing the blanket to cover herself. He'd missed her? But he was angry with her. He'd said he didn't want anything to do with her anymore.

"So, you aren't angry anymore?" Blair asked.

Derek's eyes narrowed. "I mean, I am. But I dunno. I'm tired of not being with you. I just…." He leaned in and kissed her. She let him. "I still love you, you know? I never stopped loving you. But every time I think about holding you, or kissing you, I think about how easy it was for you to take my energy away. And how easy it was for you to give it to me. And I'm scared that you'll do it again."

She had really messed up. She never should have done it.

"I still love you too," Blair said. "But what does this mean?"

Derek shifted, slipping out of bed and pulling his pants on. "I don't know, honestly. I think that I need more time. Mia asked me a while ago if I was ever going to get over you, and I don't think I will. I just need more time."

They all needed time.

"I think I do too," Blair said in a quiet voice. "You did dump me after I saved your sister's life."

Derek snorted. "Yeah. I was really angry."

"Yeah."

They fell silent. Derek continued to get dressed and Blair joined him until they were both fully clothed and staring at each other.

Blair's body burned, wanting to touch him. For him to hold her. And kiss her. And for them to get right back into bed. But she held back because he didn't want that. At least, not right now.

"Things will go back to normal," Derek said after a moment. "I think Mia misses you and Cody too. Just…we gotta wait until everyone is recovered from this summer. And maybe from last winter too. We never really processed it."

That was true. All of them jumped back into normal life, but it had been traumatic. And maybe now they could finally heal.

Blair slipped her hand in Derek's, tugging on it to pull him closer. He closed his eyes, and she kissed him. A goodbye for now kiss. Something to keep her going, because without it she was going to fall apart.

"I love you," she whispered.

"I love you too." Then he pulled away with a soft, sad smile. "Guess I'll see you at school."

"Yeah."

"Bye, Blair."

"Bye, Derek."

He left her room and she sunk onto her bed, feeling the burn of tears in her eyes. Time. He just needed time.

She didn't want to give him time. She wanted him back. Before prom. Before the end of the school year when the two of them would go off and do their own things. She wanted these last months with him.

But he wasn't ready.

So, she let him go and prepared herself to see him at school on Monday.

Chapter Twenty-Five

Mia breathed in, doing her best to keep her heart steady. All morning, Derek had asked her if she was okay, and she'd done her best to assuage his fears about her fears, but she wasn't sure she'd done a good job. And now, standing outside of school, staring up at the small building that felt massive in the moment, she wondered if she just should have *told* him about Jae. About Jae's ominous message. But she could tell him yet. Not until she fixed things with her two best friends.

After another deep breath, she did it. She pushed her way into the school and searched for Cody and Blair after having had avoided them for so damn long. She didn't seek out Chad, like she normally did first thing in the morning. Instead, she went to Blair's locker.

Blair wasn't there.

Furrowing her brow, she wandered the school in search of Cody. At the library. At his first class. The lunch room. The halls. She knew he could feel her mist, so maybe he was avoiding her, but usually she could at least *see* him disappearing around a corner. A hint of him anywhere. There was nothing.

Jae's words echoed in her mind. He'd said he would protect her from the upcoming battle, but he'd said nothing about her friends. Was the battle happening? Should she even be at school? Her body tensed as the first bell rang and there was no sign of her friends, but then she saw Derek and relaxed. He was there. If there was going to be a battle, he would be part of it too, wouldn't he? She didn't want him to be, of course, but that didn't mean the magical world was quite so kind.

The rest of the day passed in a blur. Blair wasn't at school. Neither was Cody. It wasn't that they were avoiding her, it was that they weren't there at all. Absent. For Blair, that was nothing new, but for Cody? That wasn't like him. Was it? Had she even been paying attention to him this year enough to know if that was like him anymore?

Guilt wracked her, and by the time lunch rolled around, Derek had her cornered, asking what was going on. She didn't answer him, especially when Chad walked up asking if everything was okay. The two of them remained silent. She knew Derek wanted to switch to Mandarin, to ask her more questions, but that would only make Chad worry more.

Instead, he backed off.

Instead, she went with Chad.

Chad asked her about her day, and she made up some excuse. Some lie. He saw through it and asked if she was okay. She couldn't answer.

Because she didn't know.

Finally, the day ended, and she slipped out of the building before Derek or Chad could find her. She didn't want to talk to either of them. The people she *wanted* to speak to were hiding, probably at home. Blair. Cody. She didn't know who to talk to first. Cody was closer, but Blair might be easier, but she felt like she'd hurt Cody more. She pulled out her phone and hovered over their group chat.

The last message had been sent months ago.

A sigh escaped her lips. Things really had fallen apart.

A warm, almost humid breeze rustled her hair. Her clothes. She looked up at the sky as she clicked on the group chat, preparing a message to tell her brother and two best friends that she needed to speak to them. All of them. That she had to tell them about Jae and his ominous message. The world around her was lush and alive. Green leaves danced in the wind, and flowers seemed to call out to her. She smiled.

It was the perfect day to heal. To make things right. To fix what was broken.

The perfect....

"Found her."

The voice came out of nowhere, speaking in Mandarin, but it didn't belong to anyone in her family.

Mia whipped around, phone clattering to the ground as she realized she was no longer alone. Then, her feet stopped. They wouldn't move. Darkness encased her vision and arms wrapped around her body. Her face went cold.

No. No. No, no, no, no, no!

She couldn't speak. Or move. Or fight. Her conscious faded and the last thought she had was that she needed to tell the others that it was happening. Again.

Blair hadn't been able to bring herself to attend school. To face Derek after letting herself fall into his arms with so little buildup. She could still feel him. The way his hands gripped her to his body, desperate for intimacy. How warm he'd been. How, even though he was far more built than he used to be, he'd still been soft against her.

His lips, his wandering hands, his desperate pulling and pushing.

She blushed thinking about it.

The idea of seeing him at school, knowing that he wasn't ready yet, but that he was close, hurt more than he realized. She was willing to give him space. To let him heal, but she also needed that.

Then the sky turned gray.

Now, the sky turning gray in the middle of spring was nothing new in Willow Creek. But the thing about this gray sky was it was isolated. Blair stared up at it, electricity dancing around her hair, and her eyes widened. Because it wasn't all over the amazing, clear, blue sky.

It was just over her house. Just over the school. Just over Willow Creek.

"Oh *shit*."

Blair stumbled outside, forgetting to grab her shoes in the process, and jerked her head around in search of the source. The electricity in the air wasn't thunder. It wasn't lightning. It was magic. Someone's magic. She didn't recognize who it belonged to, which made her increasingly nervous. Her heart raced, thumping in her ears until her gaze landed on a man standing at the edge of her driveway. He waited there, hooded, with the Staff of Storms held out in front of him. All of the magic energy in the air exuded from him, swirling around his body like fog.

"Shit." She took a step back, grabbing for the door.

"Blair Arbour," the man called out in a heavy French accent.

She froze. Not because she wanted to, but because his magic made her.

Shit, shit, shit, shit, shit!

"The time has come. Your crimes against the clans have grown numerous. You must pay the price for rejecting your clan and stealing our artifacts."

Blair balked. She couldn't think of anything to say in her defense except, "Rejecting my clan is not a crime. It's a lifestyle."

The man let out a low hiss, and others appeared around him. People from all over the world. Some of them were hooded. Others were not. They came from four of the five major clans, and probably from minor clans as well. Blair wanted to run. To call for Esther, but she could barely speak, must less move.

Then, she noticed something that made her stomach turn. Her eyes widen. Her jaw drop. One of the men stood there holding an unconscious Mia in his arms.

Blair gasped. "Hey, what are you doing with her? She has nothing to do with this!" Mia wasn't supposed to get involved in the magical world anymore. She didn't want anything to do with it. All she wanted was a normal life with a normal boy and normal friends.

The man with the staff reached up and lowered his hood. He was a middle-aged man with piercing blue eyes and a permanent scowl etched onto his face. With sandy blond hair and high cheekbones, he could have been handsome if he wasn't old, threatening Blair, and holding Mia hostage.

Blair's eyes narrowed, and she struggled against his magic. He was strong, and he had better control than she did, but she was a goddamn seer.

She was stronger.

She stepped forward. The man's eyes narrowed, and he slammed his staff into the ground, shaking the world with it. But not the entire world. Just Blair's house. She stumbled, catching herself on the porch railing. None of the other mages reacted, though a hushed whisper flew through the crowd. They weren't expecting her to be able to resist.

"Come with us, Blair," the man said. "Don't make trouble."

"Bite me," Blair snapped.

The man's nose twitched up into a snarl, and he stepped forward right as footsteps appeared behind Blair. They were frantic, quick and heavy as they pounded against the ground.

"Claude! What are you doing here?"

Esther appeared next to Blair, placing a hand on her shoulder. She wore an apron, hair in two braids, but pinned back to keep it out of her face while she cooked dinner. Blair looked up at her mom, eyes widening. How did she know who the man with the staff was?

"Mom, they have Mia." Blair was frantic.

Esther sucked in a breath and scanned the crowd before her eyes narrowed. "Let her go. Now."

"We warned you to keep the children under control, Esther," Claude said. "You failed. Now they pay the price."

"She's not a mage. She doesn't follow our laws. And my daughter has done nothing wrong except get on your nerves. Amahle gave up the artifact of her own free will. You know it, and I know it. She is not a child and she can make the decision about her artifact however she sees fit."

Blair's head spun. This Claude guy...the clans...they'd been in contact with Esther? Why hadn't she told Blair any of this?

But Claude only shook his head and raised his staff again. "We cannot let Blair and her friends interfere in clan politics again." With that he slammed the tip of the staff into the ground again, and thunder exploded through the sky.

When the thunder boomed through the library, a girl screamed and the lights went out. Derek jumped a foot, then glanced around, expecting someone to laugh. But it was just him and the one girl and the librarian, who was walking over to the phone. For a second, he thought that it was just a normal summer storm, but it didn't take long for him to realize that something was wrong.

Something was very wrong.

Because he couldn't feel anyone's emotions.

His breath caught in his throat. The last time this had happened, he'd been sick. He wasn't sick. He wasn't weak and pathetic, barely able to get up. No one was poisoning him. But there was something in the air. A stillness that unnerved him. An entire dimension in his life had vanished, and he needed to know why. A shudder ran up his spine. He stood, shoving his things into his backpack, and then sped walked out of the library.

The librarian called after him, probably to tell him not to leave, but he was already gone. The entire school had lost power, but that didn't stop him from rushing out of the building, ignoring all the remaining students in the halls. Ignoring the teachers trying to herd said students into classrooms to keep them safe during the power outage. None of them had emotions.

The moment he burst out of the school doors, the entire town shifted. It was as though he'd entered an alternate dimension. In fact, he was pretty certain he *had* entered some kind of alternate dimension, because when he glanced behind him, the school was no longer there.

"Oh, come on," he muttered before taking off down the road. He ditched his backpack somewhere along the way when it got too heavy for him, and he focused on finding the magical focal point controlling all of this. There were no other people. No citizens of Willow Creek, no tourists, wandering the streets. No fellow students excited for the end of the school day, jubilant to be in the few minutes after class and before homework. It was just him.

For a moment, he panicked. Was he in a dream? Had he fallen asleep? Was this Jae's doing? He grit his teeth and tried his best to focus on waking up, but nothing came of it. And then he felt it. Emotions. A few he recognized. Most he didn't. But there were a lot of them, and they surrounded him. All over town. But the majority of them had congregated in one place. The same place where the magic focused.

Blair's house.

"Shit, shit, *shit!*"

He took off running. He should have checked on her when he'd realized she wasn't in school. He'd wanted to give her space, and he'd needed space himself, but he should have made sure she was all right.

As he ran, he didn't think. He let his empathy range out, searching. Searching. Searching. Until he found he was close to a set of emotions he recognized, and he came to a stop just as Cody rounded the corner. Cody skidded to a halt in front of him. The two boys stared at each other as mutual understanding passed through them: this was not the time to fight.

"What's going on?" Cody asked, breathless.

"I don't know," Derek admitted. It couldn't be good.

"Let's go."

The two of them hurried toward Blair's house, running like they were being chased by a mountain lion. The minute they came into view, Derek halted, nearly skidding, because in the middle of the stranger's emotions, in the middle of their magic swirling together and blocking out much of his other senses, he felt one thing he'd always hoped he'd never have to feel again: Mia's sleeping terror.

Cody felt Mia's sleeping mist before he saw her cradled in the arms of a strange man. He came to a halt, grabbing Derek's arm to stop him. There was no doubt in Cody's mind that Derek would do something stupid if his sister was in danger, and they needed to think. This wasn't a group of kids. This wasn't the Natara. This was a host of adult mages who had all trained for decades in the art of magic.

Derek tried to yank his arm out of Cody's grip, but Cody slipped his mist into Derek's, holding him there. Derek gasped.

"Stop that," Derek snapped.

"Don't act rashly," Cody said. "We need to think."

"They have Mia. Who knows what they're going to do to Blair."

"You think I don't know that?" He wracked his brain, trying to think of a way to fix this. To get Mia away from them. He took a deep breath, and let go of Derek's mist.

Derek pulled away from him, rubbing his arm. "We have to do something."

"Barging in and attacking them isn't going to do any good."

"But—"

"No." Cody was not about to let Derek be irrational. "This is why we left you behind last summer. You don't *think* Derek. You just do whatever comes first to your head when it comes to the people you love. But we need to *think* here."

Derek fell silent, staring at Cody with hatred in his eyes. His gold mist fluctuated, ready for a fight, and Cody continued to think. Think. Think. Think.

They were far enough away from the mages that the group hadn't noticed them yet, but close enough that they could hear a man with a booming voice and a thick French accent say, "The children are dangerous, Esther. Unless they are taken into custody, they will continue to wreak havoc amongst the clans. Since they have become *friends*—" he spat the word "—with the Gray Spirits, everything has fallen apart. You know this."

"That's a coincidence," Esther Arbour argued.

"You don't believe in coincidences."

The boys exchanged glances. Cody needed to think of something, and fast, before they were noticed and the mages disappeared with

Mia. The last thing she needed was more trauma. Not when she was finally healing. Not when she was finally having a normal life.

"Give us the children," the French man said. "Hand over the Bowl of Transportation. End this now, or we will use violence."

Mrs. Arbour let out a laugh. "You don't want to fight me, Claude. You know what kind of mage I am."

"Were," the French man, Claude, corrected. "You've let yourself slip."

"Cody," Derek whispered, urgent.

"Dammit." He could only think of one thing to do, and he didn't want to do it.

"Dammit, what?" Derek asked.

He turned to Derek. "Get to Blair. I'll get Mia. Then we run, got it?"

"What are you planning?"

"Just go!" He tried to be quiet, but he didn't succeed. His voice carried and someone noticed them. The whispers started, and Cody focused. He focused on his mist. His purple mist, making it clear. Making himself disappear. Derek gasped as he vanished. "Go!"

Derek did as he was told, running toward Blair and Mrs. Arbour.

"Where did he go?" Cody heard as he ran toward the group. Toward Mia. He dodged in and out of mages, hoping they couldn't feel his magic. He'd hidden his mist. He'd hidden his magic. All he had to do was hide Mia too. Right? He could do that.

Right?

"Esther, make this stop!" Claude shouted.

But Mrs. Arbour had her own plans. A wave of magic flooded the group of mages. It washed through Cody, and he shivered, but it didn't knock him back the way it did those around him. The magic, her blue magic, must have gone after their mists, and his was invisible.

The man with Mia stumbled, but didn't fall onto his back like his colleagues. He gripped her tighter, brow furrowing. Cody grimaced. He wasn't sure he could keep his mist invisible and do what he needed to do, but he had to try. He reached out with his invisible mist and grabbed the man's, pulling, pulling, pulling....

He yelped, his grip loosening around Mia. She hung there, limp, and another wave of Mrs. Arbour's magic, accompanied by shouts from Claude and other mages, flew through the air. This was enough to blow the man off his balance. Mia flew through the air, and Cody ran forward, using his mist to catch hers. The moment his mist mixed with hers, she turned invisible to the world, but not to Cody.

His heart rate, racing a million miles a minute, slowed, as he caught her, and he sunk to the ground.

"Mia?" he whispered, but she didn't wake. "Mia!"

"Where'd she go? What's going on?" The gruff voice of the man who had been holding Mia came out as a shout, laced with a thick Scottish accent.

Cody lifted Mia, struggling to get to his feet, and then hurried through the crowd, careful not to touch anyone else. He could feel his magic draining. He didn't have long before he would turn visible. Each step drained him more, and it was getting more and more difficult as the mages reacted to Mrs. Arbour's attacks.

Derek and Blair had backed away, hands entwined in each other, but they hadn't run yet.

Idiots.

Cody wanted to scream at them. He didn't, but only because it wouldn't do anyone any good.

He only had a few seconds left.

A few steps.

He could make it.

He could....

He and Mia turned visible right as he broke through the crowd.

"There she is!" someone shouted in accented English. Cody

stumbled, but made it behind Mrs. Arbour.

"Go," she said to the teens. "I'll handle this."

"Mom, no." Blair stepped forward, but Derek pulled her back. Away from the crowd. Toward the forest.

"She's right," Derek said. "We gotta go."

Cody, panting, shifted Mia onto his back. He wasn't going to argue with Mrs. Arbour. She knew what she was doing. If she wanted to fight an entire group of mages by herself, then he wasn't going to stop her. He needed to get Mia to safety. He needed to make sure she woke up. And he needed to get the Iravata here to deal with this mess. He glared at Blair, who glared right back, though there was no fire behind it.

She knew she'd messed up. She knew this was her fault.

Still, he ran with her. With Derek. With Mia on his back. The three of them took off as Mrs. Arbour's magic exploded behind them, and Cody flinched, hoping that she would be all right.

Chapter Twenty-Six

Mia woke on someone's back.

At first she wasn't sure what was going on. She remembered leaving school. She remembered walking home. She remembered someone grabbing her. Is that who had her? No, the person smelled of sandalwood. It was a familiar smell. One she'd gotten used to over the years.

Cody.

Her eyes flickered open. They were in the woods. The sunlight dappled through the leaves, shining into her eyes. She groaned and shifted.

"She's awake." Blair's voice.

"Oh thank god." Derek's.

"Let's stop for a moment." Cody's voice rumbled through his back, vibrating Mia's chest. She wanted to cling to him, to hold him like she had on Jae's roof, but she knew he couldn't carry her forever. He was strong, and she wasn't heavy, but carry a feather for long enough....

"What happened?" Mia asked as Cody lowered her to the

ground. Her voice was faraway. Almost like it didn't belong to her.

When her feet touched the ground, her legs buckled and she collapsed, held up only by Cody's arms.

"Before that," Blair said, helping Cody bring Mia to a nearby tree to lean against, "are you okay?"

Was she okay? The world spun. The ground tilted and shifted. Her limbs were jelly. But she wasn't panicking. She'd been kidnapped, again, but this time she'd woken up with her friends, not with Jae. Had they already saved her? Was the fight already over?

"I'm okay," she said. "What's going on?"

Her voice was closer this time. The world still spun, but slower. She glanced between her three friends. Cody crouched before her, placing a hand on her forehead, like he was checking her temperature, while Derek glanced around, panic written all over his face. Blair looked from Derek to Mia, to the woods around them.

"Blair fucked up," Cody said.

"Hey, this is not entirely my fault," she snapped.

"Right," Derek said with a roll of his eyes. "Nothing is ever your fault."

Mia groaned and curled into a ball. "Someone please tell me what happened?"

There was a moment of silence, and then shouting from closer to town. Mia glanced in the direction of the shouts. Cody said Blair had messed up. Was this about the artifacts? Did Blair get one? Were people coming after them? Why would they take Mia? Use her as a bargaining chip?

She was no one's bargaining chip.

"Are we in danger?" Mia asked.

"Okay fine," Blair said. "I messed up. I pissed off the mage clans and now they're here to, I dunno, get revenge? They've been communicating with my mom, who didn't tell me, but they've been warning her? And they're here for us. But I don't know what they're gonna do if they get us. And it sounds like they're coming this way so we should *get out of here.*"

Mia wasn't sure she could *get out of here*, but the urgency in Blair's voice sparked her adrenaline. She pushed herself to her feet, stumbling in the process. Cody caught her, and she wanted to thank him, only to find he wasn't looking her in the eye. Was he still angry about the whole Chad thing?

Now's not the time to think of that, Poppet.

Mia blinked and looked around. "Lior?"

"No. Crazy mages," Blair snapped. "Come on, let's move."

She grabbed Mia's wrist and yanked her through the woods. Mia continued to stumble, but with each step she grew stronger until the four of them were running. They knew these woods better than the mages. They would be able to find some place to hide if they worked hard enough.

There's no place to hide. They aren't normal humans. Three of you have immense power. They can and will track you.

Mia groaned and stopped, pulling her hand out of Blair's.

"We don't have time for this," Blair said. "Come on, we have to hide."

"They'll just find us. You got one of the artifacts, right? That's why they're here? Just give it back to them." Mia did not have the patience for this.

"No!" Blair's voice echoed through the woods. Mia jumped back, startled. What had she missed?

Blair bowed her head. "Look, I'm not giving it back. The wielder didn't want it. She gave it to me and I'm going to keep it safe."

"But the clans don't want to abuse it," Cody argued.

"Seriously." Derek crossed his arms.

"I said no," Blair snapped.

"Then you leave us no choice."

A shudder ran up Mia's spine at the newcomer's voice. She

turned and found a man with more bruises on his face than Mia could count, holding himself up with a staff that she knew had to be an artifact, but she wasn't sure how.

Next to her, Blair snorted. "Looks like my mom beat you up something good, Claude."

The man snarled. "I've dealt with your mother. Now to focus on you and your friends."

Mia stepped back. She wasn't sure why she was involved in any of this. She'd systematically pushed away anyone having to do with magic. She didn't want to be part of the magical world. She wanted her friends back, but she wanted their magical lives to be separate. Something they didn't talk about. The opposite of last year. But last year felt like a million years away, and she was a different person. She'd been through too much.

Blair clenched her fist and Mia backed away. She could run. She didn't have magic. They couldn't track her. Maybe she could find the Iravata. Lior seemed up to date on the situation, at least. The others had to be as well.

So, where were they?

RIGHT HERE.

Mia spun around, coming face to face with her favorite teacher. She stumbled away from him, hearing the whispers of other people.

Lior grinned at her.

NO NEED TO PANIC, POPPET. WE'RE HERE TO HELP.

Mia looked around and most of the Iravata melted out of the woods. There were two Mia didn't recognize. Two women she assumed were Nina and Tori.

Mia glanced back at Claude, who backed away with his staff between his hands. The sky continued to thunder.

"Claude Dubois." Shubishi stepped out from among the group, smiling like always.

Claude's eyes widened. "Monsieur...."

"Confused?" Shubishi asked. "I can imagine why. It isn't often that you realize that someone in your life isn't who they say they are."

"This is impossible!" Claude shouted. "You're a normal human! I checked your magic levels myself!"

"And this is what happens when you forget that the Iravata are not human," Shubishi said with a chuckle. "You think that you can sense our magic the same way you can sense that of a fellow mage? Fool. Of course, I live my life off the backs of fools, so I suppose I can't complain."

Claude sputtered, and the mages emerging around him looked far more tense than before.

POPPET, YOU SHOULD LEAVE BEFORE THINGS GET MESSY.

She should have left. She should have taken off into the woods, run home and cried to her mother. But she found she couldn't move. All of her desire to run had vanished the second the tables had turned. No longer was it three kids against a group of fully trained mages. Now it was three teenage mages, seven immortals, and Mia against a group of fully trained mages.

NO, NOT YOU.

What? Why not?

IT'S TOO DANGEROUS.

I can handle myself.

DIDN'T YOU WANT TO LEAVE ALL THIS BEHIND YOU? FIGHT THEM AND YOU'LL STAY ON THEIR LIST.

I can't just abandon my friends.

YOU WON'T BE.

Before Mia knew what was happening, Lior placed a hand on her shoulder and her body tightened. The world around her shifted and twisted, and she tried to pull away, but his grip was too tight.

When the world righted itself again, Mia realized she wasn't in the woods, but in a room filled to the brim with books. A warm, wooden desk sat in front of her, couches behind her. She knew this place. She'd spent days in this place, listening to the tale of the Iravata.

Shubishi's study.

"No!" she shouted, spinning around to tell Lior to take her back, but he was gone, and she was alone, far away from her friends and her family.

Cody noticed when Mia and Lior disappeared. He spun around, looking for her, but she was long gone. Probably somewhere safe. He breathed out. She was safe. For the first time since everything went to shit, she wasn't in the middle of the action.

He faced Claude and Shubishi again, fists tightening at the sight of the Iravata who he was certain was his father.

"Mia's gone," Blair whispered.

"Yup." Cody didn't know what else to say.

"Good," Derek said. "She doesn't deserve to see what's gonna happen."

Cody agreed.

"Where did the girl go?" Claude shouted. "Mia. Where is she?"

"Somewhere safe," Shubishi said. "Now, we should talk about this little temper tantrum that you're throwing."

"It is not a—"

Shubishi held up a hand. "I've been alive for millions of years. I recognize a temper tantrum when I see one."

Claude remained silent and Cody marveled at the way Shubishi commanded the room. He'd thought this back when Shubishi was telling the tale of the Iravata. How easily he'd spoken. The smoothness in which he walked through life. It was nothing like how Cody lived. It was nothing like how Jae had been when Cody had met him. Nothing at all.

"You blame the children for the faults in your clans?" Shubishi called out. "But why? What have they ever done besides learn the truth about us? How could four children be the reason that your magic is waning? That your politics are dissolving? Are you sure it's not because *you* have gotten so arrogant that you believe yourselves better than?"

Cody blinked, shocked at the news. He nudged Blair and shot her a look. But she shrugged. She was still hiding things. If Cody knew anything about Blair, it was that she was *always* going to hide things. She knew *something* about Shubishi's revelations.

Something was causing their magic to wane. Their politics to dissolve. As far as Cody knew, listening to Blair talk about it for years, the clans had put together a fool proof way of keeping peace between the clans. Treaties among treaties, making rules and laws for those who were part of one of the five major clans or their subsets. He wanted to ask Shubishi what he was talking about, but he also didn't want to interrupt the conversation. Maybe Shubishi could calm the mages down with no casualties.

"All of this started when those children got involved in your world," Claude said with a stuttering voice. "I merely put two and two together."

"Hardly." Shubishi laughed. "There are variables that you are missing, dear Claude. Variables you and your clans have long since forgotten about."

"We have forgotten nothing!"

Shubishi grinned and turned around to face the teens. Cody stiffened when Shubishi's eyes landed on him. The gray eyes that were so familiar. The same gray eyes that Olivia had. Cody blinked. There had been something missing from the story of the Iravata. They'd revealed the childhoods of all of them except for Shubishi.

His story had started when he'd met Death.

What was he hiding from the clans? What was he hiding from the other Iravata?

"Enough of this!" Claude pointed his staff at Shubishi. "Hand over the children and we'll move on with our lives."

Blair was absolutely, one hundred percent, not positive that Shubishi was going to protect them. The other Iravata, maybe, but Shubishi? That man had more plans than the U.S. Government, and he had the means to carry them out. For all Blair knew, this was his plan. He'd orchestrated this to happen. He knew Claude. Granted, he seemed to know everyone, but this took the cake.

She wasn't sure what to do, but when Claude announced that Shubishi hand over Blair and her friends, she tensed, ready for a battle. It wasn't until a very familiar voice echoed throughout the clearing that she relaxed. Relaxed and let confusion wash over her.

"What exactly do you plan on doing with my granddaughter?"

The entire group of mages turned, and Claude paled. Enola Demini stood behind them, shrouded in shadows, head held high.

Blair let out a breath, but next to her, both boys stiffened. Blair wanted to reassure them, but she knew that nothing she said was going to change their minds about her grandmother.

"Enola," Claude said.

"I see you've invited every clan but mine, Claude," Enola said, voice loud and clear. Commanding. She spread her arms, gesturing to the crowd. "I also see that you are harassing my family."

"Two deserters," Claude corrected.

Blair's hands curled into fists. Only Blair got to talk to her grandmother that way.

"Regardless of their status in *my* clan," Enola hissed, "they are still my family, and I do not take kindly to you rounding up every other clan to handle this issue. That goes against the treaties."

"Your granddaughter broke the treaties the moment she set her eyes on the artifacts," Claude said.

"And what is it that you plan to do with her and her friends?"

That was a question Blair wanted answered more than anything. Yes, Claude had said he was going to deal with them, but how? Keep them locked up? Torture them? Blair had no idea what this man was capable of.

"I'm going to do as I please." Claude held up his staff and the weather shifted again. Droplets of rain fell from the sky. They misted Blair's skin, and she shuddered. Next to her, Cody muttered something about hating rain, and Derek crossed his arms.

Enola let out a hearty laugh. "You really think you can fight me, Claude? You've never been much of a fighter. My daughter, despite having had little training and four children, was still able to leave your face marred. How do you propose that you're going to fight not only me, but the Gray Spirits as well?"

"You're on the side of the Gray Spirits now?" someone shouted from the group of mages.

"Hardly." Enola glared at Shubishi who held up his hands. "But they aren't trying to hurt my family. So for today, yes."

There was a moment of tense silence, as if Enola was waiting to see what Claude would do. He didn't react at first, glaring at Enola with narrowed eyes and a furrowed brow, but the moment the staff twitched in his hands, the magic exploded.

Blair yelped as Enola's blue magic darted through the air. It smacked Claude in the chest, and he flew backward, directly toward Blair. She, without thinking, held out her hands. A shimmering blue shield fanned out in front of her. Claude smacked into it with a loud clap and collapsed to the ground.

284

R*UN*.

Lior didn't have to repeat himself. Blair took off into the woods as mages yelled and shouted. This was bad. It was so bad. She didn't check to make sure that Derek and Cody were with her. They could handle themselves, probably better than she could.

But this was bad. So bad.

It was worse than last fall. It was worse than Mia getting kidnapped. Blair had to hold back tears. She'd been so desperate to find the artifacts, to prove herself and keep Mia safe, that she hadn't thought of the consequences. She'd figured that if she didn't get any of the artifacts, then it wouldn't matter.

But it did matter. There hadn't been a fight between the clans since World War II. Who would have thought that an eighteen-year-old girl would break the peace?

R*UN*.

Derek bolted. He had no idea what was going on, or why, but he knew that he was stuck with the problems that Blair and Cody had caused for all of them. Derek had known trying to get the artifacts was a bad idea, and if he'd just talked to either of them, he might have been able to stop the madness. He might have been able to talk Blair out of all of it.

Who was he kidding, no one could talk Blair out of anything once she'd made up her mind. It was something he hated about her.

It was something he loved about her.

Lior's warning had come just in time, as the shouts grew from the forest behind them. He had no idea how powerful Enola was, but he had a feeling he didn't want to be around for the fallout.

He ran until his legs turned to jelly and his throat tasted of iron.

He skidded to a stop, looking around. Cody and Blair were nowhere to be found, though when he reached out for their emotions, he felt their panic and fear. They must have run off too. Maybe they'd gotten the same message as Derek. Maybe they'd followed his lead. He didn't care which, as long as they were safe.

Stumbling through the forest, he tried to decide if he wanted to go search for them or make his way back to town. The mages wouldn't be stupid enough to fight him with non-mages around.

Right?

As he deliberated, the wind shifted. The rain grew heavier, and he had no idea what to think. He figured it had something to do with Claude's staff, but he hadn't paid attention when he'd learned about the different artifacts. He probably should have, but the only artifact he cared about in any way shape or form was the knife he had at his belt.

The knife he hoped the clans didn't know about.

Run.

Cody hesitated, watching the scene in front of him unfold. Enola waved her hand and the group of mages scattered amongst the trees. She walked forward, holding out her hand as the Iravata vanished into the woods. Cody tensed, realizing that Blair and Derek were both gone, and took a step back.

You need to run.

He knew that, but his feet wouldn't move. They were planted in the ground, as though someone had nailed them there. He was scared. Scared that someone would attack him. Scared that someone would kill Blair's grandmother. Scared...so scared.

A hand appeared on his shoulder, but he still couldn't move.

It wasn't until Shubishi leaned in and whispered, "Time to move, Cody," that his body jumped into action.

He took off, mostly to get away from Shubishi. He stumbled in the direction of Derek's mist, sensing that he should go find Derek before they went to get Blair. He ran, hating himself for giving up on exercise these past few months. He wasn't sure for how long, or how fast, but eventually he came upon Derek's mist and slowed down, searching for him.

Searching, and searching.

Until he found him surrounded by trees, soaking wet, and staring at the knife.

"Derek!" Cody called out, breathless.

Derek looked up from the knife and replaced it at his waist. Cody knew he carried it with him sometimes, but he never knew when. Him having it now wasn't shocking, but he wasn't sure it was a bright idea to have an artifact out in the open like that.

"You get Lior's message?" Derek asked.

"I think we all did." Cody breathed in deeply, then out. "Where do you think Mia is?"

Derek scowled, which Cody didn't understand, and then he said, "Safe, somewhere. Probably pissed as hell, but I don't care."

"She's not in Willow Creek?"

"No."

Good. "What about Blair?"

Derek shrugged. "You can sense her just as well as I can. I don't know where she ran off to, but we should keep moving. Make a decision about something."

"A decision about what?"

"Where we're going to go? What we're going to do?"

"Maybe we should find Blair." Cody sought out Blair's mist and turned in the direction that she was. "Come on, we should go get her. We'll be safer together."

But Derek didn't move. Cody sighed. "What?"

"She caused all of this," Derek said.

"So?"

"So, what if I don't want to be around someone who puts everyone in danger?"

"You mean like you last winter?"

Derek flinched and looked at the ground, crossing his arms. "I...I didn't mean to...."

"And neither did Blair." Cody sighed and shook his head. "Come on, Derek. There's a literal battle happening right now. You would never forgive yourself if something happened to Blair."

"I guess."

"So, let's go find her."

Derek hesitated for a moment longer before nodding. "All right."

Cody smiled, but the smile didn't last long as a mist he recognized, a mist he hated, appeared in the woods. Nearby. Close enough that when Cody looked over Derek's shoulder, he spotted him.

Jae.

Cody immediately jumped in front of Derek, shielding him from whatever Jae had planned. Derek, clearly startled, turned around and his golden mist shifted. Jae, however, didn't move. He didn't attack. He didn't do anything except stare at the two boys.

"What do you want?" Cody asked. This was none of his business. Mia wasn't even here.

Jae reached out with one hand and pointed it at Derek. At the knife. He wanted Niran's knife. He'd tried to get it before, back when Mia was the one who'd held onto it. Cody's head spun. He'd forgotten, in all the panic about rescuing Mia back then, that Jae had also been after the knife.

"I see you've removed Mia," Jae said looking around. "I approve, though now that she's gone, the barriers around the town are open. That was rather foolish of the Iravata. They should have known that the moment she was gone, the moment I had a chance, I'd be back. They know how powerful the knife is, and how powerful it will be once I have it."

"You can't have it," Derek said. Cody hissed at him to be quiet, but Derek kept going. "You can haunt my dreams, but you cannot have the knife. It's mine, and I'll keep it, thank you very much."

Haunt his dreams? Cody glanced at him, wondering what the hell he was talking about. He didn't have time to ask questions before his body froze. Immediately, he knew what was happening. He'd felt this before. Back in the stairwell that led up to Jae's roof.

He wasn't going to let it continue.

He focused on his powers. The energy in his soul, and pushed. Pushed and pushed until Jae's grip on him lessened. Until he was able to pull away. It was like letting go of a rope during a game of tug of war. Cody flew back and Jae stumbled forward.

Derek caught Cody with a grunt. "What the hell?"

"We gotta get out of here," Cody said. "Before he recovers."

But it was too late. Jae's mist attempted to mix with his again, and he pushed it back with a force that nearly knocked Jae off his feet.

"What is going on?" Derek asked.

"He's trying to control my mist," Cody explained. "He'll go after you next and you don't know how to fight him off. Let's *go*."

Cody ran as fast as he could, but he knew it was useless. They didn't get very far before Jae appeared in front of them, looking as calm as before. The rain fell harder, soaking the ground into mud and Cody's clothes into sopping heaps. He wiped water out of his face.

"You can't run from me!" Jae shouted. "I should have come to Willow Creek years ago. I should have taken Mia before she became attached. I should have dealt with you myself instead of sending Steven and Kathleen. And today, I will."

He held out his hand and next to Cody, Derek stiffened. Cody watched as Jae's purple mist mixed with Derek's gold. A stark, but beautiful contrast. He tried to interfere, but Jae set the ground on fire between them. Cody stumbled backwards, his powers muted. The fire didn't last long, but it was enough of a distraction that Cody couldn't stop what happened next.

He scrambled to his feet as Jae walked toward Derek, holding out his hand. Derek struggled against Jae's grip on his mist, trying to keep his body from obeying as he reached to his belt and pulled the knife out of it.

It wasn't going to work, Cody told himself. Derek had to willing give up the artifact. Jae couldn't just take it from him.

Could he?

Jae reached out Derek's hand and Cody struggled to his feet, trying to get a grip on his magic to stop Derek, but it was too late. Jae gripped the knife and took it from Derek's hand right as Cody took control of Derek's mist.

Blair nearly crashed into Claude. She hadn't realized he'd run after her. She came to a stop and dodged him when he tried to grab her. He let out a growl and swung his magic in her direction. She flicked her wrist, knocking it into a nearby tree. The tree exploded, but the heavy rain dampened the fire before it could spread.

She backed away from him, holding out her hand as she panted. "Leave me alone!"

"Give Amahle back the Bowl of Transportation."

"Make me." Blair had been training for this for over a year now. Ever since she'd failed fighting Steven, ever since she'd almost gotten Derek killed, she'd been training. Learning to fight with the one thing she had: magic.

The fire came easily, spreading along the ground and burning at Claude's feet. He yelped and stumbled away from it before wiping it away with a flick of his wrist. But Blair was ready for that. She couldn't control the rain, but she could use it to her advantage, creating her own water out of the air and turning it into ice.

Claude dodged each of the icicles, but he stumbled and fell to the ground in the process, knocking the staff away from him.

Blair grinned. He very clearly wasn't used to fighting.

"You bitch," he said, spitting out the last word like it was meant to harm her in her soul. She didn't care, though. She'd been called a bitch enough times that the word meant nothing to her anymore.

"Damn straight," she said, holding her head high. "You can't just come to my home and demand I give you something that was willingly given to me. If you have a problem with that, talk to…what was her name? Amahle?"

"Blair!" Esther's voice carried above the rain.

"Mom?" Blair turned to find her mom, startled by her voice. A mistake. Claude took advantage of her distraction and jumped her from behind, knocking her to the ground. She kicked and tried to use her magic, but he pinned her wrists by her head, pressing his knee into her hips to keep her still.

"You have always been a problem, Blair Arbour," Claude snapped. "Always been a menace to society. Well, no more. You are coming with me. We are getting back the artifact, and you will live out your days in our prisons, unable to cause any more problems."

For the first time since all of this started, pure unadulterated fear overcame Blair. The rain poured down on her, making it difficult for her to focus on him long enough to use her magic. And that's when she realized what was going on. Her body went weak. Her mind grew dizzy. He was taking her energy.

"No!" Blair shouted, struggling again. "Stop it!"

As if her shouts summoned help, Claude was thrown back, slamming into a nearby tree. Blair gasped and rolled over, trying to gain control of herself. He hadn't taken all of her energy, but enough that getting up was a problem.

"Blair!" Esther fell to her knees by Blair's side. "Are you all right?"

"I'm fine," Blair said, though she absolutely was not. "Claude wants to imprison me."

Esther stood. "Over my dead body."

"And mine."

Blair looked up to find her grandmother standing there, clothes ripped, eyes alive with fire.

Claude pushed himself up and grabbed the staff. He slammed it into the ground, stopping the rain. "You two...you cannot win against me while I have the staff."

"You'd like to think that, wouldn't you?" Esther snapped at him. "But you're forgetting that my mother and I have always been, and will always be, more powerful than you. You're a pathetic excuse for an artifact wielder, Claude."

Blair, unable to move, could only watch as the two women stood side-by-side. Two woman whom Blair respected more than anyone. Two women who had never seen eye-to-eye. But they did today. They saw it because someone had threatened Blair.

Tears pricked her eyes.

"Mom, Grandma," she said. "You don't have to do this."

"We do," Esther said. "We do, and we will."

Claude charged. Esther and Enola exchanged a glance. Blair closed her eyes.

Derek wasn't sure what happened, but he felt the moment that the knife transferred powers from him to Jae. He knew the second it happened, and it zapped his energy like nothing else had before. He collapsed to his knees, panting.

The knife…he'd been put in charge of taking care of it, but Jae had done something to him. Controlled him. Made him give up the knife. He'd always thought he had to give it away voluntarily. Maybe he was supposed to, but maybe Jae was more powerful than any of them thought.

Or maybe the Iravata, and the clans, had been wrong.

He looked up as Jae walked away from him, holding the knife into the air.

"Finally," Jae said. "I have the thing that can kill an immortal. Now Mother will love me. Now Father will respect me. They have to. They *must*. When I kill the queen, everything will be good. The world will be at peace, and I can have whatever I want."

Derek struggled to his feet, finding stability in Cody's shoulder.

"I'm sorry," he whispered to Cody.

"It's not your fault," Cody whispered back. "I'm sorry I couldn't stop him."

But it wasn't Cody's fault. Derek should have been stronger. He should have left the knife at home. He should have done so many things differently this past year. He should have known that something bad would happen, with Niran warning him constantly. Now that Jae had the knife, there was no telling what he'd do with it. How much havoc he would wreak. How dangerous he would become.

"What do you think, Father?" Jae asked the air. "Am I good enough for you now? Will you finally accept me?"

There was a cracking of branches. The slosh of muddy footsteps. Derek looked away from Jae, toward the trees, and watched as Shubishi strode out of them. Soaking wet, but looking as calm and collected as always. Derek cursed him under his breath. He was late. If he'd been here only a minute earlier, then he could have stopped Jae. He could have kept this from ever happening.

Then, again, Shubishi wasn't one to interfere. He hadn't with Steven, he hadn't when Jae had kidnapped Mia.

So then…what was he doing here?

"I knew it," Cody muttered.

Knew what?

"No, Jae," Shubishi said. "As far as I'm concerned, there is nothing you can do to make me accept you."

Oh. Derek's face went cold. He glanced at Cody, who had his eyes trained on Shubishi. Jae was Cody's half-brother. They shared a father.

"Shubishi's your father?" Derek said with a low gasp.

Shubishi glanced at the two boys. "I'm surprised you didn't know, Derek. I never meant to keep it a secret."

Unlike all the other secrets he carried. Derek felt like a complete idiot. Of course Shubishi was Cody's father. They had the same ability. He'd been so angry this past year that he'd missed all of the signs.

"Now, then," Shubishi faced Jae. Jae pointed the knife at him, a manic grin on his face, eyes alight with excitement. His hands trembled. Shubishi sighed. "Put that away before you hurt someone."

"You mean before I hurt you?" Jae asked.

Shubishi cackled. "Foolish boy. You think that knife is powerful enough to take my life? It hasn't been used nearly enough. I've made sure of that."

"That's right, hiding it away so no one can find it. I know how your mind works."

"Hardly."

Jae charged at him and stabbed, but Shubishi disappeared.

"You have your knife. Now leave," Shubishi said. Derek blinked

294

and the Iravata was there, standing behind Jae who spun around to face him.

Jae twirled the knife between his fingers with a grin. "You said it's not powerful enough to kill you yet? That means it's not powerful enough to kill the queen. But there's one soul here that is very powerful. One I can feel through the knife. I wonder if killing her will make the knife powerful enough."

Shubishi didn't flinch, but both Derek and Cody did.

"Stop it!" Derek shouted, but Jae was gone, leaving the boys weak and alone in the forest with Shubishi. Panic flared in Derek's throat, so hot and white that he could barely speak. "Blair! He's going to go after Blair!"

Shubishi walked over to them and stared down at Derek.

"Yes," Shubishi said. "Yes he is."

All of her life, Blair had known that her mother was powerful. But she'd never quite understood how powerful until this moment. Claude, in all respects, stood no chance against Enola and Esther. Two women with more magic than he could ever begin to conceive, fighting together like a well-oiled machine. All those years of arguing had done nothing to impact how well they worked together.

And Blair could only watch.

Claude backed away from the two mages, still tensed as if he was going to fight them. He wiped a trail of blood from his mouth, beady eyes flickering from one woman to the other. He opened his mouth to say something. But then, without warning, his eyes went wide. His jaw slacked and he dropped to the ground, the staff clattering along with him. Standing behind him, holding a bloody knife, was Jae.

Claude's body dissolved into dust. Jae stepped forward and picked up the staff.

Blair gasped.

"Not the one I was looking for," Jae said, "but he was a nuisance anyway."

Jae was there. Jae. Oh god. With Mia gone, the wards were down. And he had the knife! Did that mean…was Derek…? Blair was too weak to seek out Derek's energy. She hoped he was all right, but Jae's grin made her forget all about him and Cody.

He stepped toward Blair.

"Don't you dare," Esther said as she stepped in front of her daughter. Blair tried to understand what was going on. What did her mom know that she didn't?

Jae smirked and held up his hands, creating two walls of fire around the three women.

Fire. Blair had been seeing fire in her visions. It was all she'd been able to see. Was this…was she going to….

Esther waved her hands, trying to control the flames, but they wouldn't listen to her. "Shit."

"Mom, we gotta get out of here," Blair said.

Esther turned and tried to help Blair to her feet, but she was too exhausted. Both of them were too exhausted.

"Now, now," Jae said, twirling the knife. "You know as well as I do that this isn't going to end well. If you give me Blair, then I'll be out of your hair in a moment. Scout's honor." He held up a hand, placing the other one on his chest.

Blair's eyes widened and she clung to her mother as realization dawned on her. Jae had the knife. He wanted *her*. A sob died in the back of her throat as she blinked back tears. She didn't want to die. She wanted to live. To have a chance to be normal. To not have all of this weight on her shoulders.

Enola called her name softly. Blair looked up, into her

grandmother's shimmering eyes. She had a small smile on her face. A knowing smile. She didn't understand. But her mind went wild with theories. With memories. It brought out every time Enola had talked to her about death.

Enola nodded at Blair and then faced Jae. "I don't know who you are, stranger, but you will do nothing to my granddaughter."

"Who I am isn't important," Jae said. "What matters is that I have a mission, and I need your granddaughter's soul to make that happen. The soul of a living seer. That should be powerful enough."

Blair couldn't believe her ears. He needed her soul? What in the world? Why? What was going on with the knife? With all of this?

Enola closed her eyes. She breathed out, and Blair's stomach dropped.

No!

"Grandma!" Blair shouted. She struggled to her feet, but Esther held her back. She was too weak to fight against her mother. The tears streamed down her face. "Grandma, no, don't!"

"You want the soul of a living seer?" Enola said. "Any living seer?"

"Doesn't matter to me who it is." Jae held out the knife. "Why, are you one?"

Enola glanced back at her daughter and granddaughter one last time. "I love you both," she said. "Never forget that."

"No!" Blair continued to struggle, but Esther held her, shielding her from view.

"Take my soul. Leave my granddaughter alone."

Jae smirked. "I can do that." And then he charged.

"NO!"

Blair didn't see the knife enter her grandmother's chest. Esther held her tight, pressing her face into her shoulder. But Blair felt her grandmother's magic vanish. She felt the moment that Enola dropped to the ground. A chord in her snapped. She hadn't even realized it was there, tethering her to her grandmother. To the only other living seer. She shoved Esther away in time to see her grandmother's body melt into ash. The rain lightened. The rain stopped. Blair sat there, slack jawed, and tried to comprehend.

Jae stood over the pile of ashes, and around them the fire flickered before disappearing.

Tears streaked Blair's face. She crawled over to the pile of ashes through the mud, hoping that she could bring her grandmother back. But she couldn't. No one could bring the dead back to life.

"You said you would go," Esther snapped at Jae. Her voice cracked. "Now go."

Jae merely nodded, and then he was gone.

Part Six

Chapter Twenty-Seven

Cody hadn't seen Blair in almost two weeks. She was home. Her real home. In Sangota, for the funeral. At least, that's where he hoped she was.

He didn't blame her for not wanting to go to school. School seemed pointless after everything that had happened. It seemed like nothing would ever go back to normal. Blair wasn't speaking to anyone, Derek was beating himself up for losing the knife, and Mia went about as if nothing had happened.

He didn't blame her either. She knew what had happened in the woods, but she'd been so detached when Lior had finally brought her home that it was like she hadn't heard anything they'd said. And maybe she hadn't. It was, after all, the magical world.

Mia wanted nothing to do with the magical world.

Still, as Cody sat in the library, trying to figure out what to do with graduation around the corner and the stack of college acceptances waiting for an answer, he couldn't help but wonder what he could do to help the two girls in his life.

Mia, who wanted to be divorced from all of this.

And Blair, who had gone off the grid.

It didn't matter, though, because he couldn't do anything. Nothing he did made anything better, and he just wanted to get through prom season so he could be done with it. He wasn't going to go. He had too much to do and little interest in a dance with no friends and no date.

He knew Mia was going. He knew that Derek's parents were forcing him to go. But he wouldn't attend, and he had a feeling that Blair wouldn't either.

The final bell rang. Cody collected his things and trudged home, not wanting to deal with his parents. Ever since confirming that Shubishi was his real father, he'd avoided Dylan, not wanting to have the conversation that he knew was going to happen. All he wanted to do was go back in time. Before any of the past year and a half had happened.

When he got home, he set his book bag down and looked around for his mother, knowing full well she was back in the hospital. She hadn't tried to kill herself this time. Cody had convinced his dad to get her in the hospital before that happened. Maybe "Dr. Smith" could help her again. Could make her better permanently.

Or maybe this would be what it was like for the rest of her life. In and out of hospitals, always having her memory messed with.

He closed his eyes and breathed in.

"Cody?"

He hadn't expected Dylan to be home. Cody tensed and turned toward his dad.

"Are you okay?" Dylan asked.

He had to do it. He had to tell his dad what had been going on. It wasn't fair to keep him in the dark, even if telling him about magic and the magical world was going to make things worse for him. For everyone.

He deserved to know.

"Dad," Cody said, "I have something to talk to you about."

Cody's dad gestured toward the kitchen and the two settled in the kitchen chairs. Cody's hands shook. He didn't know how to start this. He'd never told anyone about his magic who didn't already have it themselves. He didn't...he didn't know how to get the words out. How to explain to the man who had raised him and loved him that not only was magic real, but that he wasn't his actual father. That Dylan Velt, a normal accountant, didn't have a normal son. That he didn't have a son at all.

"Cody?" Dylan reached out and touched Cody's shoulder.

"Dad, I...I uh...." He breathed in. "I have magic." Dylan's face fell. He removed his hand from Cody's shoulder and sat back in his chair.

"Oh?"

And from there, the words tumbled out. A jumbled mess. Nothing like what he'd wanted to say. He didn't really know why he was telling Dylan all of this. It wasn't like Dylan needed to know. Or maybe he did. Maybe he deserved to know the truth about his wife and son.

He told Dylan everything. From Cody's magical abilities, to the traumatic events of last winter, to the real story of last summer, to two weeks ago. Then, finally, he told Dylan, his dad, that Shubishi was his real father. That his mother might be a mage. And that Cody wasn't entirely human.

And when he finished, Dylan sat there, staring at the wall as though he'd just had his mind blown. Cody tensed.

"I know," Cody said before Dylan could say anything, "that it's a lot to take in. I just...I thought you should know what's been going on. Especially with Mom in the hospital again and me going to college and...."

He trailed off when Dylan looked down at him with a smile. "Oh, Cody, I've always known about magic."

Shock. Utter shock. Cody stared at his dad, jaw dropped, unable to think straight. His dad…knew? Dylan knew about magic?

"Huh?" was all he could get out.

Dylan held up his hands in defense. "I mean, I didn't know about everything. I didn't realize it was so wide spread, but I knew you had strange abilities. When you were little, you'd talk about colors that no one else could see. Ava…your mom told me not to encourage it. That it was dangerous. Sometimes she'd know, sometimes she wouldn't, like something was protecting her. I wanted to talk to you about it, but I thought that if we brought magic into the house, it would make Mom worse. Every time I brought it up with her, she'd get angry, and take out that anger on you, and I was trying to protect you both from whatever was going on. I just…I didn't realize it had become such a large part of your life. I'm so sorry if I made you feel like you couldn't talk to me about what's been going on."

Dylan gripped Cody's shoulder. "I hope that from now on, you *can* talk to me about this."

A tear dripped down Cody's cheek and he wiped it away with the back of his hand. "You've known?"

He didn't know how to feel. Angry? Betrayed? Frustrated?

"Of course. How could I not know how special my son is?"

"I'm not your son," Cody whispered.

Dylan smiled. "You *are* my son."

"But–"

"Ava was three months pregnant when I met her. The fact that I'm not your *biological* dad doesn't mean I'm not your *dad*. And it doesn't mean I don't love you. This man…Shubishi? Where was he when you wouldn't take a bottle? When you fell and had to get three stitches on your forehead? When you learned to read? When you struggled to make friends at school? Where was he all of these years? He's not your father, Cody. He may be the man who got your mom pregnant, but I'm the one who was there. Who is here. I'm the one who loves you more than anything in the world, and I will do whatever I can to protect you."

There were more tears now. Cody hadn't expected this. Dylan had done his best. He really had. With work, and Ava, and all of the complications that came with her mental health, it was hard for all of them, but there Dylan was, assuring Cody that it didn't matter who Cody's father was. Dylan was his *dad*.

Dylan pulled Cody into a tight hug, squeezing him until it was hard to breathe.

"You are my son. You are special. And I'm glad we can talk about all of this now. I'm so sorry I haven't been the best dad to you, especially the past few years. But I'm going to try harder now, all right?"

Cody nodded, squeezing his dad back, but said nothing in return.

Chapter Twenty-Eight

The night was beautiful. A picturesque moment of glittering streamers and dancing balloons in all shades of silver and black. The gym was filled to the brim with people laughing and dancing as music thumped through the air, vibrating the walls and people's hearts. Teens clumped together, chatting with their friends. With their partners. Some danced, gyrating to the music like they were lost in the drop of the beat.

And through it all, through all of the excitement and cookies and punch, Mia stood in her beautiful ocean-blue, floor length dress, ankles hurting from the heels she'd yet to take off, staring at door, and waited. She waited for it to open. For it to reveal the people she wanted to see.

Cody, whom she knew wasn't coming.

Blair, whom she hadn't spoken to in two weeks.

Next to her, Chad, dressed in an awkward tux with a blue tie and a silver boutonniere that paired with the elegant corsage on Mia's wrist, chatted with his friends. He gripped Mia's hand, like he was trying to keep her pinned to the moment, but it wasn't working.

Her mind flashed back to two weeks ago. Over, and over, and over again. She imagined herself back in Shubishi's beach house, frustrated, crying, not sure what she wanted to do. She'd called for Lior to bring her back. To take her to her friends. To protect them in some way, but she'd known that she couldn't protect them. Not in the way they'd needed to be protected.

But maybe, just maybe, if she'd been there, she could have talked Jae out of his plan. Maybe she could have convinced him not to take anyone's life. That he didn't need to do this. After all, she was his angel. She was the one he wanted to protect. To make happy.

Killing Blair's grandmother made no one happy.

No one at school talked about Blair being gone. Mia hadn't seen her since waking up in the forest, before Lior had handled her. By the time Lior had brought her back to Willow Creek, the entire Arbour family, along with all the mages, were gone. According to Derek and Cody, the Bowl of Transportation had been returned, and peace had been brokered. She didn't ask more questions. She'd wanted to know about Blair.

No one would tell her about Blair.

"Hey, Mia," Chad said, gripping her hand, "wanna get something to drink?"

Mia glanced up at him. Chad. Chad Rogers. A sweet boy who had done nothing but make her feel warm and welcome. Who had helped her recover from her week of hell last summer. He was everything she should have wanted. But she found herself so distant from him. As far as he knew, Blair's grandmother had died suddenly of a heart attack. That's what Mrs. Arbour had told the school. He didn't know about the magic. He didn't know about the clans or the Iravata or the artifacts.

He didn't know about Jae or the connection that Mia had to a world she could never escape from. No matter how hard she tried, she couldn't....

"I think I need some air," Mia said. She pulled away from him. He let her go, tilting his head. She should have wanted him. But what she wanted was his normality. The lack of magic. It wasn't *him* that she wanted, and she didn't understand why. Why she'd never wanted to date before Steven. Why, even when she thought of her first love, of the fact that she'd kissed him, it had all felt off. All felt weird looking back. She'd been under some kind of spell.

But here, there was no magic, and Mia felt nothing.

"I'll be back." Mia smiled at Chad and then turned to head out into the chilly evening.

On her way, she passed Derek, who leaned against a wall. They made eye contact, and Mia dropped her gaze. Derek had been very distant the past two weeks. Mia didn't blame him. He had been in charge of the knife. Enola's death wasn't his fault, but he blamed himself the way Mia blamed herself.

She walked through the doors, mentioning to the teacher in charge that she would be right back, and then headed off toward the woods. She didn't know why she went that way. It wasn't like there was anything there this late at night. But she wanted a moment of peace, and the woods brought her peace. Or, at least they used to. But as she walked underneath the trees, moon lighting her path, she realized that the memories here weren't good anymore.

They were ones of blood. Of fear. Of losing control of her body. Of her world being twisted and turned. Of betrayal and heartbreak.

She shivered, rubbing her hands on her bare arms. Everything was wrong. This wasn't how her senior year was supposed to go. How prom was supposed to go. It was supposed to be fun. Exciting. Her with her brother and two best friends having the night of their lives as they prepared to go their separate ways for college.

Breathing in a sob, she turned to head back into the gym. Chad would be wondering where she was, and she didn't want him to follow her. But the moment she turned around, she paused, heart stopping for a second.

Blair stood there, leaning against the nearest tree. She didn't wear a dress, but instead one of her stupid t-shirts with a silly quote on it, and a pair of jeans. Her hair was in braids again, hanging long past her shoulders, and in the light of the moon, Mia noticed that she wasn't smiling.

Mia's first instinct was to run over and hug her. She quelled that instinct. Blair didn't look pleased to see her, and Mia wasn't sure how pleased she was to see Blair. Yes, she'd been worried about her, and Mia felt partially responsible for the death of Enola Demini, but at the same time, Blair was also one of the reasons it had happened. Blair, who had stolen the artifact. Blair, who had caused problems.

Blair, who was the reason Mia had been almost kidnapped, and then handled.

She'd pushed all of those feelings to the side, knowing that Blair was grieving for her grandmother, but now, standing there, staring at her best friend, Mia couldn't stop the anger flushing her veins.

"You're back," Mia said quietly.

Blair pushed away from the tree, dropping her crossed arms to her side. "For now."

"For now?"

Blair glanced over her shoulder. At the gym. "I have nothing here anymore. Mom's staying in Sangota with Dad and my brothers. Derek won't look me in the eye. Cody is Cody. And you...."

When she trailed off, Mia's heart thudded. "What about me?"

"You'll be happier when I'm gone."

"That's not—" Mia couldn't get out the full sentence. Because... was it true? Would she be happier of Blair went away and took the world of magic with her? For the past eight months, Mia had pulled away. Trying to find normality in a peculiar world. She'd barely spoken to her brother. Ignored Cody's anger at her dating Chad.

Dated Chad.

And Blair. Her best friend. Who had lied to her. Who had pushed her into a world of magic. Who had done something selfish that Mia hadn't wanted.

Her anger swelled.

"That's not what?" Blair asked. "True? Because we both know it is."

Mia said nothing.

Blair snorted. "God, you're so selfish. Pushing everyone away because you had a little bit of trauma."

At this, Mia snapped. "A little bit of trauma? Are you fucking kidding me? I was *kidnapped* and *held hostage* by a crazed man who tried to *kill me*. But sure, call me selfish. Call me spoiled or whatever you want. We both know that's just you projecting."

She hadn't meant to say the last sentence, but when it came out, she didn't regret it. She held her head high as Blair's eyes widened.

"Projecting?" Blair asked in a quiet voice.

"Yeah." Mia crossed her arms, feeling defensive. "You're the selfish one, Blair. Always doing what you want to do without regards to anyone who might get caught in the crossfire. We didn't need those artifacts. But you had to go and get them. Why? To prove that you're awesome? Well, you aren't."

"At least I was trying *something*," Blair snapped.

"And I wasn't?"

"No, you were ignoring everyone else's trauma to hide in your stupid little shell!"

"I was trying to recover!"

"You were being a bitch!"

"Takes one to know one."

Both girls were panting, their yells echoing in the forest. Tears streamed down Mia's face as all of her frustrations and anger at Blair over the past two years came to the forefront. All of the lies, all of

310

the secrets, all of the danger. It burst out of Mia's chest.

And then, Mia realized that Blair was also crying.

Blair.

Strong, resilient, sarcastic Blair, was crying.

Mia wiped the tears from her cheeks, sniffling, and bowed her head. "I'm sorry."

Blair didn't speak at first. The two of them stood there, the only sound their sniffles. Then, Mia heard Blair's footsteps and she looked up in time for Blair to place a hand on her shoulder. Her eyes were red, dark circles almost the same color as her pupils. She opened her mouth, as if to say something, when her gaze flickered to over Mia's shoulder.

"Shit," Blair said. She shoved Mia behind her. Mia, too shocked to fight it, let her. Standing aways in the woods was a woman with long, wavy red hair and crystal blue eyes. Mia didn't recognize her, but knew who she was deep within her gut.

There was something there. The way that Enya grinned at her. Like she knew something Mia didn't. Something about Mia. And Mia wanted to run. She wanted to run until she couldn't run anymore. But her legs froze. Her heart stilled. Her breath caught in her throat.

Why?

"Evening, ladies," Enya said in the smoothest voice Mia had ever heard. "What are you doing out here when there's a lovely party going on behind you?"

"Leave before I call the Iravata," Blair snapped.

Enya's smile faltered. Then it returned, more of a smirk than a grin. "Don't worry, Blair. I'm not here for long. I just came to complete the task my son failed to do."

"What are you talking about?" Blair asked, voice shaking.

A bead of sweat trickled down the back of Mia's neck. Her chest tightened. Jae had always had it out for Derek. Was she here to kill Derek? There was nothing they could do against her. Against an immortal. But she was out in the woods. She wasn't in the party.

Mia's eyes widened as understanding washed over her.

"Blair, run!" Mia shouted, but it was too late.

Enya raised her hand. Snapped her fingers. Fire erupted around Blair's body, consuming her.

Mia screamed.

Chapter Twenty-Nine

"Fire!"

Derek didn't know what happened. One second he was in the gym, watching people around him act like high schoolers, and the next everyone was panicking.

Someone shouted fire, and everyone herded toward the exit.

He made to follow, wondering if this was some kind of prank, but when Adelia appeared in front of him, she grabbed his wrist and disappeared them from the room.

His heart sunk into his stomach.

Cody smelled the fire before the Iravata arrived. It was Eran and Tori, an interesting couple for sure. He tried to ask what was going on. Dylan tried to ask what was going on, but Eran grabbed Dylan's arm, and Tori grabbed Cody's, and disappeared them from their house without a single word.

Mia screamed and reached into the fire, trying to save her best friend. She ignored the way her hands wailed in pain. She ignored how dangerous this was. She ignored the smoke rising into the sky and how Blair was nowhere to be seen. She merely screamed, tears running down her face as Lior appeared behind her and grabbed her. He disappeared her from the forest, and the last thing she saw was Enya's vicious smile.

Chapter Thirty

D erek arrived at Shubishi's beach house in one piece, but his mind was ablaze with curiosity. The fire hadn't been natural. Why else would the Iravata have taken them from their home? Why else would his parents be there? Would Cody be there? Would....

He looked around, searching for Mia. But he couldn't find her. He couldn't sense her. At least, not well. Mia's emotions were muted, as if someone else was putting a damper on Derek's powers.

"What the hell is going on?" he asked no one in particular. The Iravata all gathered in the room. All of the adults looked around, confused.

"The fire...." Cody looked at Derek. "It wasn't an accident, was it?"

"No," Lior said. "Enya set it."

Derek's eyes widened. Enya. They hadn't heard from her in almost a year. What was she doing in Willow Creek? Why had she set a fire? And where...?

"Where's Mia?" Cody asked, voice stern.

"She's in the other room—"

315

Lior didn't get his full sentence out before Derek bolted, followed closely by Cody, Liang, and Intira. He didn't care about anyone but his sister. He remembered the look in her eyes as she'd exited the gym. The lost, confused, desperate look. He recognized it as the one he had whenever he looked in a mirror.

He pushed his way into the room where her emotions emanated from, and found her sitting on a chair, sobbing. Bandages covered her hands and Flora spoke gently to her. Derek came to her side, crouching next to her.

"Mia?" he asked. Her emotions were still muted. "What's going on? What happened?"

"Blair," Mia sputtered.

Derek blinked. "Blair?" Blair was in Sangota. Wasn't she?

"She was…she…she…." Mia broke down into more tears.

Derek knew what Mia was going to say. He always knew what Mia was going to say. But he couldn't believe it. Because he could feel her. Out there. Blair was still alive. Her emotions were alive and well. Like a ghost….

"Oh god," Cody said from behind him. An onslaught of negative emotions burned Derek's skin. He tried to rub them off, but they dug in, clinging to his bones.

Mrs. Arbour broke down into tears, and Derek flinched. What was Mrs. Arbour doing there? Why had the Iravata brought her too? Weren't she and Blair safe in Sangota?

"What's going on?" he asked, frantic. "Why are you here? Where's Blair?"

Mrs. Arbour shook her head. Intira pulled her into a hug, rubbing her back as everyone's grief bombarded Derek. But he remained confused.

Lior came into the room. He wouldn't look at anyone. "Blair was in the fire. We couldn't save her."

But that didn't make sense. Blair was in Sangota. Focusing, he

316

searched for her emotions. At first, he found nothing, which wasn't abnormal because she was in freaking Sangota, but then, without warning, he did feel them. Her emotions were there, waiting for him to find her and show her off to everyone. They were dulled, but present. He breathed out, relieved. Dead people didn't have emotions.

"You're wrong," he said. "Blair's fine. I can feel her."

But the Iravata looked at him with pity, and Mia dissolved into sobs. Underneath her bandages, Derek noticed the charred flesh.

"What happened?" he asked, spinning around. "What the hell happened?"

No one spoke, and they didn't need to for Derek to understand. Enya had set a fire. Around Blair. But she wasn't dead.

She wasn't.

Because he could still feel her.

He could still feel her.

Chapter Thirty-One

Cody was numb. He stood in the apartment his dad had found in Denver, staring at the television reporting on the fire that had decimated Willow Creek. It ran a list of names. Of deaths. One of the deadliest fires in all of Colorado history. He watched it because there was nothing else to do. All of his books, all of his things, had burned up in the fire that had destroyed his home. The home he hadn't wanted to go back to.

Well, he'd gotten his wish. He could never go back there. Not with the fire raging throughout the mountains. It wasn't safe. Even as he sat there, he knew that ash fell outside the window. They were having trouble putting the fire out. He wondered if it would ever go out.

He couldn't imagine a world without Blair. He'd tried many times when they were younger, when she'd been particularly nasty to him, or he'd snapped at her for something. He'd pictured his life without her always butting in. But in the end, he'd decided that she was meant to be there. She was meant to be a thorn in his side, keeping him honest about his feelings.

A knock at the door distracted him. He glanced over at it, wondering if it was a delivery man with another package. With a sigh, he turned off the television and headed to the door, opening it without much thought. He would sign for the package and go back to the news.

But it wasn't a delivery man.

Cody blinked. The young woman standing in the doorway wasn't looking at him, her gaze focused on the ground, and she tucked a piece of short hair behind her ear.

Short hair. She'd never had short hair.

"Mia?"

Cody hadn't heard from her since Flora's cabin. She'd been in an almost catatonic state, unable to process anything said to her. Grief. She was grieving, just like all of them were.

"Hi," she said in a low whisper.

He reached for words, but none came out. Swallowing, he tried again, searching for a greeting or a question. Instead, what came out was, "You cut your hair."

She reached up and nodded. "Yeah."

"It…uh…looks good." He mentally smacked himself.

She looked up at him, her brown eyes making his breath catch in his throat. "Can I come in?"

"Of course." Cody stepped to the side. She looked around the empty apartment, taking in everything. He was glad to see her. Glad to hear her speaking. But he didn't know why she'd come. He'd figured she would go off to college and put all of this life behind her. He honestly never thought he'd see her again. Her parents had already moved back east, and while Derek was staying in Denver to finish high school and attend college, he'd figured Mia would have gone with her parents.

But maybe she was staying? Maybe she and Derek had worked something out?

"I'm moving."

Well, there went that. He breathed in. "Where?"

"China."

Cody's jaw dropped. The world went white for a second as he processed the news, and then came back with full force. "What?"

She didn't look at him. Instead staring at the wall. "I can't be here anymore. Everything reminds me of Blair. When I walk down the streets, I imagine I'm with her. And I just need to go. I need to get away from everything. I have nothing keeping me here. I'm sure you know that my parents moved to New York to be closer to The Met, and Derek…." She sighed. "He's Derek."

Cody didn't know how to respond. She couldn't move to China. He'd never see her again.

"Don't go," Cody said. All of a sudden, his courage kicked in. He stepped forward and grabbed her arm, turning her slowly.

There were tears in her eyes. "Why should I stay?"

He'd never told her before. He'd never had the guts. But the idea of her leaving spurred him into action. He placed both his hands on her shoulders. "Because I love you."

Mia's eyes widened. The tears stopped. "What?"

Cody breathed in, then leaned in and kissed her gently. She didn't push him away, but she kiss him either. "I love you, Mia. I always have. Stay here. Stay in Denver. Stay with me."

Mia stared at him, cheeks coloring. "I…I…."

He kissed her again. He tried, so hard, to show her that he was serious. That if she just gave him a chance, she would be happy with him. They could be happy together. If she just stayed.

This time, she kissed him back.

He briefly remembered her getting up to use the restroom. He briefly remembered waiting for her to come back. But then he'd fallen asleep again. And when he woke, he found the apartment empty. No Mia. Just him laying naked in the twin bed in his empty room.

Her mist was gone. He sat there, staring at his door, trying to comprehend that she'd left. Him. She'd left him. She'd left Denver. Colorado. The U.S.

She was gone. Just like she'd said. And he wanted to throw up.

Epilogue

Derek sat in his empty apartment, staring at the wall. He could have gone with his parents. He could have moved back to China. Instead, he stayed in Denver. He'd told his parents he was going to finish high school and go to college. He wasn't sure they'd believed him. He didn't care if they'd believed him. It was all a lie anyway. The high school part, fine. But college? No. That wasn't for him. Not anymore.

Now he had a mission. School couldn't help him with it. He had to do it alone.

He had to find Blair.

Everyone kept insisting she was gone. That the fire had engulfed her.

He knew better.

Her emotions were out there, calling to him. They weren't in his head. They weren't his grief trying to justify his loss. They were there, whispering on the wind. Tickling his skin. They were too soft for him to make out, but he knew they belonged to her.

He was going to get to work. All of their things had burned up in the fire, so he would have to start anew. He would have to find the books, read the papers, and build up an arsenal of knowledge to find her. He wasn't going to let her float wherever she was. Someone had taken her. Enya hadn't set her on fire. Someone had taken her.

He was going to find out who.

He was going to find out where.

And he was going to bring her back.

To Be Concluded in...

THE
RISEN
QUEEN

Acknowledgements

This book.

What do I even say about the formation and creation of this book? I said in *The Children of Death* that it was the most difficult book to write of the series. Boy was I wrong. It had the most moving parts, yes, but emotionally, this book was a disaster from start to finish.

You see, when I wrote the first book, I had an idea of where the series was going to go. Book 1 was an intro. Book 2 Mia got kidnapped. Book 3 is the history. Book 5 was the end. But book 4? This book? What the hell even is it?

Honestly, I didn't know how book 4 would go until I wrote the outline. It was a risk for me, personally, to do this because I was so out of my wheelhouse. I knew the beginning. I knew the ending. I knew nothing about how to get from Point A to Point Z. I'd outlined book 5 before I even started book 4! So, that was a whole thing.

Then I did write it. And I didn't know if it was good. Thank you Karen for assuring me that it was not terrible and horrible and that I needed to rethink the entire plot. Thank you Kathleen and Ashley for listening to me in main chat rant endlessly about how much

I hated creating this book. And thank you Chika for pushing me to write one of the hardest scenes in the series. If you've read the book, you know the one.

This book was a nightmare. But I think it's one of the best of the series. I'm very proud of what I managed to put together, especially considering everything in the world trying to keep me from finishing it. From Book 5 calling, to other projects taking center stage, to people screwing me over when it came to beta-reading and making me question not just this book, but the series as a whole, to moving across the world. This book was a struggle.

But it's out in the world. I'm proud of it. I'm proud of what I've learned as a writer through writing and revising it. I'm proud of who I am as a person after all the set backs. I persevered. I didn't give up.

Thank you Jules, who worked so hard to bring this beautiful new cover into the world and managed to shift through my complicated explanations and moods and timelines to create something so freaking beautiful!

Thank you to everyone who helped me along the way. Whether it be critiquing and listening to me vent, like with Karen, Kathleen, Ashley, and Chika, or *still* putting up with me and my website (love you Cas), or giving me the faith I needed in this book after all the delays and frustrations, as Lilli did this past fall.

You are all fantastic. I love every one of you and am so excited to put an end to the saga that is *A Hollow Secret*'s creation.

About the Author

A Colorado native, Linn Coldiron spends her time reading, writing, and studying languages. Her love of language and culture has led her to live a peripatetic life filled with inspiration from all over the world.